DEATH ON DEMAND

DEATH ON DEMAND
Jim Kelly

Severn House Large Print
London & New York

For Bernard
A connoisseur of memories

This first large print edition published 2017
in Great Britain and the USA by
SEVERN HOUSE PUBLISHERS LTD of
19 Cedar Road, Sutton, Surrey, England, SM2 5DA.
First world regular print edition published 2015 by
Crème de la Crime, an imprint of
Severn House Publishers Ltd.

British Library Cataloguing in Publication Data
A CIP catalogue record for this title is available from the British Library.

ISBN-13: 9780727895110

Severn House Publishers support the Forest Stewardship Council™
[FSC™], the leading international forest certification organisation. All
our titles that are printed on FSC certified paper carry the FSC logo.

MIX
Paper from
responsible sources
FSC® C013056

Typeset by Palimpsest Book Production Ltd.,
Falkirk, Stirlingshire
Printed and bound i
T J International, Pa

Blackpool Council

PAL
1/17
RL

30 MAR 2017

Sheridan
Haugh
Hordle
Threlfall
Gough
Wilkinson

− 3 JUN 2019

Please return/renew this item
by the last date shown.

To renew this item go to :
www.blackpool.gov.uk/libraries
or phone : **01253 478070**

One

The first glimmer of the rising supermoon appeared as a star of light on the marine horizon at a point, according to DI Peter Shaw's iPhone compass, five degrees from magnetic north. Its intensity brightened by the second, until a beam broke free, sweeping across the sea, as if from some unseen polar lighthouse. Within a dozen heartbeats the lunar curve was revealed, tracking east, gliding perhaps on watery rails.

Shaw checked his watch. Moonrise had been predicted at 7.08 p.m. precisely; it was now 7.09 p.m., revealing the precision of celestial mechanics. The crowd on the beach, in contrast, was chaotically human. Small groups broke into applause; a strange, neo-pagan welcome for the phenomena they had all come to witness: congratulating a lump of inanimate rock, if a spectacularly beautiful one, for succumbing to the universal laws of physics.

The speed of ascent into the night sky was extraordinary, clearly visible to the naked eye; the moon's rise heavenwards accentuated by the warm layer of air just above the sea, the result of a day of unrelenting sunshine, which had, in effect, created a giant lens, an atmospheric magnifying glass. The crowd whooped and clapped, urging the moon along its inevitable path.

One of the party groups on the sand had a

portable speaker and, on cue, it began to broadcast the opening bars of Strauss's *Also Sprach Zarathustra* – the closest, it was clearly felt, that several thousand years of human evolution had yet come to the music of the spheres. Shaw, sitting on the bottom rung of the ladder which led to the lifeguard's high chair, recalled that the opening bars of the musical poem were entitled *Sunrise* – and were therefore spectacularly inappropriate.

Rising, the moon accrued a pink-orange luminescence, giving the orb a subtle shadowing, a three-dimensional quality, a sense of untold mass often absent from the usual white, cold disc. Shaw was moved, not by the grandeur of the phenomenon, but by the way in which this ball of rock gave to the flat sky an astonishing depth, so that he sensed that he could reach out a hand and cradle the great sphere in mid-air, turning it if he wished to see the hidden dark side.

Sixty-five seconds after making its first appearance the moon finally let loose the bounds of earth and was free, launching itself into a silent voyage which suggested the verb *sailing,* a spinnaker billowing out at the leading edge, perhaps, with flags trailing, and a wake even, like a stream of stardust. Camera lenses clicked in a chorus behind him, on the crest of the dunes, where a line of photographers had set up their tripods to catch the event: the crowded beach as foreground, with its flickering barbecue fires, mobile phones flashing, and a single Chinese lantern already lit, a child's hand away from its own free flight.

A family twenty yards down the beach from

2

Shaw examined a large lunar map spread out on the sand, a father-figure excitedly pointing out the principal features to a ten-year-old boy, while his toddler sister stood, transfixed, dead arms hanging loose at her sides, watching this strange apparition as if bewitched by a hypnotist's pendulum watch. The 'Man in the Moon' had never been more apparent, the 'eyes' of the Mare Crisium and the Mare Serenitatis like giant sockets in a pumpkin skull. As the colours bled away, the orange and red, the green and the blue, slipping from the surface as the moon rose, a lifeless white took their place, suggesting not just the bones and teeth, but the deathless quality of outer space.

A cheer rose behind Shaw, prompting him to look back up the beach to *Surf!* – the beach bar and café run by his wife, Lena. The dozen picnic tables had sold out for a special 'Supermoon Menu' of smoked eel, Hunstanton fishcakes (squid and hake) and toasted marshmallow pie; plus a house cocktail dubbed 'The Moon Riser', which fortuitously included shots from several untouched bottles on the shelf behind the bar (including a Japanese whiskey, a Basque sloe brandy and a vile Czech liqueur with the consistency of axle grease). The result was nothing if not potent, and Shaw wondered how many of the diners were applauding just the one moon. Several of the sky-watchers stood on picnic tables, but all faces tracked the magnificent progress of the light in the sky, like upturned sunflowers. A pleasing symmetry seemed to create a tension between the watchers and the watched: the giant

3

face looking down, the hundreds staring back in reply.

Lena, meticulous in everything related to her clientele, had included a fact sheet on the back of the menu, pointing out, among other things, that no less an authority than NASA had estimated that a supermoon (the coincidence of a full harvest moon with the point at which the earth's lone satellite is at its closest to its parent planet) would appear in the sky fourteen per cent bigger by area, seven per cent wider, and – best of all – thirty per cent brighter, than its every-night self. This was the moment of perigee-syzygy, according to the scientists. Shaw memorized the spelling on the one-in-a-million chance he ever got to use it in a game of Scrabble with his daughter.

The cheering persisted as three waitresses, employed by Lena for the occasion, dispensed a further round of the lethal potion.

Down by the water's edge, a group had gathered around a quad bike loaded with an entire consignment of Chinese lanterns. Shaw, in his role as a crewman for the local lifeboat a mile south at Hunstanton, had been involved in making sure that *Surf!*'s supermoon event used bio-degradable lanterns, and would only proceed to a mass launch if an off-shore wind was blowing. Shaw planned a two-hour coastguard shift on top of the lifeguard chair, tracking the lanterns, making sure any real life emergencies didn't get lost in the drifting light show.

'Peter.'

Turning quickly at the sound of his name, Shaw

found himself face-to-face with his chief constable, Kieran Joyce, in shorts and Irish rugby shirt, cradling a large Moon Riser. Twenty yards along the beach he noted Joyce's personal driver, in dark suit and tie, sipping an orange juice, and looking bored. For a moment Shaw felt a distinct sense of doom approaching. At the same instant he realized that this was probably due to the supermoon itself, supposedly a sign of imminent disaster, for as the moon controlled the tides and the drifting tectonic plates of the earth, its super counterpart was said to trigger tidal waves, earthquakes and all manner of biblical dangers.

'Sorry to creep up,' said Joyce. 'You were miles away. Makes you think, a sight like that.'

Shaw dutifully considered the giant moon with his one good eye, the right. He'd lost the sight in his left on the beach one day, ten miles to the east, when he tried to get a toddler away from a pool of toxic waste which was bubbling out of a discarded drum of industrial effluent. The kid, waving a stick, had panicked as Shaw scooped her up in his arms, the tip of the stick catching his right sclera, injecting the poison waste into the soft tissue. Lena always said it was like a beauty spot, that it simply served to accentuate how handsome the rest of his face remained. Echoes again: this time the rising moon and the white, lifeless pupil, a contrast to its water-blue twin.

'It's very big, I'm very small, that's as philosophical as I get, sir,' he said.

The former deputy chief constable of Northern Ireland, Joyce, a high-flyer at forty-eight years of age, found himself widely tipped as a potential candidate for the biggest job of all, with the Met, if the politics went his way. He'd been in the new job for six weeks and so far had taken the *softly-softly* approach. Shaw wasn't fooled, for when he looked into Joyce's eyes he saw echoes of the Irishman's past: a vicious sectarian childhood spent in Belfast's poorest Catholic neighbourhood – the Short Strand. Joyce had seen his father shot dead by a gunman at the height of the Troubles in 1976; a fleeting grey figure in the newsreel, hurling a petrol bomb over a barricade of burnt-out cars. According to one interview Shaw had tracked down online, ten-year-old Kieran had watched from his bedroom window as the fatal shot found its target, his father clutching at the throat wound that would drain his life away. Twenty years later his son was at the heart of the negotiations which had laid the foundations of the peace process. Shaw tried to imagine what that felt like inside; sitting across a conference table in an anonymous room, pouring out tap water into crystal glasses for men, any one of whom might have been behind the cross hairs of a rifle that day, adjusting the telescopic sight to bring his father's outline into focus.

'Just a couple of things, Peter.'

Shaw's sense of augury deepened, so that the sounds of *Surf!* – the high-decibel chit-chat, the Beach Boys soundtrack – seemed to fade away. The world appeared to contract into a sphere of warm air, containing just the two police officers.

Joyce was compact, slight and wiry, with a

thick head of hair prematurely silver-white. There wasn't a single half ounce of fat on his bones, and he gave the appearance of someone who could drive a nail into a plank of wood with the flat of his hand.

'Sir.'

'Walsingham, Peter. I'm at the Home Office tomorrow. I'd like to reassure Whitehall we have this under control. I'm sorry, I know this is a social event. But we're coppers, not bank clerks, so we don't really do down time. I'd like an update.'

Every year, several times a year, thousands of pilgrims joined forces to mark the old paths which led to the shrine of the Virgin Mary, at Walsingham, a town ten miles inland from the coast. The so-called 'National' pilgrimage was the biggest, held in the spring; but this year a special one was planned for the August bank holiday to mark World Pilgrim Day, organized by an international committee and expected to attract thousands. The so-called 'World' had spawned a counter-pilgrimage, a coalition of largely Left-wing protestors, keen to challenge what were seen as the forces of reaction. The West Norfolk Constabulary was solely responsible for public order on the day.

Earlier, in the back office in their cottage behind *Surf!*, Shaw had checked out TV footage the team had downloaded from *BBC Look East*. A crowd of about two hundred were shown processing along a narrow country lane, following a priest and an icon of the Virgin Mary decked in flowers. The faithful, to either side, had crossed

7

themselves as the icon passed, or knelt to say a prayer. A lone uniformed constable had made an entirely symbolic effort to keep the way ahead clear by preceding the procession, arms outstretched. The pilgrims were still a week away and security was the responsibility of the Cambridgeshire force. As soon as they crossed the county line they were Shaw's problem.

It wasn't a new problem. They'd been coming for a thousand years, interrupted only by the Reformation. Way back, a Saxon noblewoman had seen a vision of Christ's mother and been given the exact cubic measurements of the 'Holy House' of Nazareth, the site of the Miracle of the Annunciation. Shaw, the unwilling recipient of a Catholic education, knew his scripture: the Annunciation was the moment Gabriel told Mary she'd give birth to the Christ-child.

After the Saxon noblewoman saw the angel, she promptly built a replica of the Holy House as instructed. (Or, it was miraculously constructed overnight by Gabriel: you took your choice.) The noblewoman's son built an abbey over the house. When the Holy Land was invaded by the Infidel, places like Walsingham were ideally placed to mop up the medieval tourist market. Millions made the trip to what became known as 'England's Nazareth'.

Henry VIII tore down the abbey, despite having been an enthusiastic pilgrim himself. The shrine was rebuilt in the 1920s with its replica *replica* of the Holy House tucked inside. As a result, Walsingham survived as an exotic, one-off remnant of pre-Reformation England, an Italian

8

hill town cast down, it seemed, on the greensward of protestant Norfolk by a flock of passing angels.

But the chief constable wasn't interested in Walsingham's heavenly past – he feared an infernal future. In recent years the pilgrimage had attracted various protest groups, from the Far Right, enraged at Marian idolatory, to the Far Left, eager to air liberal views on women priests, gay rights and a Woman's Right to Choose. Joyce, haunted by his own sectarian past, wanted to make sure north Norfolk didn't spawn its own unique marching season.

It was Peter Shaw's job to ensure the 'World' went ahead without incident. It took him less than a minute now to outline the measures he was taking: all leave had been cancelled for the force's uniformed branch on the day, two helicopters would be on stand-by at Fakenham – seven miles south – while CID officers would be in the crowd. All official protest groups had been contacted and allocated agreed 'protest points'. Six CCTV sites had been planned on radial routes and at the shrine.

'OK. Good,' said Joyce, looking out to sea. 'Keep on it, Peter. It's a bag of worms, so let's keep it tied up nice and tight. This is a one-off. Next year we'll be back to the National. We can handle that.'

All the lanterns were aloft, a string of more than fifty, drifting up and out to sea, the candles flickering. Shaw was struck by the contrast between this joyful pagan worship of the super-moon, and the fervent, pious passion of the pilgrims, on their way to Walsingham.

9

'I better get back to my table,' said Joyce. 'My wife's not safe left alone with one of these . . .' He shook the cocktail glass. 'You've got a good business here. You've built something.'

'It's my wife's business – lock, stock and barrel.'

'Right,' said Joyce, but he hadn't heard. 'Oh. The other thing. DS Valentine's medical didn't go well.'

George Valentine was Peter Shaw's partner, his sergeant. They'd been a team, a reluctant duo it had to be said, for nearly six years. Valentine had been his father's partner back in the eighties. DCI Jack Shaw was a legend in the West Norfolk Constabulary – although Joyce had probably never heard of him. To the outside world, Valentine was an old-fashioned copper, a dinosaur roaming the brave new world of CSI, community relations and equal opportunities, not to mention health and safety. At fifty-nine he was in the last furlong before retirement. A widower, smoking sixty Silk Cut a day, he had never felt the need to plan for the time when he didn't have to go to work. Dying on the job wasn't a possibility – it was George Valentine's goal.

'He's got an appointment with the force doctor, Scrutton, at St James' to review his test results. They made him take a scan to track emphysema. Unfortunately, the picture told a different story – lung cancer. Looks bad, I'm afraid. If he wants some time off to think, he can have it. His pension lump sum comes in at just under £130,000. He could see the world. I don't know. Whatever spins his wheels. Right now he'll be feeling fine. In

10

six months he'll be on his knees. This isn't something that's going to go away.

'That's all entirely *entre nous*. You didn't hear it from me. It might be an idea to take him out and get him pissed after he's seen Scrutton. You need to break through, crack the complacency. Miracles aside, this is going to kill him.'

Joyce spilt the dregs of his Moon Riser into the sand and waded off towards the lights of *Surf!*. On the way up the beach he passed a slim, black woman in a white bikini holding two full cocktail glasses, which meant Shaw had less than thirty seconds to manufacture a smile to greet his wife.

Two

George Valentine descended the uncarpeted stairs to a familiar sound; the cat flap flapping as Zebra made his customary early morning exit. The cat had been Julie's as a kitten, and with her death the animal had seemed to take a violent dislike to her bereaved husband, as if the disease which had killed her so swiftly was in some moral sense his fault. Standing in the kitchen he lit the gas ring under the kettle with the match he would have used to fire up his first cigarette of the day, if he hadn't promised himself that today was *the day*. Valentine was a stubborn man but he didn't fight losing battles. Emphysema was making him increasingly breathless. The quack at St James' had made him take a scan at the Great Eastern Hospital, an experience so alien, antiseptic, and claustrophobic he'd vowed to quit for good while his old bones were still inside the machine, his head outside.

'I've quit,' he announced to the kitchen, although his eyes flitted across the Formica table and worktops until he remembered he'd thrown his last packet of Silk Cut into a bin on the Boal Quay the night before. Outside the cat caught his eye, treading its sinuous feline path along the fence, paw in front of paw, like a tightrope walker. The movement of featherweight bones apparent beneath the skinny flesh reminded Valentine that they were both of a certain age. He noted that the cat's bowl was still full of yesterday's food.

While the aluminium kettle fidgeted on the gas ring he walked to the front door to pick up the paper, only remembering when he'd got to the end of the gloomy hallway that he'd been persuaded to cancel it. The *Daily Mail* – apparently – enhanced a cynical tendency, a mean view of the world, dominated by a morbid anxiety towards the concept of change. He stood for a moment, looking at his black slip-on leather shoes, and thought that while that might be true, what were the alternatives? He'd rather be suspected of necrophilia than being a *Guardian* reader. He'd have to do without. Something else he'd have to do without. It occurred to him that life had a certain symmetry, because you spent the first twenty years doing things for the first time, and the final twenty years doing them for the last.

Back in the kitchen he found a new chopping board and a loaf of bread wrapped in slightly greasy tissue paper with a watermark, which must mean it was organic, and therefore almost certainly inedible. He cut some, noting with distaste the embedded shards of gritty husk, and popped it in the toaster, beginning to count the seconds before the slice was launched briefly into orbit. Outside, distinctly, he heard a child's voice in play; so pellucid, so sharp, she could have been in the room. Whitefriars' primary school was a street away and ran a breakfast club for kids with working parents. He'd grown up in these streets, between the river and the London Gate, and the playground simply provided part of the soundtrack to his life. If he'd been born in the country it would have been birdsong.

Upstairs, the shower unit cut out, the sudden silence emphasizing the loss of the buzzing electric motor. He imagined the woman standing beneath the final drops of water, eyes closed, hands covering her mouth, and felt the stab of guilt that it wasn't Julie he saw, that the water drops didn't slide over her skin. The bathroom door opened and footsteps ran to the bedroom. In less than a minute she was coming down the stairs, with a smart *rat-a-tat-tat*; and then, there she was in the black-and-white uniform: creased trousers, polished shoes, a black-and-white chequered scarf, body belt, summer tunic, radio: Probationary Police Constable Jan Clay.

She was the only thing in the kitchen that wasn't stale, including the organic bread.

'Morning, Constable,' he said, thinking that

when she got out of bed she never left an impression; no nest-like whorl, no crumpled, nightmarish shroud. There was something light and luminous about her, which he hoped wasn't simply a facet of being temporary.

'Detective Sergeant,' she said, her brown eyes checking both his hands, left then right, for signs of the first cigarette.

Satisfied, she turned her back to face the mirror; neat blonde hair, cut short, with that happy habit of always falling into place. *Neat* wasn't quite right but it was the word everyone used. Tidy perhaps, compact even. And brisk. The uniform was as yet unfamiliar, and she re-jigged the scarf, readjusted the cap, tucking in a stray hair.

Valentine had long harboured the fantasy that the mirrors in the house stored the images from the past which only he was blessed, or cursed, to see. If he stole a glance over Jan's shoulder now, would he catch Julie's face looking out; assessing, disappointed, approving?

Jan's husband, DC Paul Clay, had been Valentine's partner in what he liked to refer to, with a Churchillian flourish, as his 'Wilderness Years' – when he'd been banished from the CID unit at Lynn to the north Norfolk coast after making a spectacular hash of a murder inquiry, fetching up finally at Wells-next-the-Sea, to spend a decade going quietly to seed, investigating petty thefts, Saturday night brawls, second-home burglaries.

DC Clay hadn't been his kind of copper, or his kind of man; but he'd envied him his life, the teetotal rectitude, the easy good humour, the

14

dutiful wife, the two children. He'd seen the kids grow up, leave home. Then DC Clay's health had started to decline, marked by a long series of vaguely mysterious ailments, and his wife had begun soliciting for odd jobs to supplement the single salary, now bereft of overtime. She'd taken in washing, offered to clean houses, and so Valentine's bedsit had been one of her first tasks. She'd seen the minutiae of a widower's life: the single Christmas card from Valentine's sister, the armchair in front of the TV, the empty bottles, the takeaway cartons.

How different, he'd thought at the time, it must all be to Jan Clay's own home, but time told a different story. DC Clay, it turned out, was a secret alcoholic who died of liver cancer after a long, final illness which was anything but bravely borne, and Jan had spent their life together, she later confessed, envying him his job; policing it turned out, was in her blood at just about the same concentration as alcohol was in his.

'What's on today then, Georgie?' she asked, pulling down the front of her tunic and opening the fridge to retrieve a yogurt pot.

Valentine yawned. The fact that she wanted to talk about The Job wasn't a problem. The problem was that she wanted to talk about it at seven fifteen in the morning. But he liked being called Georgie; it made him feel twenty years younger, and it was thrillingly intimate after nearly twenty years of watching other people's lives, as if through a half-open door. Flattered too, as almost any fifty-something widower would have been, by an attentive lover. Pressing his left foot down

15

hard on the lino, he made an effort to straighten his back and felt the visceral 'click' of his vertebrae reshuffling, his spine uncurling.

'Walsingham, planning for the pilgrimage,' he said.

Valentine had a head like a hatchet – two-dimensional, so that when he turned it now to track the disappearance of Zebra over a rooftop, his face seemed to move from light to dark with no intervening shadows. 'Meetings all day. Tea cups. Biscuits. Agendas. God squad. Vicars – worse, monks. Neighbourhood Witch. PowerPoint presentations. Can it get any better? Especially when we've still got two GBHs and an attempted murder on the books.'

It was his turn to let his image fall upon the silvered glass and it gave him a moment to recover: jet-black receding hair, narrow features fighting a losing battle with gravity, grey eyes with an icy splinter of reflected light.

Jan blew on her tea. 'I went once,' she said, 'with the kids on the railway.' Wells, Jan's old home town, was five miles from the shrine by a narrow-gauge tourist line which just about kept up a year-round service. 'They'd just held a service in one of the old churches and the nave and the aisles, every bit of the floor was covered in fresh herbs – rosemary, thyme, mint. They'd processed up and down with the icon and crushed the herbs underfoot.' She met Valentine's eye. 'It *was* amazing Georgie. Put the kids in a trance. Like breathing perfume.'

Valentine looked dubious. When they'd taken a weekend break to Paris, Jan had tried to get

16

him to join her inside Notre Dame, but he'd just walked away to watch the riverboats sliding past on the Seine. It wasn't that Valentine didn't believe, he later explained over an ice-cold litre of Normandy cider, he just reasoned that he'd find out one way or another soon enough. Life was a game of poker, why show his hand now?

Munching the cast iron crust of his toast, he switched on the local radio news: haystack arson at Gayton; an affray on the Tuesday Market; weather fine. He worked a finger under his stiff white shirt collar. 'Who you with today?' he asked.

Jan would be a West Norfolk Constabulary probationer for two years. She'd got through her initial training and was now spending time with various units, learning different aspects of The Job. She'd just completed two months on foot patrol.

'DS Chalker. Shoe squad.'

'*Shoe squad?*'

She took Valentine by the arm and led him into the living room: sixty-inch flat-screen TV (with Sky Sports), ironing board and a mantelpiece crammed with pictures of Jan's grown-up children. Parting the net curtains to look out in to Greenland Street, they found the world outside was bathed in mist, lit a rather beautiful lemon-yellow by the pale disc of the risen sun. Briefly it reminded Jan of the supermoon they'd glimpsed the night before, floating free of the rooftops, capturing Zebra in silhouette.

A milk float tinkled past with a whirring electric motor.

17

The house stood at a T-junction so that they could see down Whitefriars' Street directly opposite. The telephone wires were strung between poles in a zigzag pattern into the distance. About a hundred yards down on the left a pair of trainers had been lobbed up over the lines, dangling in the air like a set of South American *bolas*.

'Shoes,' said Jan.

'Right. They're illegal, are they?' said Valentine. 'That'd be the Dangerous Sneaker Act, 2008.'

'Listen,' she said. She'd brought the yogurt pot with her and quickly took another teaspoonful. 'Joyce has got some expert coming in to give us all the lowdown. It's billed as a *lecture*, no less. It's nothing new, I know, but there's definitely something afoot . . .'

She smiled at her own joke. 'Twenty, thirty pairs a day out on the estates. And here in town. If you don't look up, Georgie, you'd have missed them.'

Valentine's eyes rarely left the pavement.

'Some of it's art, vandalism, but criminal gangs use them too, drugs, gambling, prostitution. The Met's had a spate around White City, West London that *was* drug related. Apparently there's a lot of interest in the *international policing community.*'

An ability to talk in italics was only one of the gifts Valentine admired in PPC Jan Clay.

'We're going out with the cherry picker to take 'em all down,' said Jan, valiantly attempting to instill a sense of urgency into the project. 'I saw a pair last night on Greyfriars right opposite the nick. Cheeky bastards. And we'll have those

18

too . . .' she added, nodding down Whitefriars' Street. 'Last thing we want is the local PTA on our backs. Street drugs outside the primary school playground, not nice.'

'It's a craze,' said Valentine, suddenly short of breath. 'You take them down the kids will put some new ones up. I'd leave 'em. Ignore it. It's graffiti in the sky. So what?'

'You haven't got Neighbourhood Watch to deal with, or the police committee, or the press. Or, for that matter, Facebook and Twitter – both of which are awash with pictures every time a new pair goes up. Social media, Georgie. It's the new street.'

She waved her iPhone at him, in its trendy polka-dot case.

They both heard his mobile buzzing on the kitchen table, doing its bee-waggle dance on the Formica top.

'See ya,' she said, fleeing.

The mobile screen when he snatched it up said simply: SHAW.

He knew what he'd hear before he picked the mobile up: that weird sonar-echo of wide open space, a seagull or two, the soft rise and fall of the waves on the beach – *his* beach.

'George?' The voice was much higher than he ever expected, and tuneful, suggesting an ability to hit a note first time.

'Peter.' In public, and especially in front of the CID team, they kept it formal. It was DI Shaw, or just 'sir'. But he'd known Peter Shaw for thirty years; in fact, Valentine had been young Peter's godfather, although this had never been mentioned

19

since the whizz-kid had returned home to join the West Norfolk Constabulary from the Met.

'I know you were looking forward to a three-hour planning meeting on Walsingham, George, but . . . How about you jump in the Mazda. I'll meet you on the coast road outside Marsh House, that's a private residential care home about two hundred yards east of Brancaster Church. I'll be outside. I'll wait. We'll walk in.'

'Give me something for the journey,' said Valentine, reaching for his coat and automatically searching the pockets for the packet of Silk Cut. He knew why Shaw liked to play it like this: no details, no theories, the walk-up routine. If Valentine had no idea what he was heading for he'd have no preconceptions. He'd be what Shaw needed: a pair of objective, experienced, investigative eyes. 'Cold eyes' was what Shaw had called them once, and they knew each other well enough for Valentine to recognize the compliment.

'Murder, George. That's usually good enough to get you out of bed in the morning. But here's the thing: our victim's a rarity. A one-off. All set to meet the postman this morning she was, expecting her card from the Queen. She'd have been 100 today, George, if she'd lived. Alert apparently, had all her marbles. But you'd think, after *one hundred years*, that all passion was spent. What's the point in killing someone who's lived a century? What possible motive could justify that?'

Three

A great yew tree, its rickety zigzag branches obscuring the second-floor windows of Marsh House, spread its fingertips out in the grey mist, like hands reaching for the warmth of an unseen sun. Shaw had expected the usual brand-image cypress trees, which seemed to lurk above the manicured lawns of every care home. He'd never quite grasped the psychology of such a choice. The cypress was an evergreen, and therefore a symbol of immortality, and so grew in every churchyard and graveyard – thus, surely, becoming, at least for the skeptical, a potent symbol of the very opposite of eternal life, a signpost instead to a kind of evergreen, picturesque, death.

At least the yew, by contrast, was unambiguous: toxic, with blood-red sap, indelibly linked to death and pain. Christ, it was said, was crucified on a cross of yew, the carpenter of Nazareth, finding death, nailed to wood. It too only grew in churchyards, because the surrounding walls and hedges guarded its lethal leaves and berries from becoming food for children, or worse, precious cattle. A symbol too of longevity, living two thousand years, three thousand years, or more. Which made its choice for the care home garden as unintelligible as the cypress. To complete the cemetery gloom a willow bowed its head, the ultimate icon of mourning.

21

The mist nudged inland, as warm and damp as the fetid interior of a launderette. Somewhere, out in the phlegm-white gloom of the North Sea, a coaster boomed its foghorn. Marsh House itself seemed to crouch in its grove of manicured gardens, just glimpsed – a whitewashed Napoleonic mansion with playful naval features: double bay windows, a maritime lookout tower, a flagpole, the whole estate behind a Norfolk stone wall. To one side of the gate stood a blue-and-white police squad car. Out on the marsh, just visible in the gloom, lay the wreck of a wooden boat, its toast-rack beams set in a line like a broken ribcage.

The Porsche's passenger side window was down so that Shaw could smell the sea, the wind-choked marshes, the drying sands inundated by an advancing tide; a spring tide, drawn up by the very supermoon the crowd had applauded the night before on the beach. He checked his diver's watch – good at sixty fathoms – and noted the time: 8.21 a.m. He'd give Valentine another two minutes.

The landline call to Shaw from the control room at St James' had made it clear a uniformed constable was at the scene of the crime, but like most detectives he felt that the quicker he could actually see the victim, the better chance there was to catch the killer. It was an odd irony but the scene of crime – especially of a murder – was in itself a living thing, which began to age from the moment of death, giving up its vital clues to the passage of time.

A hearse, in deadly black, purred past twice on

22

the coast road before slipping down a side-entrance into Marsh House past a sign marked: DELIVERIES. As it slowed to turn, Shaw noticed a particular sound, a kind of oily clicking, which he'd heard before when walking beside his father's casket as it was driven to the crematorium: the finely tuned motor idling perhaps, like a clock ticking. The engines of hearses must be strangely pampered mechanisms, polished and oiled, calibrated and recalibrated, for the occasional stately journey.

A sign opposite, across the misty deserted road, read:

MARSH HOUSE
REST HOME
STRICTLY PRIVATE

Another, much larger, warned with no obvious irony:

DEAD SLOW

George Valentine's fate loomed: later that day, at the hands of the workmanlike Dr Scrutton, he'd learn that his life had just been irrevocably altered. Shaw had woken with that one thought, perfectly formed, like the lingering anxiety of a nightmare. Lung cancer; two words which seemed to suck the life out of the day ahead. Would Valentine embrace the diagnosis as inevitable, greet death as a friend, or fight against it? Shaw had checked online with the medical unit at St James' and found the DS's appointment was at three that afternoon. What was best? Let him walk into the room, sit down, hear the news, or warn him first? The problem with the second option was the near certainty that Valentine would simply not attend the medical. He needed to hear the truth, unvarnished, from a doctor.

Shaw's phone, true to north Norfolk custom, showed no signal at all. Drumming his fingers on the steering wheel, he adjusted the rear-view mirror so that he could see the road to Lynn, the dotted white line disappearing into a floating world of white mist. A line of telegraph wire looped into the distance, distinguished by a single pair of old shoes thrown high over the road. He caught sight of his own face: broad, tanned; a nomad's face, always searching for a wide horizon. An outrider, a lone horseman perhaps, scouting ahead of the Mongol Horde. Blinking, he could discern that his early morning swim had left his good eye slightly bloodshot, even clouded.

Patience was Shaw's short suit. He kicked the door open, locked the car and considered Marsh House. It was important to Shaw where he lived, but it had never occurred to him that he might be able to choose *where* to die. Had the victim, as yet unknown, chosen Marsh House as her last home? Or had they hoped for something else? Shaw loved the beach where they lived because he'd played there as a child. The emotions he'd felt then, as a ten-year-old, had become imprinted on the landscape itself, as if it was a solid-state tape which he could replay by simply returning to the scene. Emotions dominated by a sense of freedom, because the world lay behind him, while ahead lay the sea – limitless, empty. And he lived on the edge between those two worlds. But where did he want to die? What would be the last image to fall on that one, blue-water eye?

Valentine's Mazda emerged from the mist, executing a modest skid on the grit, the engine dying with two pulmonary coughs and a backfire. By the time the DS had extricated himself from the driver's seat, Shaw was there, waiting, emitting that vaguely electrical buzz that indicates excessive good health. His short-cut hair stood up in spikes, as if powered by static.

'Let's walk,' said Shaw, already halfway across the road. Small talk wasn't something they ever shared, let alone convivial welcomes, and on this particular morning Shaw was keen not to allow any subtle changes in his persona to alert Valentine to his impending rendezvous with Dr Scrutton. The relationship between any DI and his DS was bound to be close; theirs was complicated by a shared past, and compatibly dry senses of humour, but personally it was generally cool, at worst tetchy, antagonistic, or even hostile – studded nonetheless with moments of almost familial intensity. For the rest of *this* day Shaw was going to keep their personal lives firmly separated from the case at hand.

Stopping on the broken white line, he looked up and down the foggy narrow coast road. To the east the village ran on, stone cottages on each side, summer lets and second homes. To the west lay the church, and the road down to the distant beach at Brancaster Staithe. The top of the church tower was lost in the mist.

25

'What do we know?' asked Valentine, wrapping a raincoat around his narrow thighs.

'Local community copper attended an emergency call at just after 6.55 a.m. this morning. Name of Curtis – that's the copper, not the victim. Patient missing from her room. No name. He arrived at 7.20 a.m. As I said, George, no details, but murder according to Curtis. He told the control room there was no doubt.'

Marsh House's driveway ended in a turning circle, surrounding a stone fountain depicting a dolphin, from which a dribble of water splashed into a mossy basin.

Valentine filled his lungs. 'You know as well as I do this isn't going to be a sodding murder. Some old dear will be dead at the bottom of a set of two steps and the house busy-body will have fingered a suitable villain. Motive? They've been bickering over the custard creams. It's all they've got to think about, isn't it? Food, and other peoples' deaths. Takes their minds off their own.'

'I think we should give PC Curtis the benefit, don't you? Until proved otherwise.'

Valentine's tendency to theorize on crime in the absence of evidence was just one of the aspects of being an 'old-fashioned copper' which tested Shaw's patience.

'You're the boss,' said the DS, stubbing one of his black slip-ons against the base of the fountain.

'Yes, George. I am.'

A notice on the front door directed them to a side entrance, which lay down a short path behind

26

a gaudy blue hydrangea, the blooms studded with mist drops. A glass porch held an entry phone and a security keypad, while overhead a remote-controlled camera chattered quietly, panning left and right, until it locked on Valentine.

'You've scored, George. Big smile.'

The lock sprang with an audible release ten seconds before a woman appeared to greet them: dark suit, white blouse and a name badge which read: Julia Fortis: ADMINISTRATOR. Shaw estimated she was twenty-five, dressed like a fifty-year-old. The faux-tweed suit didn't quite conceal the trim figure beneath. She had a silver brooch depicting lilies of the valley – symbols again, thought Shaw, this time of innocence.

'Inspector,' she said, offering Valentine her hand.

'DS Valentine. This is DI Shaw. It's an easy mistake to make,' he added, smiling for the first time that day.

Shaw noted the briefest eye movement as she clocked his absent tie. Then she saw the mooneye, which seemed to unsettle her sufficiently to force a quick switch of attention back to Valentine, betraying a strange sensitivity for disability in a manager of a nursing home.

'Sorry,' she said, flustered. 'It's been a dreadful few hours . . .' She waved a hand, the fingers shaking, although Shaw was pretty certain this little bit of theatre was pure am-dram, because there wasn't a bead of sweat on her tanned, taut skin.

The hallway, dominated by a double sweep staircase, was decorated with purple and white balloons.

'This was all for Ruby . . .' Fortis' eyes went down to the carpet, as if hiding an emotion. Loss, anger, irritation? There was something calculating in the soft green eyes when she did look up, as if the real her was simply looking out through someone else's face.

'Her party,' offered Fortis.

'One hundred today? Ruby . . .?'

'Yes. Sorry – Ruby Bright. Our Ruby . . .'

They appeared to have become becalmed in the echoing hallway. 'First thing,' said Shaw, 'no one leaves. Not until I say so – or DS Valentine does. OK. Absolutely nobody.'

'Yes. I've spoken to the staff.'

'How many staff?' asked Valentine.

'Eight. Nurses and catering.'

'Cleaning staff?' asked Shaw.

'Not yet. They're in at nine.'

'Tell them not to touch anything. Keep them here, please, in the lobby, until our forensic team arrives. No work at all; no carpets, no floors, no bins, no washing up . . . Nothing,' said Shaw, looking up the stairs to the first-floor landing.

'And the rest of the residents are all accounted for?' asked Valentine.

'Yes. Nineteen in total. They're all well, thank God.'

A sitting room had been cleared for a reception and a large iced cake stood in one corner on a gold disc: the lettering said 'RUBY – A FINE CENTURY!'. There was a single bottle of champagne standing in a dry ice bucket.

French doors led out on to a terrace, slightly raised above a green lawn as unblemished as a

28

snooker table. Shaw noted half-a-dozen discarded cigarette ends by a stone seat and an empty wine glass on a white-painted iron table. Several wicker reclining chairs stood on the stone patio, plus a large telescope with a tarpaulin cover and a fire pit full of damp ashes.

Dense sea mist lay over Brancaster Marsh, an expanse of reed infiltrated by channels which formed the watery maze between the house and the beach. On the map Shaw always thought the marsh looked like a cross section of the human brain. Into this wilderness ran a path of beaten bark between wooden boundary boards.

'Someone pushed her wheelchair down this path,' said Fortis, shivering now, without a coat, as the mist caressed her shoulders. 'Ruby was still active and she could get around the house on the ground floor, on the lino and the parquet – but there's no way she had the strength in her arms to use the path alone. Absolutely no way.'

She led the way into the mist for two hundred yards, each hand clutching opposite elbows. Ahead they could hear the open sea, still building towards high tide. The air was freighted with ozone, the scent of white water. The marsh channels were brim full, trickling and sighing, as the sea edged its way into pool after pool, with a gently rhythmic surge, as if the ocean had a pulse of its own. The path took an artistic, looping curve, then a double twist before decanting into a circular area marked by a set of three iron benches. Another telescope stood here, mounted on a concrete base.

'Residents come here for the view,' offered Fortis.

Valentine used his hand to wipe away a sheen of water droplets from his face. The damp seemed to reach down his throat and into his lungs, prompting a rib-wracking cough.

The viewing circle was slightly elevated above the marsh ahead, enough, in this flat world, to allow them to see over the blanket of mist, which hugged the earth. Ahead, like the distant rounded peaks of some fabulous mountain range, a line of humped-back dunes floated on a skein of fog. Also poking through stood a line of rotting wooden mooring posts, marking the passage of the main channel.

A sea breeze stirred and the pale disc of the sun broke through, lending a pink tint to this white world.

They could see Ruby Bright's head and upper body about thirty yards ahead: a visual shock because Shaw, unforgivably, had presumed she'd drowned. He'd braced himself to find her corpse curled in a tidal pool, a nightdress tugging with the current. Or lying in a black muddy creek, the body half-submerged. But there she was, still in her wheelchair – the high metal back visible and catching the light – her back to the house, looking out to sea. The lower curve of the wheels and her body were lost in the mist. Beside her stood a partly disembodied police constable, visible above the belt, also looking seawards, the sudden glow of a mobile phone in his hand as if he was checking for a signal. The scene was oddly theatrical, as if the curtain had just gone up on an outdoor stage. The sun, brightening, began to burn off the mist as they watched, revealing with each passing second more of the chair, which was set slightly at an angle, so that Ruby's head too was tilted to the right, like Christ's on the cross. Wisps of shredded mist rose up, twisting in the sunlight.

The constable must have heard a noise because he turned, saw them watching, and began to pick his way back through the grass. They waited, and he didn't hurry, which was impressive in itself. No more than twenty-five, his movements were nonetheless deliberate, measured, as if he moved underwater.

'Sir. PC Curtis. I can give you what I've got, but frankly, I'd recommend you take a look first.'

Shaw led the way, the view widening, the sea filling more and more of the way ahead as the channel widened and the sun shone, until the thought surfaced that if he had to pick a place to die this might be a contender. It was an aspect of the coast, of this edge of England, that he'd never confronted before, that it might delineate the border between life and death. Some half remembered tale of mythology came to mind, of a boat being rowed away, carrying the dead to hell, or heaven.

Ten feet short he stopped to consider the victim from behind: the head tilted at perhaps ten degrees from the vertical, arms tied behind the back of the wheelchair with what looked like a dressing gown cord, knotted round the wrists. A baby-blue housecoat showed at her neck and there was a glimpse of a naked foot to the left.

One hand showed a wedding ring, a gold charm bracelet and a bright pink charity band; and, vividly, in the loose skin below the elbow the little purple bruises of a series of injections. She might have been asleep, dreaming of her party cake, but for the ugly angle of the dangling foot. Her hair – fashioned into a tight helmet of crimped grey – seemed to glisten, reflecting the sky and the dancing sunlight, as if she might be wearing a shower cap.

Taking three steps past her, Shaw stopped and turned on his heel. Valentine held back, with PC Curtis. In the far distance Shaw could see Fortis, looking east towards Wells, as if she couldn't bear to watch the moment.

Ruby Bright had most certainly been murdered. Her head was completely covered with a plastic bag, bunched below her right ear. The bag's open edge was arterial red – zippered, like a freezer bag. Shaw was vividly reminded of a painting, not a subtle north Norfolk watercolour but Edvard Munch's *The Scream*; except that this tortured face was embellished with a pair of large, rather stylish glasses, the lenses still misted with what must have been Ruby Bright's last breath.

Four

PPC Jan Clay clung to the safety rail on the cherry picker as it rose in a series of heart-stopping judders towards the high telegraph wire.

She'd been nominated for this role because, stupidly, she'd revealed a lingering anxiety over heights. As an aspect of the police force, this constant, laddish humour was beginning to wear her down. Not that she couldn't cope; she'd been a policeman's wife for twenty-one years, and played that secondary, supporting role, with aplomb. The police force was institutionally sexist, but she'd always seen that vice as a reflection of wider society. It wasn't an excuse, but it was an explanation. Faced with prejudice, she'd fight back, but she was no whistle-blowing mole. Instead she'd developed a memory capable of coolly filing away slights and – especially – the patronizing tone of the middle-aged man. When the time came, she'd be happy to take a timely revenge. She was slightly disappointed, however, to find that DS Chalker, in charge of the shoe squad, was her principal protagonist.

'Come on now, PPC Clay. Let's see a smile on that pretty face.'

Chalker, thirty feet below her, beamed.

The hoist engine whirred, operated by a council workman in a Day-Glo jacket, who seemed to find the sight of an airborne woman police officer fabulously amusing.

Jan was in the narrow, enclosed 'basket' of the cherry picker. So far that morning the shoe quad had retrieved six pairs of shoes/trainers/boots from various locations across the North End, the network of terraced streets once home to the town's fishing community, including the dock road leading down to the Fisher Fleet. None of the trainers were actually shop new, but several

33

were high quality designer shoes which *could* have been resold, or passed on to new owners. There was one pair of boots, Army issue, according to PC Goldsmith, who was in the Territorials. All had been expertly lobbed over so-called telegraph wires, mostly phone company cables, and a few power lines. So far they didn't have a single witness to the actual act itself, what DS Chalker, who had a way with words, referred to as 'galosha tossing', but which Jan knew the kids called 'flying kicks'. The town had a network of CCTV cameras, but so far the budget allocated to the shoe squad did not stretch to having the tapes retrieved, or an officer detached to watch several hundred hours of tedious, indistinct footage.

This particular pair of trainers, now six feet from Jan's grasp, had not been on their original list, but their location had been phoned in by a squad car. This pair was unique; in that the shoes weren't hanging from telegraph wires, but from a power line slung through a road tunnel, which had once lit a series of overhead lights. The 'tunnel' itself ran under a railway bridge, was no longer than fifty yards, and was now largely disused, as it had been dug through a high embankment to provide access to Parkwood Springs – a Victorian suburb, now in various stages of dereliction. A skip, full of building waste, stood to one side in the shadows.

Jan's grandmother, Iris, had been born and raised on what everyone called the Springs. An old manor house had once stood on the site, she'd told Jan many times, but all that was left was an old iron water-pump, the origin of the name. The old estate had found itself cut off from the town by the railway, the new Alexandra Dock and the muddy silted creek of the Crab Fleet. A Victorian speculator called Lister bought the land for thirty shillings (Iris' version stipulated the precise amount, which Jan suspected was a fiction, designed to equate the hated entrepreneur with Judas Iscariot). Issuing shares in a private company, he raised the capital needed to tunnel through the great embankment and liberate the lucrative real estate beyond. A picture of the work in progress had hung in Iris' front room: a wooden cradle holding up the earthern roof and track as half-naked Irish navies toiled below with picks. Once Lister had his access he applied for planning permission to build houses, complete with two corner pubs, two corner shops and other amenities. In an act of public charity he allocated one plot for a Methodist chapel, a gesture which earned him an alderman's seat. Complete, the Springs was a miniature walled city state: with one way in and one way out through its single gate, the Lister Tunnel.

For a while, as Iris grew up, got married, rented a house on the Springs and raised a family of her own, the neighbourhood thrived; the nearby docks providing enough jobs to pay the rents, which were set just below the level of those in the rest of town. The tunnel-back houses, fetid in summer, churned coal-smoke into the sky in winter in a doomed attempt to eradicate the damp. But the community had been close, safe and self-contained. Jan recalled the rent book in Iris' kitchen: tea-stained, dog-eared, set always on the sideboard, held down by a glass paperweight, which kicked up a snow storm around a miniature church if you turned it upside down.

As Jan grew up the Springs began its long decline; first the docks closed, then the bus company's new double-decker buses couldn't fit under the Lister Tunnel. Finally, a run of dry summers dried out the marshy ground, so that large cracks began to appear in the red brick houses. By the time Iris died – at home, in the front bedroom – the Springs was a slum, the pubs closed, the shops boarded up.

The council, according to the local paper, was considering blocking Lister Tunnel, while they vetted various plans put forward by developers keen to emulate Lister's original, lucrative coup. Top of the list was a new 'out-of-town' Tesco, with an ice rink offered as planning gain.

As soon as she'd seen the hanging trainers in the gloom of the Lister Tunnel, a strange image had come back to Jan. Back in the first year of her marriage to Paul Clay they'd gone away for a weekend break in York, cashing in on a deal at the Marriott, leaving the car at home. She'd bought a guide book and recalled standing under one of the city gates – Micklegate Bar – and reading how the heads of traitors had been spiked over the portcullis. It had been dusk, orange street lights casting a lurid light, and she'd imagined walking under and feeling the gentle splash of dripping blood from above. Paul had said that was the difference between then and now, that in the past they'd lived in daily sight of death, a condition as real as life.

White-knuckled now, Jan held on to the cherry picker basket as it edged towards the old power cable, black with soot, and grease and what looked like rotting pigeon droppings. The Victorians seemed to be synonymous with the concept of grime. The air itself seemed heavy with soot, nearly half a century after the steam trains had run their last services in and out of Lynn.

She was close enough to see the brand name on the trainers: a Guggenheim '87 – whatever that meant: Guggenheim '87 *Sportfire*. The laces had been tied together and the weight of the two shoes had twirled them into a single strand. The trainers were decorated with random red flashes of colour and a silver panel on the sides, with 3D hologram lettering. They didn't look worn out, or even worn at all. Most trainers collapse slightly to fit the foot that wears them, these looked stiff, even shop-new.

The council operator must have pulled the wrong lever because the basket suddenly dropped six feet. Jan's stomach did a flip but she managed not to scream, although her audience below, the six other members of the shoe squad, whistled and clapped. A group of local children had already gathered and were catcalling, telling Jan to hold on tight.

Jan, looking down, noted, as did none of the rest of the so-called shoe squad, that these local kids wore trainers of nothing like the quality of the pair she was trying to retrieve; just battered Slazengers, old Nike and gym shoes.

At the second attempt the operator got her within three feet of her prize, so she had to let go of the basket rail to try and untangle the laces, which meant she wasn't looking at the shoes until they were jiggling in front of her eyes. It wasn't what she saw, it was what she smelt, that made her stop. She'd expected a kind of changing-room sweatiness, but this was earthier – with a hint of iron and seaweed. Then she saw that the chaotic red flash design wasn't chaotic at all, but consisted of stripes and that the other red marks, little fireworks of crimson, weren't random either, they formed a very particular pattern, one she recognized from her forensic science block course as spatter marks. So it was the smell of blood and maybe urine and – her heartbeat was running hard now – fear; although she realized that she might be the source of that.

One shoe had held a lot of blood. It was pooled inside at the heel. One of the laces was smeared pink too.

From her breast pocket she extracted her smartphone and took a picture, using her thumb to add the caption: PARKWOOD SPRINGS, then turned it into a text message and sent it to Valentine's phone.

Then she took a pair of forensic gloves from her belt bag and three evidence bags.

The chorus below booed enthusiastically.

'No, no, no – Christ – Clay. This is the shoe squad not CSI fucking King's Lynn. You bag them the paperwork's all yours, darling . . .' DS Chalker advanced on the cherry picker. 'D'you hear me? I'm not effing doing it.'

38

'Second, Sarge,' she said, keeping her voice light.

She swiftly got the bloody shoe into an evidence bag and then, with a gloved hand, used it as the stationary point around which she could unwind the other. When the second was free, she lightly tossed it in with its partner, encompassing the laces.

For a moment she stood still trying to think of anything she might have missed. Dimly, distantly, she could hear Chalker's voice and the laughter of the kids, who'd started to jeer. She felt the cherry picker engine beginning to change gear, ready to pull away, and in the moment before it began to retract she took a piece of chalk from her pocket and left a dash of white calcium where the laces had looped the power line: adding a quickly scrawled JC on the brickwork above.

Five

The press had arrived at Marsh House, not because Ruby Bright had been murdered, but to cover her one-hundredth birthday; just a reporter and a photographer from the *Lynn Express*, with a bunch of flowers, which Shaw thought was a nice touch. The residents, not including those suffering from dementia and confined to the upper floor secure unit, were gathered in the breakfast room. Shaw glimpsed them through the glass doors and could tell that despite the absence of any official announcement they seemed acutely aware of events: three elderly women stood at the window looking out over the marsh to where a white scene-of-crime tent now stood over Ruby's wheelchair. Two men sat at a chessboard, but none of the pieces had made a move. A flat-screen TV set in one corner showed *Breakfast Time*, volume down, but nobody watched. Outside the sun, its attendant mist burnt away, blazed down on a wide panorama of marsh, beach and sea, the SOCO tent like a sugar cube dropped by a giant.

Shaw and Valentine, in forensic boots and gloves, edged into Ruby Bright's room, No. 4, on the ground floor, its two windows facing seawards. In delicate silence, like a pair of deep-sea divers, they seemed to struggle through the thick air, examining only with their eyes, sweeping the surface of things for each telling detail. Jack Shaw, Shaw's father, had always told him that the secret to conducting an efficient murder inquiry was to imprint the scene of crime on the mind's retina, so that it was as familiar as a family snapshot. In Ruby Bright's case this was not difficult; her face, distorted into its Munch-like scream, was indelible. Despite himself, Shaw had stepped over the threshold of Marsh House with a set of preconceptions, expecting – at worst – an insipid, half-hearted death; a feeble capitulation, perhaps, to a more vigorous assailant. But the frozen scream told a very different story.

So he'd have no problem conjuring up that scene in detail. But the wider picture – the care home and the marshes – presented a greater challenge. They'd decided to start with the victim's room, her only personal space, in the hope it would yield instant results. All murder inquiries were overshadowed by a ticking clock. The chances of finding the killer were falling by the minute. Shaw tried to breathe in the room, to inhale its precise coordinates; its aromas, colours, shadows.

He'd always been fascinated by lives led in single rooms, packed into a limited space, like the contents of a trunk for a trans-Atlantic voyage. During his time on the Met two men had been found stabbed to death in one-room flats in Hammersmith. Shaw's degree had been in art at Southampton University, including a year out at the FBI college at Quantico. He'd come back with a diploma in forensic art; able to produce facial reconstructions from bones, build ID pictures from witness statements, age the faces of missing persons, or produce 'lifelike' wanted posters from the morgue. He was one of less than fifty officers in the UK with the qualification. The murder squad had called him in to try and create a 3D artist's impression of the killer by interviewing two men who'd survived similar attacks and seen their assailant. Dubbed the 'Bedsit Killer', the press were eager to print Shaw's portrait. Shaw decided to interview the witnesses in situ, in the rooms where the would-be killer had struck. His FBI training had taught him techniques to extract memories, to tease out details, eking out half-remembered fragments. The key was that memory could be accessed gradually, it wasn't a binary substance – either present or absent. One small detail could lead to the next.

Those who live in houses, where rooms are stacked in layers, with attics, glory holes, cellars, can hide facets of their personalities in different parts of the building. So much can be concealed, whereas a single room reveals the gritty details of everyday existence: an ashtray by the pillow, a plate smeared with ketchup on a bookcase, a discarded dirty sock, the shredded utility bill. Shaw's forensic eye had noted something SOCO had missed in those two bedsits; both survivors took prescribed medication, one had a pillbox by the bed, the other on top of a cabinet in the loo. Shaw backed a hunch, took a note, traced both prescriptions to the same chemist in Ravenscourt Park. When he'd turned up with a uniformed constable and one of the DSs on the murder squad, they'd found a corner shop, a young Asian woman behind the counter and a small 'serving hatch' into the chemists' dispensing room in the back. The face looking out at them through the hatch was identical to Shaw's 3D sketch of the killer. While he'd never stood trial due to mental illness, the chemist did tell the murder squad he'd chosen his victims because they'd 'leered' at the Asian girl, to whom he felt protective. The addresses of all four victims were on the pharmacy's digital records.

Ruby Bright's room was no threadbare bedsit, but it held the same sense of a life condensed.

A few charred logs lay in a stylish fireplace, behind a mesh guard, while a rocking chair had been set very close, a large-print novel on the seat: *Slaughterhouse 5*. The mantelpiece carried a series of framed photographs; Shaw recognized the victim's glasses, rather than her face. In each of the five pictures she was with the same companion; a woman her junior by possibly ten years or more, taller, almost stately, with a ramrod back. In one, an artful composition, they reclined on a terrace overlooking a Tuscan landscape: stone pines, a distant villa, a wedge of sea between hills. Shaw noted their hands entwined – double-clasped, in an almost fierce grasp.

The room also held a desk, clean-lined in a business-like pine. He left Valentine to sort the drawers and moved off to check the en suite bathroom which, by contrast, could have doubled up for any in a four-star hotel, as anonymous as an airport departure lounge. It wasn't clean, it was antiseptic, the clinical ambiance rammed home by the Greek-white walls. The shower room had an entrance wide enough for a wheelchair. It was a mark of the dehumanization of the room's scrubbed efficiency that the only object which Shaw felt was personal was the victim's toothbrush, its slightly crushed bristles reminding him that he was dealing with the brutal murder of a frail human being.

Back in the bedroom, Valentine had begun to bag relevant documents: a solicitor's letter, a cheque book, some handwritten letters in a pale blue ink signed simply 'Beatty', a photograph album, various files marked with the date by year – the oldest 1993, all containing correspondence, insurance claims, AA membership.

'I'll try the lawyer – see if we can cut to the

chase . . .' said Valentine. Taking out his phone, he saw Jan's text and brought up the picture, the bloodstained trainers and the caption PARKWOOD SPRINGS. He gave that five seconds of thought and then rang Ruby Bright's solicitor: engaged, a smooth female voice requested he leave a message, which he did.

Shaw considered the artwork on the walls: four canvasses, oils, in frames of pine, all hung on the unpapered white, south-facing wall. Picture frames leave a mark where they've protected the paint, or plaster, from sunlight. One of the four pictures was smaller than the mark on the wall, which extended both to the left and right beyond the frame. With gloved hands Shaw checked behind the other three frames, all were mismatched with their 'shadows'. The pictures were, on close inspection, photographs of originals: high-quality, digital images. He didn't recognize the painter, but he could guess the movement – the Norwich School, the Victorians inspired by the Dutch to capture the light and space of the East Anglian landscape. In the corner of one of the canvasses, an evening study of moonlight on a beach, a postcard had been wedged into the narrow gap afforded by the frame, a National Portrait Gallery postcard. Shaw gently eased it free, studied the face portrayed, and then flipped it over, to read a legend on the reverse: *Henry Bright: 1810-1873. Self-portrait.*

'Which means?' asked Valentine, breaking the silence.

'Who knows, but at least it's a personal touch.

I think these are hers, the pictures, she's had them copied. The originals are probably in Norwich Castle with the rest of the school. Shows, perhaps, an interest in landscape, light, water, sky. A famous ancestor perhaps? A fellow Bright?'

The image came again unbidden; the wheelchair on the edge of the marsh, the view ahead of the sea, the misted freezer-bag scrunched tight below the ear.

Shaw turned the picture frame over and noted a small gold sticker marked Phoenix – with the motif of the mythical creature rising from the flames. The framer, perhaps? There was a telephone number and website address.

'We know there's money,' said Valentine. 'Fortis gave me a brochure,' he added, waving a glossy pamphlet. 'This place charges a basic fee of £1,200 a week. *A week*, Peter. If there's money on that scale, there's a will. If she's dead there are beneficiaries. I'll make a start once I've got through to the solicitor.'

Technically, Ruby's body probably still retained traces of its original heat, and yet here was DS Valentine constructing motives, preparing to close in on possible suspects. It was the way he worked, the way Jack Shaw had operated too, fitting suspects to the scene, not vice versa. It was a modus operandi which deeply troubled Shaw. The great miscarriages of justice could all be traced back to this one, intensely human, vice; the need to find a pattern before the picture was complete, an inability to live with chaos.

'Why don't we collect some facts first, George, before we name the killer. You'll have him, or

45

her, swinging on a rope before the victim's in the ground.'

Valentine wordlessly continued to search the bedside table, a chest of drawers, a fitted cupboard.

Shaw perched on the windowsill and summarized what they had discovered so far from Fortis and her staff.

In two hours they'd assembled a bare framework of verifiable facts. They'd worked as a team for five years and this had become a key part of their modus operandi – they'd take it in turns to *vocalize*, to say out loud what they knew, what they didn't know.

'First – the victim,' said Shaw.

Ruby Rose Bright had outlived her relatives, a husband, son and daughter, and received no regular visitors. Her next of kin was listed as a great nephew resident in Belfast, from whom Ruby received a telephone call on Christmas Day and a birthday card. She had twenty-seven cards waiting to be opened beside her cake, the vast majority from staff and residents. One had a stamp, postmarked Northern Ireland. Her medical file listed eleven daily medications, for a range of conditions from diabetes to shingles. None of her ailments were life-threatening.

'Second,' said Shaw, 'Ruby's last twelve hours alive.'

She'd had dinner in her room last night at six thirty: chicken chasseur, pilau rice and fine beans, followed by apple crumble with single cream. She'd then been wheeled out on to the terrace by one of the nurses to join other residents. Fruit

46

juice and wine were served, with cheese. All residents were back in their rooms by eight.

'Third – security.'

Ruby's suite had one exit door, which was never locked. The first (upper) floor of Marsh House was restricted to patients suffering from dementia or Alzheimer's and was entirely secure: one locked stairwell provided access, with double doors, both with keypads. Two fire escape doors were opened by special keys kept by the resident nursing staff, one of whom was on duty 24/7. The ground floor was less restrictive, but all exits were keypad controlled. The residents did not have the code.

CCTV cameras were mounted over each outside door. They operated overnight from eight till six and the recordings were kept for thirty days, in line with Whitehall guidance. During the day they could be activated from the nurses' station, but were generally shut down in the interests of patient privacy. Marsh House boasted a high nurse–resident ratio. The CCTV was a security system, not a replacement for personal care.

DC Mark Birley, one of Shaw's team, was an expert in CCTV evidence and was already on his way to the site. A picture, however murky or blurred, was their best hope of putting together a description of Ruby Bright's killer – or killers.

Given that the human body's ability to sleep through the night declines with age, Shaw felt that the freedom to wander at night would be a *necessity* of old age. The residents of Marsh House paid the fees, why did they want to be locked in? If Shaw had the money to pay £1,200 a week he'd have found a way to get the keypad code and bribed the night nurse to look the other way. It was possible staff – and patients – came and went; but impossible that they did so unrecorded on the CCTV film.

Valentine knelt beside the desk. There was a blotter and a small pile of A4 paper with the Marsh House heading and a pencil, laid neatly – almost mathematically – at ninety degrees to the blotter, alongside a blue biro. The DS held the biro up to the light. 'No top,' he said. They both examined the carpet around their shoes, but there was no sign of the missing blue cap. On a small 'bureau' style shelf there were envelopes, stamps, a few postcards unused – each one identical, showing the self-portrait of Henry Bright.

On stiff knees, Valentine tried to get low enough to see if the thin light revealed any marks on the blotter. 'I'll get SOCO to bag the lot once they're on site,' he said.

Shaw continued with a summary of what they knew, this time – the discovery of the victim's body.

Overnight there was one nurse on duty, while two others slept in the resident staff wing, which was over a pair of twin garages, separated from the main building by an open-air passage. The night nurse was Xavier 'Javi' Copon, a twenty-eight-year-old Spaniard. He had been relieved at the nurses' station at 6.15 a.m. by Senior Nurse Kay Richmond.

Catering staff had begun arriving at 6.20 a.m., and one of them – Gill Butcher – had taken a tray of tea to Bright's room at 6.40 a.m. Her bed was empty and, indeed, still made-up, complete with crisp hospital corners. Richmond organized a search of Marsh House's public rooms, and then asked Gill and two of the kitchen staff, to check the grounds. They spotted Ruby's distant wheelchair at 6.55 a.m. The police – in the form of PC Curtis – arrived at 7.20 a.m. from Hunstanton.

Tom Hadden, head of forensic services, appeared in the doorway. Energized, flushed, his green eyes catching the light, Hadden was as motivated by murder as the detectives themselves. A former Home Office adviser, who'd taken early retirement and fled a messy divorce for the north Norfolk coast, Hadden brought a first-class intelligence to the application of science. The thin sunlight made him look pale, receding red hair little more than an amber stubble. Several skin cancer lesions had been removed from his face, giving it a pitted, rugged look.

'Peter, George. Victim's room?'

He took a step over the threshold. 'Justina's with the body now,' he said. Dr Justina Kazimeirz was the force pathologist.

'But some things are clear, if not set in stone,' said Hadden. 'Someone put a freezer zip-bag over her head and held it twisted at her collarbone until she was dead.'

He held a hand to his own head above the left ear.

'Her hands were tied, a slip knot. She's used one foot to try and spin the chair round during the attack. Time of death? Tricky. The outside temperature was fairly chilly last night – so let's

49

say eight in the evening until two this morning. Justina may narrow that down, but it's a six-hour window, so think yourselves lucky. As I say, we'll know when she's back at the Ark.'

The Ark was West Norfolk's forensic laboratory, built inside an old Methodist chapel, next to police headquarters on St James' in the centre of Lynn.

'One detail: her hands are clean, so that supports the theory she was pushed out there. The bark pathway picks up peat and grass, and she'd have soiled her palms if she'd propelled herself forward. Two nails broken, but still clean.'

He was about to go but turned back, eyes closed, a mannerism which indicated he wanted to say something that might be important. 'Justina wanted you to know that she put up a fight. Her words. Like in the poem: *Do not go gentle into that long good night*. Certainly nothing gentle about this. A fighter, our Ruby, despite her age.'

Shaw went with Hadden to examine the outside doors, leaving Valentine to finish in Ruby Bright's room.

Shaw had left one of the watercolours against the wall and as Valentine lifted it back on to the hook he saw that an envelope had been taped to the back with two neat strips of sticky tape. Sitting on Ruby's high, counter-paned bed he held the painting on his knees and extracted from the envelope a single sheet of paper. The slightly waxy paper allowed him to guess what it was before he had it open: a death certificate, dated eighteen months previously. The name, Beatrice Hood, meant nothing. She'd been eighty-seven

50

years old and the primary cause of death was stated badly as 'old age', while the contributing factors were obscured by the peculiar tortured Latin of the medical profession. But the address listed under 'place of death' was plain enough, and the coincidence made his skin creep – because coincidence was, as Jan often told him, God's way of remaining anonymous.

32 Hartington Street, Parkwood Springs.

Six

The Porsche, touching ninety miles per hour, breasted a hill and Shaw enjoyed the fleeting sense of weightlessness. In his rear-view mirror he could see the sunlit sea, while ahead the low hills were shrouded in threatening black clouds, boiling up as the summer heat rose. For a mile the road ran parallel with the narrow-gauge railway, and he drew level with a train, a line of wooden open carriages, mostly empty at this early hour, the small, gleaming engine ahead, emitting white puffs of toy-town smoke. Drawing ahead effortlessly he found the scene oddly comic, as if he'd been transposed into a black-and-white thriller of the silent movie era, racing for the spot where the heroine lay tied between the rails.

On the passenger seat his mobile still held the chief constable's latest text: *Shaw. Keep me posted on Walsingham op. I'm at Home Office overnight.*

51

Shaw, whose temper was rarely, if ever, sighted, slammed the palm of his hand against the Porsche's thin, leather-bound, steering wheel.

For the next hour the murder inquiry would have to do without him. Walsingham was Joyce's priority, not the brutal murder of a frail, elderly woman. He'd despatched Valentine back to St James' to organize the murder team, and to ensure that he was on hand for his appointment with Dr Scrutton. The squad needed to find a relative of the dead woman and details of her last will and testament. Meanwhile DC Paul Twine – smart, graduate-entry, with an eye for meticulous detail – would stay at Marsh House to organize interviews and monitor forensics. The private trust which ran Marsh House had declined Shaw's request for access to the staff records on the grounds of data protection, and the application for a warrant from a magistrate would take at least an hour, if not more.

Uniformed branch had been drafted in to track down Javi Copon, the Marsh House night nurse, and deliver him for interview to St James'. The West Norfolk Constabulary's records office was tasked with finding documentation on Beatrice Hood, the woman whose seemingly innocuous death certificate had been discovered sticky-taped to the back of one of Ruby Bright's luminous Norfolk landscapes. The coroner's officer had agreed to check the files to see if Hood's body had undergone an autopsy.

The tourist train was now in the far distance behind him and he had to slow as he slipped through the sleepy outskirts of Walsingham, dipping down into the town – in effect a large village – with the narrow leaded spire of the church ahead, along with the neo-Byzantine campanile of the thirties' shrine. The summer storm was close to breaking, the light inky and damp beneath gunmetal clouds.

The Friday Market, the Georgian square at the heart of the village, would be crammed with trippers and pilgrims for the festival of the Virgin Mary and the arrival of the pilgrims, but this morning it lay deserted but for a flock of seagulls. Shaw's appointment was with a representative of the Walsingham Alternative Pilgrimage (WAP) – an umbrella organization for left-wing protest groups from gay rights to A Woman's Right to Choose, determined to make their voice heard on the big day. They had offices on a boat in Wells harbour, but also a protest 'rainbow bus', which would be their HQ on the day the pilgrimage arrived.

WAP was just one of the reasons Joyce was so jittery about the pilgrimage, now only a few days from arriving in the town. The annual 'National' had its own tensions, which had grown over the years. A decade ago several hundred visiting Christian Tamils from London had made the journey north and ended up on the nearby beach at Wells, many worse for drink, prompting a 'riot' by brandishing ceremonial knives. A middle-class backlash had filled the local press with complaints of yobbish pilgrims urinating over garden fences.

The following year the police had stopped and searched pilgrims' cars, after being tipped off some were carrying guns. None were found.

53

Large numbers of Irish travellers had begun arriving for the event too, across-country from the ferry ports of Wales and Liverpool, adding to the inflammatory mix. The addition of WAP, keen to pick a theological punch-up, brandishing banners and eager to engage the pious in debate, had raised the temperature a little further. Most of the local publicans planned to shut up shop on the big day.

The jittery atmosphere had never engendered genuine violence, but the new chief constable felt the 'World' might just provide the spark necessary to light the powder keg. Most of the resident CID officers thought this view alarmist. The vast majority of annual pilgrims were very young, or very old, devout or peaceful. There was no real reason to think this pilgrimage would be any different, except for a sprinkling of foreign visitors, but Joyce was taking no chances. Pilgrims on foot were converging on Walsingham, not just with the main body, but along other, ancient routes. Their every footfall was being monitored at police headquarters.

The protestors' rainbow bus was difficult to miss, a seventies charabanc painted using the entire psychedelic spectrum, standing on an acre of tarmac otherwise deserted. By the time Shaw was out of the Porsche, a woman was climbing down the bus steps, clipboard in her hand.

'Nano Heaney,' she said, holding out a pale hand, a natural extension of a pale, slender arm. The name Nano, surely, an ironic nickname, must have had its origins in her height, which had to be six feet, possibly even an inch more. Her stature was the dominant feature of her outward appearance and surely stood in comic counterpoint to Nano, the Greek diminutive, the root of nanotechnology. The name suggested, Shaw thought, a classical education.

The neat, luminous face was perched on a particular body shape, which reminded Shaw of the classic Pierrot – the sad clown of the comedy theatre, the fool, with a tear perhaps marked on the cheek, dressed in white, with wide hips and silver, silk pantaloons. The effect was enforced by the loose white trousers, a baggy white T-shirt, both hung on a kite-shaped body: even the motif was in a shade of almost unreadable grey: *Sweet toleration*.

She held a West Norfolk Constabulary card between two fingers, flicking it deftly. 'DI Shaw? The radio said there's been a murder; I thought you'd be busy . . .'

'We've got more than one detective,' said Shaw.

Heaney's pale whiteness seemed to glow in the deepening gloom under the storm cloud. She looked like a daytime angel, fallen to earth. There was something about the make-up-free face, felt Shaw, which invited trust.

'I'm chair of WAP,' she said. 'The chief constable asked me to cooperate, which I'm happy to do. I understand you'd like to know our *plans*?' She smiled, suggesting any anxiety might be misplaced. 'I'm afraid they're modest and hardly command the attention of a DI . . .'

'This will be brief, Ms Heaney,' said Shaw. 'I think you've been liaising with uniformed branch, but I just wanted to get a quick overview. The chief constable is anxious to avoid flashpoints, if I can put it like that.'

'A tour d'horizon?' she asked, managing to imbue the phrase with the hint of an Irish accent. And again, an educated allusion. She swung her arm out over the view below, the little town a choppy seascape of rooftops.

'Precisely . . .' agreed Shaw, noting that this horizon, a black sinuous line of surrounding hills, was already blurred by falling rain.

A random hail stone fell between them, then twenty, then a hundred. The air filled with the alien aroma of ice and the sound of a million miniature percussions. The source of the falling hail, the blue-black cloud, slid away south, the sunlight flooding in behind, a rainbow vaulting the valley. But the hail still fell from a clear sky and another bank of clouds threatened.

Shaw expected Heaney to retreat to the bus, but instead she ran, dodging the icy pellets, over the old level crossing towards a clapboard building which looked as if it had once been the town's old mainline station. It was only as he ran up a set of entrance steps that he saw, improbably mounted on the roof, an onion-dome surmounted by a cross: no ordinary cross, but the triple-cross of Byzantium.

Inside, beyond a glass porch, the darkness was velvety and it took a moment for Shaw's eyes to pick out the gilt, glimmering in the light from a single, guttering candle. They were in a room divided by a wooden partition, decorated with a series of icons, Mary, Christ, various saints, all in the distinct style of the Orthodox Church.

Crosses, crowns and statues stood in niches. Beyond the partition a lead-grey candelabra hung in what must be the priest's vestibule, partly hidden by a decorated wooden double-door.

'Welcome to St Seraphim's,' said Heaney, shaking her head like a dog, so that melting hailstones flew out, catching the light. 'There's a lot of interest within the Orthodox churches in the shrine. I think the Russians have been here fifty years. Mind you, the priests are discreet. I hardly ever see them.'

'I'd have put you down as a lifetime atheist,' offered Shaw.

'The attraction's entirely aesthetic,' said Heaney. 'I've had enough of religion and I suspect the feeling's mutual. I was expelled by the Sisters of Mercy, Inspector, and that's an All-Ireland record.'

'And the crime?' asked Shaw.

She bit her lip. 'I stayed home, nursing my mother in her final illness. They said I should have been in school learning the pluperfect of *amo*, an irony which, believe me, totally escaped them. They said God would take care of Mother. I suppose he did, but not in the fashion I'd hoped. Still, that's all done now.'

Shaw, examining the little church in the half-light, found the icons strangely unsettling. Was it the foursquare penetrating eyes, seeking out the watchers' own? And what eyes; always lidded, full and hooded, as if searching for an image within as much as without.

'I have to visit Walsingham a lot,' said Heaney. 'There's an old people's home over the back of the new Catholic church and two more on the outskirts. Occasionally, I like to have a few minutes on my own. I can thank St Seraphim for that, if nothing else. Sorry, I didn't say. I'm in health care, just another bloody bureaucrat of course, based up at the Great Eastern.

'It's the oddest place, Walsingham. The shrine itself down in the town is a total horror, and the church isn't much better. I was brought up a Catholic, County Mayo, and even I think it's over the top. Talk about smoke and bells. Meanwhile, the Slipper Chapel, which is RC, feels like the C of E – so work that out. But St Seraphim's is rather wonderful by comparison.'

She reached out a hand and let her fingertips brush one of the icons, a small statuette of the Virgin. 'I can come here and just sit, and I don't get that claustrophobic feeling I do in the other churches, that someone's trying to sell me an idea. I had enough of that as a kid.'

She gave Shaw a mischievous smile. 'And, to be frank, the absence of priests and nuns or – God help us – monks, helps a lot.' The smile deepened and then saddened. 'Priests, Ireland's gift to England, just when you'd got rid of them.'

In his back pocket Shaw felt his mobile buzz.

A text from DC Twine: *Night nurse not known at address given.* Shaw considered the implications and a possible scenario for murder. The elderly often formed strong attachments to their carers. It was not unknown for wills to contain bequests. The will, if it existed, was the key.

'Look,' he said, meeting Heaney's eyes, 'we do need some rules. The National's big enough, this could be much bigger. The numbers are pretty much fiction at this stage but it might be six, seven thousand. We need to be vigilant. We can't have any surprises with those numbers of people in narrow lanes and streets. Any protest needs to be well controlled, and above all, static. How many will WAP bring, and where will you demonstrate?'

'This is for police use only, not the press?' asked Heaney.

Shaw nodded.

'Three hundred, that's our target, but I think we'll fall well short. Gay rights is strong, and there's a bus load coming from North London, but the rest is' – she broke something unseen with her narrow hands – 'fragmented. Pro-choice is committed, angry even, but I really don't think we're a threat to public order, Inspector, although that is not to say there are not strong feelings here. The Christian Right, up close, can be an infuriating theology.'

She took out a photocopied Ordnance Survey map and laid it out on a table which held a visitors book, and across which the candlelight fell. 'We'll be in town at dawn, or earlier,' she said. 'Our bus will be up here, where it is now. There'll be someone on board all day. That's the plan. The rest will go down to the war memorial at the top of the short hill from the shrine. I marked it all up on a map at one of the preliminary meetings. We'll be in position by ten. Shouting, chanting, a bit of dialogue with those who want to engage. That's the long and the short of it.'

'It's a long day,' said Shaw. 'People get hungry, thirsty.'

'The bus will be stocked up with food and drink. We're not going near the pubs.'

'Well, good news for my DS, at least. He's on duty and he can't stand a queue at the bar.'

The sound of hail on the roof seemed to change gear, becoming a thunderous percussion.

'That's our dispositions,' she said. 'Not exactly the February Revolution, is it? Or Bloody Sunday, St Petersburg or Derry for that matter.'

Shaw was glad the chief constable wasn't present for that particular allusion.

'Bloody Sunday, an uprising led, if I recall A-level history correctly, by a Russian Orthodox priest,' said Shaw.

Over their heads the hail suddenly fell silent and sunlight beamed through a rather grimy window into the priest's cubbyhole.

'I'd like a promise, Ms Heaney. Let's swap mobile numbers. If I ring on the day, please answer – OK? I'm happy to trust you, and your organization, but it only takes one individual to create a confrontation of a more physical nature. If you ring me I'll answer too. I'd like to be able to communicate quickly if there's a problem . . .' They handed each other their phones and keyed in the numbers: she entered hers under NANO, his went under SHAW.

She got up close to another icon, a saint, with dark hair and asymmetric eyes. 'They worship these, you know. This isn't just art. Windows on heaven. Portals on the divine. On heaven and hell.'

The image of Ruby Bright's scream suddenly pulsed in Shaw's mind. He tried to push it aside,

60

aware that considerations of heaven and hell had little part to play in a twenty-first-century murder inquiry.

'I need to get back to my team,' said Shaw.

By the door there was a full length, life-size image of St Seraphim himself, if Shaw was correctly transliterating the elegant Cyrillic script. He paused on the threshold, feeling the need to get close. Six inches away his good eye struggled to maintain focus, a few inches closer and he felt the surface of the picture buckle, and swim, as if it was a borderland, a thin film of paint and canvas, or a fragile lath of wood, beyond which lay the unknown, or at least the unknowable. Perhaps the power of these images lay in this sense that they were simply windows, flimsy barriers between the present and the past, the living and the dead.

Seven

As Javi Copon walked out of the sea, summoned by Shaw's loudhailer, the detective tallied up the value of his surfing gear: a £1,000 Megaseaweed winter wetsuit, a £500 Studer FlexTail surfboard, and a pair of £150 sand shoes – brand unknown, but they looked like top of the range Tribords. Not bad for a care home nurse.

Copon emerged from the waves reluctantly, as if the salty sea was his chosen element and that he resented this summons to return to the gravity

61

of the earth. Around him stretched Holkham beach, six straight miles of open sand, backed by pine woods, facing the North Sea. In high summer a crowd of several thousand could be entirely lost on this vast swathe of pristine beach. Shaw had been delighted after seeing *Shakespeare in Love* at the cinema in Lynn with Lena to discover, in the credits, that the final breathtaking vistas of Viola stepping ashore in the untouched New World of the seventeenth century had been filmed right here, a few miles along the coast from *Surf!*. (A still from the film was now framed over the bar.)

Copon began the long wade out of the shallows.

According to Fortis, the Marsh House administrator, Copon lived at Flat 18, Houghton House, South End, Lynn. Uniformed branch had checked the address out and found it occupied by an elderly couple who had been in residence for nearly thirteen years. They'd never heard of Javi Copon, but they did think immigrants were ruining the country, although Spaniards weren't as bad as Portuguese, or Romanians. DC Twine had asked around, finding Copon had several friends on the staff at Marsh House. One, a Spanish woman who made beds, had told them where to find him if the sea was running a swell.

If Shaw had been alone he'd have joined Copon in the sea rather than dragging him out on dry land. How many more days as good as this would there be before winter blew in from the pole? The offshore breeze was creating perfect waves in a moderate swell. Surfers called such waves A-Frame – ideal, high-backed, curling breakers, offering the expert the chance to stay up on his – or her – feet for several hundred yards.

Javi was compact, muscled, with a good set of surfer's teeth, which disappeared when Shaw flashed his warrant card and told him everything he needed to know about the death of Ruby Bright.

'Why the false address?' asked Shaw.

Javi worked a hand round his neck and slipped the zip on the wetsuit, shrugging himself out of the top half, so that it hung loose, making him look like a multi-legged pond-skater. Steam rose off his flesh, which was strangely pale, with black hair matted in swirls.

'You need an address to get the job. I make it up, they don't check. No one ever checks, right? Otherwise I never get work nowhere. I live here, in a camper van, and go up and down the coast. November I'll drive home. Three years now I come back to Marsh House. It's a lifestyle, the whole . . .' He waved his arms around to indicate some invisible over-arching structure. 'The whole corporate world, it can't handle people like me.'

He produced a small oilskin package from the suit pocket, within which was a crumpled pack of Gitanes and a lighter.

'Where's home?' asked Shaw.

'Zarautz,' he said, drawing in the nicotine.

Shaw knew of the town, a surfer's paradise on the north coast of Spain, once patronized by the royal families of Europe, keen to escape the searing heat of the south. Shaw suspected that

Copon was a middle-class boy, drawn to radical, anti-capitalist politics.

'I need to wash the suit down,' said Copon, and so they set off towards the woods, a path opening out, leading due south.

The Spaniard's VW Camper, no doubt parked illegally, was in a glade of ageing Scots pine. Copon introduced his girlfriend, Gail, who lay sunbathing on a towel, a paperback in the grass beside her.

Copon had rigged up an outside 'shower': a ten-gallon water container wedged between the branches of a pine, with the tap downwards. Letting the water gush out, he rinsed the salt off the suit.

Gail said she'd make tea although no one said they wanted a drink. Shaw, taking his chance, followed her up the steps and stood at the door of the camper van, so that he could see a double bed, crumpled and unmade. The rest of the interior looked like a surfhead's workshop: boards of various widths and lengths, wetsuits, waxes, beach shoes, a folded surf kite.

Most of the walls carried what looked like radical labour posters, stylized Stalinist images of men forging steel, or women tending the sick.

But one image stood out.

'Who's that?' he asked, indicating a poster of a man's face: salt-and-pepper stubble, the slightly bloated skin of someone immersed in water during daylight hours and cold, dead, jet-black eyes. He looked like the kind of surfer whose heartbeat could stay flat on a thirty-foot wall of water.

'That's the great hero,' said Gail in a mock whisper, the kettle already pinking on its gas ring. 'Garrett McNamara, rode a seventy-eight-foot wave. That's the world record. I know all the facts, like I have a choice.'

'Hawaii?' asked Shaw.

'Portugal, Hawaii's ankle-busters up against the Atlantic.'

'And the old man?' Shaw had spotted another portrait, this one was framed, but otherwise the grizzly, wrinkled skin of the subject staring out was oddly reminiscent of the wave-riding surfer king.

'That's my grandfather,' said Copon, climbing the steps, the wetsuit on a hanger. 'A fisherman at home, he died in his boat, I think his heart went. I was with him, pulling in the net. He folded up, was gone in a minute. A good death, I think. You?'

'Yes,' said Shaw. 'A good death, if he loved the sea.'

The woods echoed to the staccato rattle of a woodpecker.

'Let's talk in the sun,' said Shaw.

They waited while Copon stowed his gear and Gail ferried out mugs of tea.

'I'm sorry Ruby's dead,' he said, reappearing. 'I like her a lot.' His Spanish accent came and went like a radio signal. 'I saw nothing, for sure. Nothing in the night.'

Shaw thought about taking him back to St James' for a formal interview, in a cell, a world away from his vast, spectacular, comfort zone. But Twine had reported that Copon was well

65

known at Marsh House for a kindly, caring approach to his patients, and especially the aged Ruby Bright. Shaw wanted him to talk freely, because he might know a lot, and he judged there was no better place for that than here, in the dappled woods, within earshot of the sea.

'How did she get out of Marsh House, Mr Copon? How did her killer get in? This doesn't make sense. The killer would have to get in through the keypad door. She'd have to get out through a keypad door. The nurses' station is on the ground floor, and you heard nothing? Saw nothing? There's a bank of six CCTV screens. It's your job to keep watch, yes? You were on shift from eight – when everyone went back to their rooms – until 6.15 a.m. And you saw nothing – really?'

Copon licked salt from his lips and tossed the damp towel to Gail. He had a curious face, with wide brown eyes, high cheekbones and black hair; but the components were undermined by a sickly complexion, the skin blotched and without surface tension. Shaw had seen this before, the way constant immersion in the sea undermined the surfer's image: tanned, blond, toned. Most of the real fanatics looked like something goggle-eyed on a fishmonger's counter.

'Look. I not tell you this. The keypad code is 1818, since the day I come, my first season. If the residents have this' – he tapped a forefinger just below his right eye – 'they know this too. 1818. Now you know. How do you say? Join the club. So it's easy to come and go. But I make rounds, on the hour, and see nothing. I don't

66

check, I don't open doors, unless someone rings a bell, or I hear something.'

'It's part of your job to monitor the CCTV?' asked Shaw.

'I make rounds. I don't watch TVs. It will be on the record, yes. But I don't see.' He licked his lips, tasting salt. 'You look at film?'

'We're doing that now. But it's several hours and there's six cameras,' said Shaw.

'Last night busy too,' said Copon. 'The medical log will have this in the writing, yes? I go up to the secure wing to help patient there, Mrs Blanchard, she needs regular medication, every four hours. And Mr Eyres, he thinks I am room service. Ring for this. Ring for that. Really, he wants to talk, about diamonds and gold and silver, because he was a jeweller, and he wants to think about anything he can that isn't what the doctors say: that he will be dead this year. I'm a nurse. So I listen. It's better than the pills. I don't see Ruby, not once, although she is a friend.'

He actually placed a hand over his heart, on his bare chest; a gesture so theatrical that Shaw felt, intuitively, that it must be genuine. Copon shook his head to dislodge sea water from his hair, the movement of the neat skull on the muscular shoulders fluid and easy and strangely reminiscent of Nano Heaney's attempts to dislodge Walsingham's hailstones.

'There are pictures in her room of Ruby with a woman, the staff told us she was an old friend, but they didn't know her name. They seem close, was she a relative, a sister?'

Copon took his time answering, blowing on his

67

tea. Somewhere overhead a paraglider flew past, the material of the great single wing crackling.

'She was yes, she died, a year ago,' said Javi. 'Beatrice. Beatty Hood.'

Shaw kept a poker face: Beatrice Hood was the woman whose death certificate they'd found Sellotaped to the back of one of Ruby Bright's paintings.

'Great woman,' said Copon, the jaw hardening as if to emphasize the weight of the word *great*. 'You know, dying I see very often. Often, almost always, it is not like that . . .' He clicked his fingers. 'An event. No, a process, yes? And sometimes this process begins when people fall alone. A husband dies, a wife dies. The downward path begins. Then – sometimes – they find someone else. Ruby, she has Beatty. Not a resident, no. But for many years a friend. They share this passion for art, for paintings. They cling together. Very close. Lost souls . . .'

Gail, who'd sat down on her towel, hugged her knees.

'They make death wait these two. They want to live, this I'm sure is the secret; they want to live to spend more time with each other. They love life together . . .'

He held out a hand and, as if by telepathy, Gail rummaged in a large leather handbag and gave him a smartphone. Scrolling into a photo album, he showed them a shot of Bright in a wheelchair on the front at Hunstanton, pointing out to sea, where a line of breakers was dotted with wetsuited surfers.

Copon pressed a button and the picture became

68

a video, revealing Bright's animated face, a wide – genuine – grin, which crumpled into a laugh. The wind, blustery, wrapped a scarf around her neck and blew her hair into a wind-sock, but she looked delighted just to be outside. The contrast with Shaw's only previous image of this woman was shocking.

'Mr Copon,' said Shaw, handing the phone back to Gail, 'can you think of any reason why Ruby would have ordered, and kept hidden, a copy of Beatty Hood's death certificate?'

Copon massaged his left shoulder and Shaw thought he detected a minute hesitation, a half-second break in the smooth manipulation of the pectoralis major, the thumb pressed into the flesh.

'Death certificate? Where?'

'I'm asking the questions, Mr Copon. Is there any reason why she'd have her friend's death certificate. She died last year. Any idea?'

Copon looked at Gail. 'No. Beatty died at home, I think, in her bed. A house in Lynn. She was a good age too, mid-eighties, maybe more. I don't understand.'

'Can you think of anyone who might have wanted Ruby Bright dead, Mr Copon?'

'She had no enemies,' said Copon. 'Very popular. Full of life, still.'

'We'll need a statement,' said Shaw, looking back down the track towards the sea. The rhythmic fall of the breakers was clearer now, the percussion just discernible through the sand.

Copon caught Shaw's eye. 'If the tide is right, and the waves, I swim, surf. Always. One day I will be too old. Or death will come early. I know this. One day I will be gone. So I take each day's waves as they break. The sea is god – yes?'

Eight

Pushing out through the revolving doors of the West End Community Health Centre, Dr Gokak Roy felt an immediate sense of relief: the night air was cool, the car park deserted, while behind him lay a pressure-cooker of stress and responsibility. At one point in the shift he'd had to immunize a four-month-old child; inserting the needle into the vein had required a clinical magnifier and the steadiest of hands, the wrist was less than thirty centimeters in circumference, the vein as narrow as a fibre-optic cable. The child – Bibiana – was being monitored by her father, who sat, masked, rigid with anxiety, his face so close his breath left the ghost of condensation on Dr Roy's glasses, so that he felt his own stress levels climbing, the blood rushing in his ears. He'd taken his break in the canteen and had actually started awake, even though his eyes were open, to find himself watching a silent TV.

And this was his day off. It followed a ten-day stretch as a GP. The workload here was crushing and chaotic. He'd always wanted to be a doctor, and he'd always worked hard. In a real sense he was living his dream, but in an equally real sense it had become a nightmare. The frenetic schedule was shredding his health. But he'd found a way to cope, although, cruelly, that only meant he had to work even harder to afford his special remedy.

That afternoon he'd slipped into a toilet cubicle at the health centre at four o'clock and taken a codeine tablet, two temazepam and an upper. For thirty seconds he sat on the toilet seat and looked at the four walls. Each day now he passed through a room like this, a kind of portal, linking his life on one side (anxious, stressed, panic-stricken) to the life on the other side (relaxed, omnipotent, heroic). In a humdrum way such cubicles had become a symbol of his survival. After twenty seconds he felt the codeine hit his nervous system, so that his neck muscles were able to slip from the tendons at the top of his spine, relieving the pressure on the base of his brain stem. Within a minute the stress had pooled in his feet, then bled into the floor, which was a blue-grey lino flecked with colours. As he stood he was conscious of his body, of the bones in their skeletal frame, his blood pumping smoothly now, like a power supply.

The rest of the shift had been serene until six thirty when the codeine had begun to falter, so that during that last hour he'd been jumpy and brittle, manically completing the paperwork for a new drugs trial. A slamming door made his joints contract as if he'd been stricken by a seizure; the jangling music in the overhead speakers frayed his nerve ends. When his shift ended he'd had to stop himself actually running for the lift to the basement. Its blue walls, winking buttons and reflective mirror walls always provided an instant haven. Alone, he popped a pill. He caught a glimpse of himself then in the mirrored walls; European bone structure, from his Goan Portuguese grandfather – dark, sub-Continental skin, as dry as parchment. Only, perhaps, his eyes betrayed him, the brown irises wide and watery, like a fish glimpsed in the shallows, and with the same fleeting impermanence.

He'd parked the second-hand BMW soft-top in its usual spot. Once, a year earlier during his training, he'd let a diazepam tablet confuse him so much he'd spent forty-five minutes searching for his own car. But he walked directly to the BMW tonight, and driving at a modulated fifteen miles per hour, headed for the exit, his hyper-awareness acute, so that he watched a bunch of teenagers on a street corner opposite, sharing a cigarette, the lit butt glowing brightly on its downward trajectory to the concrete forecourt. Beyond the barrier-exit a police patrol car sat purring in a layby, so that his heartbeat picked up, and for the first time that day he felt globes of sweat prickling along his forehead. As he drove away he checked the rear-view mirror to make sure the police weren't following.

Lynn's Vancouver Centre shopping complex, refurbished this year in vibrant pastel shades, had been re-designed to incorporate a small block of 'luxury' flats, behind a gated car-bay. Planners, caustic about the deserted shopping malls of the 1980s, wanted people like Gokak Roy – young, salaried, single – to reinvigorate the town. He was only inside the flat for ten minutes: time enough for a shower, clean jeans, T-shirt and

72

trainers. Then he was dancing down the stairs, his ankles sending little jolts of joy through his bones.

His uncle's restaurant was three streets away and empty when he put his head in, so he said he'd eaten at work. Then he ran, laughing, down Eastman Street, to Ja-Ja's – a basement bar, full of friends. He had four shots of vodka with a pint of lager and Sean, the barman, said he was on a roll, although the words seemed to float into his head as if they were falling leaves. At one point a girl, in white shorts and a ripped T-shirt, had licked his ear and he'd said something and she'd simply walked away. The disappointment, the frustration, felt like it might bloom into anger so he went to the toilet and popped two more diazepam. When he got back to the bar Sean had lined up three shots, each a kind of petroleum blue in colour, which he downed to the sound of applause.

Back in the flat, in the small hours, he forced himself to re-engage with his daily routine, setting up a saline drip by the bedside which would rehydrate his body overnight, so that when he woke up he might feel physically as if he'd been hit by a truck, but there'd be no actual pain, no headache, no nausea. The headlong chaos of his interior life could continue, masked by its crisp, carefully nurtured, facade.

Sitting on the bedside, naked, he'd seen the envelope on the distant mat at the end of the corridor. He must have walked straight over it a few minutes earlier.

On the outside it said simply GOKAK in an

eccentric curling script he'd come to know well. Inside, he would find a date, a time, but no indication of place, because that was always the same. Sitting on the floor, he began to cry, the envelope on his knees. He knew that if he failed to rip open the letter his life would be over, but that if he *did* rip it open this simple action would set in motion a lethal series of events, which would begin in earnest after he parked the BMW under a street light as he always did, and slipped into the shadows beneath the Lister Tunnel.

Nine

The desktop PC glowed in the suburban dark of midnight. Nothing moved in the silent cul-de-sac outside the curtainless window as DC Mark Birley stretched until his bones cracked. Pushing the heel of his right hand into an eye-socket, he massaged the muscles, seeing a kaleidoscope of colours dance across the darkness, before forcing himself to re-focus on the screen's six mini-images.

CAMERA A: looking west, showed the 'tradesman's' entrance to Marsh House, consisting of a tarmac parking area, surrounded by hydrangeas, reaching up more than fifteen feet. A bird-feeder, with fat balls, took up part of the foreground in sharp focus. There was an exterior light, which lit the scene in a bleak monotone.

CAMERA B: mounted over the original front

74

door, facing inland, covered the drive, the turning circle, the gardens and offered a brief glimpse of the coast road beyond the closed iron gates, all lit by a single floodlight in a flowerbed.

CAMERA C: one of three cameras mounted on the north-facing, seaward side of the building. This door was for the kitchen and served as an emergency exit. The view consisted largely of a close-up of an extractor unit, a series of three wheelie bins and a small iron bench. The scene was lit by an emergency-lighting, low-voltage bulb.

CAMERA D: mounted over the French windows, showed the view from the main lounge on to the terrace. Tables, chairs – all ironwork, and a fire pit of steel, the lawn stretching down to the edge of the marsh grass. Also, bone white, the stone bench: the whole scene illuminated by the only floodlight on the rear of the property.

CAMERA E: set over a back door, accessed from a corridor leading back to the stairwell and the nurses' station, showed a limited view north; the edge of the terrace and the lawn, including the pole for a large parasol. Unlit.

CAMERA F: showed the main entrance, to the side of the building, crazy-paving, the narrow path and surrounding shrubs. A mock-Georgian gas lantern hung in the top right of the picture and was sensor controlled, giving light during darkness.

Birley thought he heard his daughter cry out in the room next door, so he stood, carefully edging back the desk chair, and went out into the corridor. The neighbourhood, an estate on the edge of Castle Rising, was deep within its communal sleep, a spell-like slumber. Edging the bedroom door open he turned a dimmer switch to produce a thin white light; his daughter's mouth hung open like a fish, her limbs splayed on top of the duvet as if she'd fallen into the bed from a parachute drop.

Back at the desk he cradled a mug of lukewarm coffee and looked out into the street: all over again, absolutely nothing moved. They'd watched *Harry Potter and the Philosopher's Stone* the week before and Birley had noted how excited his children were that the adventure began in Privet Close, a cul-de-sac just like their own. A celestial motorbike might easily have appeared from the stars to touch down on the family driveway.

Birley switched to a full-screen image of CAMERA A: the timer in the bottom left corner skipped along at thirty times its normal speed. He'd already watched all six CCTV digital downloads for the night of the murder, individually. This was the start of the second round.

It was 1.35 a.m.

His plan this time was to reduce the speed so that each camera download took an hour to view. The prospect was strangely comforting, because he knew he was good at this: the painstaking, the meticulous. Most of all he knew he was trusted with the task. A large man, who'd played rugby for the force, he stretched his arms and legs, joining fingers over his head to pull the joints to produce a satisfying series of clicks.

Yawning, he heard his jaw bone crack, and simultaneously the bedroom door creaked open. His wife, Helen, shuffled past without looking into the spare room, en route to the bathroom. The word: 'Tea?' floated back to him before she closed the door. He was in the kitchen, filling a kettle, when he saw Shaw's Porsche trundle into the drive. The DI shut the driver's door with the softest of mechanical clicks.

Birley opened the door in boxers and T-shirt, filling the doorframe like the Michelin man.

'Mark, sorry. Thought I'd check for a light. Couldn't sleep,' Shaw said.

This was only half a lie; he'd been ringing George Valentine's mobile since early evening. Checking with Dr Scrutton, he'd confirmed that the diagnosis had been passed on to the patient. The CID team had logged their DS back in at the office in St James' at five, and he'd left at seven, saying he was off to check out some background, a form of words which usually indicated he was heading for the Red House, CID's boozer of choice. Since then he'd maintained radio silence. The only comfort was that Shaw couldn't raise Jan Clay either, which suggested that they might be together.

Birley made an extra mug of tea and grabbed a biscuit tin marked in homemade capitals: MITTS OFF!

'Helen's up, she's in her winceyette nightie, so you're in luck.'

'I'll look away.'

But the landing was deserted.

The spare room held the desk, a chair, a single

77

bed and a dismantled fold-down cot. Shaw noted an exercise bike in the corner, a set of dumbbells on the carpet.

Shaw's theory was that Birley's keep-fit regime, which included a daily 5K run, burned off excess tension and stress, leaving him able to collapse in on himself physically, freeing his brain to run a detached and unruffled computer-like programme of observation. The DC had an almost saint-like patience.

CAMERA A was still running, the clock past 4.30 a.m., the little clock hands whirling.

'I made a plan,' said Birley. An A3 sheet held the outline of Marsh House expertly rendered, with each camera vista shown as a cone extending out from the building. If the view was finite, for example CAMERA B's of the extractor chute, then the cone's open end was closed off, delineated in black. If the view was effectively unlimited, such as CAMERA D's of the marsh, the cone extended on, bounded by increasingly feeble dotted lines.

This was everything Shaw expected: organized, clear, focused.

'You've watched all six?'

'Yes, at times thirty normal speed.'

'Over what period?'

'The whole record, from eight to six, which is what the nursing staff refer to as "lockdown", although I'm sure they don't put that in the brochure. All six cameras film continuously, the image comes up in the nurses' station, and then the digital record is stored. During the day the cameras are dormant, only activated by staff in emergencies. They want the residents to feel safe, not watched, apparently.'

'What have we got?'

Birley's stubby fingers moved over the keyboard and CAMERA C came up, scrolling forward automatically to 2.21 a.m. Birley pressed PLAY and the film rolled at normal speed, in time to reveal the arrival of a small fox, which circled the bins, carrying what looked like a rat in its jaws. The eyes, catching the moonlight, were alien, unblinking.

'Supermoon,' said Shaw, tapping the screen where the white light caught the metallic surface of the aluminium extractor.

'Yup. The emergency lighting is on too, but it's just very weak,' said Birley.

The fox ambled away and Birley switched to CAMERA B at 4.09 a.m. On the distant coast road a car swept past, the headlights picking out trees and telegraph poles, and briefly the stone walls of St Peter's church.

'Traffic picks up after that on a regular basis, but there's nothing up the drive at all until Curtis arrives on foot, his squad car up on the road.'

Birley put his arms behind his head. 'And that's it, Peter. Nothing.'

'How can that be?' asked Shaw, immediately holding up a hand in apology; these were the facts, if Shaw didn't like them it wasn't Birley's fault.

The problem was that other facts didn't fit these facts. 'Someone got into Marsh House and pushed Ruby Bright down to the waterside. Or someone in Marsh House pushed her down to the waterside. Either way she went through one of these six doors . . .'

Birley nodded. 'Yeah. Tricky . . .'

Shaw sipped his tea. 'Pathologist confirms Tom's estimate of the time of death and has narrowed it slightly to between ten p.m. and two a.m. We'd like it narrower still, but Justina won't play ball. Outside, at night, under a cloudless sky it was fifty Fahrenheit, inside it was a torrid seventy. That makes calculating the time of death an art. Justina does science. So, if Ruby's not on the cameras, we have a problem, because she was in her room at eight p.m. and dead by two a.m. Either she got out (with her wheelchair) without using any of the six doors, or, both her and her killer got out without using the doors, with the added probability that the killer got in without using the doors.'

Shaw stood, looking out at the amber-lit street. 'Tomorrow we need to crawl over every inch of the place: cellars, windows . . . the garage? Can you get into the garage direct from the house?'

Birley shrugged. 'It was *her* wheelchair?' he asked.

'Good question. We may have assumed that, I'll check . . .' Shaw got out his iPhone and typed himself a message.

'Or . . .' offered Shaw, 'she's on the film and we've missed her?'

Somewhere in the house there was a single cough, then a bedspring creaked.

Birley considered the question: could he have missed her? 'If the killer got a door open and pushed her quickly away from – say CAMERA

D – she'd be gone in thirty seconds. So that's roughly a second viewed at this speed. I might have missed it. I'll check – now. But I didn't, Peter. You can take it from me, she's not on any of these tapes.'

'We're missing something,' said Shaw, thinking now, too late, that he should have slept when he had the chance. This puzzle would be just as intractable by daylight. Now the concept of oblivion, of resting his mind, seemed impossibly remote. His sense of unease was not helped by the near certainty that he'd seen something today, on his arrival at Marsh House, that he should have questioned. Something out of place, something incidental . . .

'One question,' said Birley. 'Why is it necessary to mount six security cameras on an old people's home on the north Norfolk coast? There's only twenty-two residents max – they might as well put them all under twenty-four-hour surveillance. They've got keypad doors. A nurse on duty. Two more on the premises. What's that all about?'

Shaw stood and felt the cool air closer to the curtain-less window playing on his skin. 'I suspect it's about a woman called Irene Coldshaw, Mark. Two years ago, when you were on traffic and in a uniform, she went missing from Marsh House, at night. George remembered; he's got what the top brass like to call an institutional memory, although that never gets mentioned during the salary round. Anyway, Irene was seventy-three years old, and she'd been in Marsh House for two years, ever since her husband had died and she'd suffered a stroke. Her medical notes recorded rising levels of anxiety, the emergence of some kind of internal tension. She lost weight, couldn't sleep, and became irritable. She decided to take back control of her life.

'She left one morning before dawn and walked to Burnham Deepdale. It's what? A mile? She let herself out at six o'clock in the morning, no CCTV then, although there were security pad exits and twenty-four-hour nursing cover. Next thing we know, she's hiring a car, a Volvo estate, at the garage at Deepdale, paying by credit card.

'The coroner presumed she was heading back to Scunthorpe which is where she'd been born, and where she still had a niece. She was fine until she got to Lincoln, but then she hit the motorway system. Problem was the last time she'd driven was 1962, the day after she passed her test. She'd jumped a red light and knocked down a pedestrian, causing him serious injuries. There were plenty of witnesses and she was banned for two years. She never got back behind the wheel again until the day she fled Marsh House. So motorways were a mystery to her.

'She took the A1(M) north, but for some reason got syphoned into the M62 and ended up circling Manchester. By this time fatigue had set in. Spaghetti Junction sucked her in and then spat her out on the M6 heading for the West Country. By now the petrol tank was low and she'd started to panic. When she came off the motorway she went down an up slip road – back on to the motorway but travelling the wrong way. By now it was dark and traffic was light. She clipped two cars, then caught an oil tanker head-on. The explosion actually melted the tarmac; she died instantly, the driver of the lorry badly burned.'

'I remember now,' said Birley. 'But like, that's a freak accident.'

'West Norfolk social services ran an inquiry. Marsh House found itself severely criticized. Don't be fooled by all this talk about "the trust" – it's not a charity. The Starlight Trust is owned by a listed company that runs nearly 200 homes, and operates under more than thirty NHS trusts. The inquiry report wiped thirty million quid off the company's share value. They promised an overhaul of security. That's why there's six cameras, Mark.'

Birley swilled the cold coffee in his mug. 'Makes you wonder what was suddenly so bad about Marsh House that she was prepared to take the risks. That age, I'll need a good reason to get out of an armchair.'

Shaw filed that thought away, because it was a good question: what had driven Irene Coldshaw to escape from the warm comfort of Marsh House?

Ten

Shaw found Valentine in the alley behind the Ark, actually a stretch of long-forgotten street, a hundred yards of city-centre tarmac overshadowed by the back of Iceland, a multi-storey car

83

park and an electricity sub-station. The sign said *Clennam Street*. Valentine sat on the kerb, a favourite perch, his knees up, facing the rising sun, a single cigarette stub in the gutter. He found the forensic lab, and the morgue beyond, unsettling on a good day. Today wasn't a good day.

Shaw let the fire door clang behind him. 'George. Tom's ready.'

Valentine didn't move.

'Scrutton said you knew the diagnosis. You and the CC.'

Shaw walked out into the middle of the street, his feet set as far apart as his shoulders. 'I thought you'd want to hear first from the doc. Get the facts. It's what I would have wanted.'

Valentine began to stand, twisting slightly to take the pressure of his knees. 'Good call. Thanks. I've certainly got the facts. And it's hardly a surprise, is it, Peter. Or a mystery. Pretty much an open-and-shut case. Lung cancer; a particular kind of lung cancer by the way, which is common in non-smokers. Scrutton seemed to think the irony would cheer me up.'

'Self-pity's understandable, but you might like to think of Jan,' said Shaw. 'She's probably had enough of it given her first husband's death. Least the booze didn't get you.'

'I knew there was an upside. It was only a matter of time until some fucker found it.'

Shaw refused to rise to the bait. 'You don't have to do this, George. Take control of what you *can* control. Take leave, right now. Think about surgery – chemo, radiotherapy. Tackle it, deal with it. What did Jan say?'

'What you've just said.' There was a slight sheen of sweat on his face. 'Not precisely the same words, but the underlying message was on the money.'

He took a big breath, his ribcage rising. 'She said liver disease, which got her old man, isn't a bag of laughs. Death by cancer is, by contrast, a walk in the park. Well, she said something like that.

'Some quack on the radio she heard said cancer provided an ideal death, what with the morphine and all. It's only a guess, but I bet *he* didn't have it at the time. No. Apparently cancer affords an opportunity to say goodbye, time to do stuff, get ready for the end. Then there's whiskey.'

Valentine rubbed the skin on his face with both hands.

'I've been thinking about this other bloke,' he said. 'When I went in for the scan the guy before me was called Juan Roberto Valenciana, a Portuguese migrant worker. He had a shadow on his lungs too. We worked it out quick enough, that the appointments are alphabetical. I've been thinking about what his scan showed. Emphysema, I bet. He'll have to give up cigarettes, take more exercise, build a new life.'

There was a silence and Shaw knew instantly they were picturing the same scene: the room his father had died in at the family house at Hunstanton, the nurses busy changing beds, his mother ferrying tea cups, and George Valentine a bedside companion, with a glass of whiskey. Shaw had been training at the Met at the time, and had been reduced to weekend flying visits, so that when the end came he missed it, having to take a call from his mother in the early hours. But Valentine had been there at the end, at the bedside.

The DS shot the cuffs on his suit. 'For now, Peter, for today – a week, maybe a month, I'm going to work. Scrutton's trying to get a date for surgery. When he's got it, I'll decide.'

Valentine stood, a hand to the small of his back. 'I checked with the coroner last night. Beatty Hood, the victim's best friend, and the subject of the hidden death certificate? Well, everything's in order according to Furey. No inquest required. Died in her sleep, at home. Her medical records show she'd been ill for a while. Loads of things going wrong. He called it "complex morbidity".'

Dr Furey was the district coroner, a sociable Irishman with a commendable academic interest in deaths amongst Lynn's homeless community. Hood's death sounded routine, mundane, a fitting end to a quiet life.

Valentine held the fire door open, but Shaw didn't move. 'Jack would have fought if he'd had a chance,' he said. 'But he didn't have a choice, the diagnosis was too late. It's not the same, it's not like it has to end like that. You've got a chance, George. More of a chance than he ever had.'

Eleven

Inside the Ark they found Tom Hadden, in a laboratory white suit on the phone, so Shaw commandeered one of the hot desks and spread out a copy of Birley's hand-drawn plan of Marsh House and what cartographers liked to call its 'environs'.

Shaw had texted Valentine on the latest CCTV news overnight, so the DS was up to speed.

'I met Fortis at six thirty this morning,' said Shaw. 'We walked the boundary of the building. There has to be another way into, and out of, Marsh House.

'She did confirm that the wheelchair was Ruby's. They're all coded with a punched metal tag. Which means either she got out alone, in the chair, or the killer got her out, by means other than the six doors, with the chair. It is technically possible to open two windows and step out of the building without being caught on camera – here and here . . .'

Valentine, standing, curved his back over the plan to get a closer look. 'Height of the sills?'

Shaw put a boot on the desk top, judging the height. 'Three foot six plus. So it's hard to imagine. But even if she got out, with the chair, she couldn't move away from the building because she'd have to cross the line-of-fire – so to speak – of one of the CCTV cameras.

87

'There are two possibilities, George. If you were a gambling man, which you are, I'd say they're both 1,000–1 long shots. There are twin wooden shutter doors here, outside the French windows, which lead down to the old coal cellar. We'll get Tom to check, but you'd have to get into the cellar down a narrow staircase, and then climb out. In a wheelchair? Or, you can exit the building from a second-floor window on to the roof of the covered passageway which leads to the flat roof of the garage. I'll leave you to work out the pitfalls in that little scenario. But I can't see it, can you?'

Hadden, off the phone, led them up a spiral metal staircase to what had been the organ loft of the old Methodist chapel. From the minstrels' gallery they could gaze down the length of the church; the view reminded Shaw of the derivation of the word 'nave', from the Latin *navis*, for a ship. The body of this vessel had been divided, amidships, by a glass wall, separating Hadden's laboratory from the pathologist's morgue beyond, overseen by a single stone angel, its face covered with both palms, as if unable to look upon the dead below. A pair of glass doors provided access from morgue to laboratory. Valentine tried not to let his eye catch the image beyond the reflective glass, but it was too late; the grey corpse of Ruby Bright lay on the aluminium table, the only colour the yellow name tag attached to the right ankle. On any other morning of his life he'd have been able to keep this glimpse of mortality in perspective, but today it held a fatal attraction.

'Here she is,' said Hadden, extracting a small

88

machine from the wooden chest once used for bibles. The ESDA (Electrostatic Detection Apparatus) had been hidden away – there was no other word for it – beneath several file boxes. The size of a small photocopier, constructed of glass and blue steel, it held the brand name: ESDA-Lite.

'Don't get a lot of call to use it, so might as well save the space,' said Hadden, but he had the decency not to meet Shaw's eye. They all knew why this particular machine had been slipped into a wooden chest: why remind everyone who came through the door of the Ark of the one single device that had done more damage to the collective reputation of the British police in the last century?

Valentine and Shaw helped Hadden inveigle the ESDA down the spiral stairs and on to one of the hot desks. To make room, the scientist removed a plastic bag containing a pair of blood-spattered trainers.

'What's the story here?' asked Valentine, examining the shoes through the murky plastic and the label marked: PC Clay 34671.

'Pig's blood,' said Hadden. 'Someone's idea of a joke, or a warning.'

Plugged in, the ESDA began to hum, an internal pump sucking air through thousands of small holes in the brass 'table' which formed the flat top of the machine. Over this Hadden placed the sheet of paper found on the blotter of Ruby Bright's desk. On top of that he stretched a polymer sheet, effectively a piece of cling film, sealing the 'sandwich' below.

'Now for the magic,' he said, picking up the electronic 'wand' attached to the side of the table. 'You might want to stand back a bit, George, this can generate a potential of 5,000 volts. I wouldn't want it to wake you up.'

He drew the wand across the blotter. Shaw knew the science from his Met forensics' course: the 'corona discharge unit' – the wand in Hadden's hand – was inducing an electrostatic current to pass down through the brass table. The charge was higher in any indentations made in the blotter such as the little – minute – valleys in the paper made by the downward pressure of a pen or pencil on the sheet above, and it was in these dips that the positive electric charge would linger.

Hadden returned the wand to its holder, having primed the sheet, and then gently tilted the brass table on its hinges, clicking it into place at an angle of about thirty degrees. Down this gentle slope he now poured carbon granules from a glass beaker, 'lubricated' by tiny plastic spheres mixed with the powder. Slowly, inevitably, the carbon began to gather in the dips, attracted by the positive electrostatic charge. In effect, the ESDA operated as a sophisticated form of brass rubbing.

It always took a few moments for any traces to appear. The three of them stood, stupidly, watching the brass table vibrate. Shaw wondered what the forensic staff had felt on that day in 1982 when a very similar model of the machine was used to discover that the West Midlands Serious Crime Squad had tampered with evidence in their inquiries into the Birmingham pub bombings; or the day the New Scotland Yard lab staff operated their ESDA to uncover police fraud in the case against the killers of PC Paul Blakelock – hacked to death by rioters at Broadwater Farm. Before those two cases, a majority of the public thought the police never tampered with evidence; after them a majority thought they did. And all because of the innocent practice of taking notes in an interview room by leaning on a pile of fresh, unmarked, paper, so that each page, inadvertently, held an impression of its forerunner. The technology allowed them to compare *original* statements with their doctored, fraudulent successors, presented in court to secure convictions in high-visibility cases.

'Nowt,' said Hadden, giving the ESDA slope a light tap. Or rather, too much: they could see traces of written lines, each at a slightly different angle to the horizontal. But the result looked like spaghetti, and was unreadable.

'Let's try the top sheet from the headed notepaper.'

As Hadden prepared the machine they heard the pathologist, Dr Justina Kazimierz, working on the far side of the glass divide: sluicing down a table, running an electric saw for thirty seconds, so that Valentine's teeth seemed to vibrate in his narrow skull.

Shaw stared at the ESDA's brass table as it began to vibrate again, unable to slough off the image of George Valentine out in the street, sat on the kerb, head down. A detail of that picture was important, but he couldn't see how. The scene

91

appeared to his mind's eye as if drawn for a Victorian newspaper, a morality tale like so many others; the fallen woman plunging from London Bridge into the Thames, the urchin stealing a loaf of bread. A black-and-white picture complete with a moral caption.

'That's strange,' said Hadden. The cascading carbon had adhered quite distinctly to a small area of writing: three lines, set in a narrow space three inches by one-and-a-half.

'It's an address,' said Shaw instantly, trying to turn his head to read the sense of it.

Hadden applied an adhesive sheet to the cling-film layer to preserve the ESDA 'lift', and then slid the sheet out to reveal the writing, in so doing demonstrating one of the machine's great bene-fits, that it didn't in any way corrupt the original evidence. Such an experiment could be repeated in court with no deterioration in results. A forensic scientist could test the veracity of the evidence a thousand times, using the original on each occa-sion, even in court.

It was an address of sorts.

Gordon Lee
Chief Reporter
Lynn Express

The three lines were set at a wide angle to the horizontal.

'So,' said Hadden, 'like this.' He took a roll of address labels, tore off one, set it on a sheet of A4, and wrote an address, the paper at an angle to allow his right elbow to support his right hand.

'It's perfectly natural to set something this small at an angle to suit the hand-writer. She'll be right handed, absolutely no doubt.'

'So, it's possible the last thing she wrote was this label,' said Shaw. 'Where's the letter?'

'Perhaps the killer's the postman,' said Valentine, already keying in the number of the *Lynn Express* news desk to his mobile. 'I'll check it out . . .' he added, retreating back towards the fire doors and the sanctuary of Clennam Street. The image flashed again behind Shaw's blind eye: the cigarette stub, Valentine's feet in the kerb, and he knew then what he'd missed.

Twelve

Mark Birley, sleepless, in his gym kit, was at his desk in the CID suite, a wide-screen PC showing the six camera feeds he'd transferred from the Marsh House CCTV database: Cameras A, B, C, D, E and F.

Shaw had ordered in a dozen Costa coffees and a round of sticky buns, so he had the team's undivided attention, gathered round the desk. Hadden, still in his white forensic gown, completed the audience.

'Mark, run me Camera D, please. Pick any time you like, but in darkness, please, and on the night of the murder.'

The screen showed a single image of the terrace of Marsh House.

Shaw let the images flicker forward for thirty seconds.

'Mark, stop it there. Now, here's the stone bench on the terrace . . .' Shaw leant forward over Birley's shoulder and touched the image. 'George and I were on the scene first thing and there were half a dozen – maybe more – cigarette butts under that seat. There's nothing in this shot, not one.'

Birley had a set of notebooks open, flicking through pages of neat notes. Finding what he wanted, he ran the shot on Camera D forward to 5.36 a.m.

'Here, right there.' A marsh bird was visible on the terrace wall for a second, maybe three, before flying out of the halo of the floodlight. As it took to the air, the wings flapped once, twice, three times before it entered an effortless glide.

'Marsh harrier,' said Hadden. 'The shallow "V" of the wing position marks it out – plus its size.'

'Rare?' asked Shaw, guessing where Birley was taking them next, sure that the detective had guessed the implications of those missing cigarette butts.

'Maybe three hundred breeding pairs in the UK. Doing well now, but still on the amber list. Rare, certainly, a precious bird.' Hadden's own flight from London to north Norfolk had been, at least in part, an attempt to indulge his passion for birds.

'We've got thirty days' worth of the digital record,' said Birley. 'I was going to watch it through for the previous night at least, just in case the killer cased the joint. Here's Camera D again, but twenty-four hours earlier.'

They all watched as he entered 5.35 a.m. in the digital time counter: in the minute that followed Shaw imagined silent wings over starlit water, and then it was there, the marsh harrier, taking its identical three second bow, and then – one flap, two flaps, three flaps – sliding away on its effortless glide.

'Same tape,' said Birley, covering his eyes.

'We both missed it, Mark. It was the night of the supermoon, and yet the marsh, and the pathway shown in Camera D, are all in darkness. The floodlight obscures it slightly, but you can see there's no moon, nothing. Once you know what you're looking for, it pretty much shouts at you.'

'Obvious next question,' said Valentine, knowing Birley was already after the answer, fingers tapping smartly on the keyboard, selecting from a folder a twenty-four-hour file for Camera D for a date a month earlier.

The footage looked identical but they all waited dutifully for the minute to pass before the marsh harrier made its scheduled landing yet again.

'So, not just for the night of the murder, or the night before, but every night. Mark, ideas?' Shaw asked.

'My guess is there's an automatic programme which simply runs this one night's footage, including the bird, over the actual film, or possibly, the camera's blind and the footage just replaces a blank image.

'I'll check, but my guess is that it is just this

95

one camera, not all six. Either way, it takes a degree of computer technical knowledge to set up the override. Question is did the killer set it up, or did he, or she, just know that camera was blind and take advantage?'

Shaw chose a team of six to go back out to Marsh House with Valentine in charge; they needed to re-interview all night staff and find out who knew about the false camera. It suggested Bright's killer may well have deliberately used the door under Camera D between eight and six.

Shaw had one more job for Valentine. 'George – stop off at Copon's camper van en route. If he's there rope him in, if the girlfriend's there, try to get his passport. He's worked in that nurses' station for three years, there's no way he didn't know the camera was blind. And he's a smoker. I think he's just become our first prime suspect.'

Thirteen

Lena was clearing one of the picnic tables outside *Surf!* when she spotted a man picking his way along the sands: grey suit, black shoes, a briefcase, wading through the dunes above the high-water mark, zigzagging a path between sunbathing bodies and families camped out around cool boxes and shell tents. By the time he'd reached the bar his thin hair was damp with sweat.

'Mrs Shaw? Norfolk Coastal District Council.'

He offered her a photo ID in a see-through wallet. 'Daniel Richmond.'

'It's Braithwaite, not Shaw. The name's over the door.' She nodded back towards the bar and the small brass plate over the lintel which held those magic words: 'licensed to sell' . . .

Fumbling with his briefcase he spilt the contents out on the sand. 'Sorry – of course. My mistake.'

And what a *revealing* mistake, thought Lena. The council had clearly decided she was the wife of DI Peter Shaw, rather than Lena Braithwaite, licensee of The Old Beach Café, Hunstanton – aka *Surf!*, north Norfolk's newest beach hotspot. She couldn't work out if that was good news or bad news. Now that the government had removed magistrates from the licensing process, the local town hall was judge and jury on her opening hours.

'I'm making coffee, or tea?' She considered offering a glass of white wine but there was something of the petty bureaucrat about Richmond which held her back.

The clock on the veranda read 11.32 a.m., so they were open to sell alcohol, and Leo D'Asti, Lena's business partner, was behind the bar. A chef and two trainee cooks were already preparing sandwiches and salads. Fran – the Shaws' daughter – was on a day trip to London with friends, so the pace was professional, a note of commercial tension in the brisk activity. The supermoon party had boosted takings by a clear £2,300 – cashflow, not profits, but a triumph nonetheless. If Lena could come up with an event a week in the summer, the business model would be

97

transformed from a 1950s tea-shack to something much more exciting: a template for a string of bar/restaurants perhaps, on some of the country's finest beaches.

Over a pot of tea, they dealt swiftly with introductions. Richmond was Assistant Licensing Officer for the council, based in Hunstanton. They'd received an application to allow *Surf!* to sell alcohol over the bank holiday weekend, three days, from 10.30 a.m. to 11.30 p.m.

'Quite a place . . .' said Richmond, trying not to look at two women sauntering by, topless. *Surf!* was a clear country mile from the family beaches at Hunstanton, and the atmosphere was cosmopolitan, more Chelsea-on-Sea than kiss-me-quick. Lena's chin came up, proud of what she'd created, letting her eyes flit over the twenty picnic tables, already crowded with customers crumbling saffron cake, or pouring Nicaraguan blend from glass cafetières. One couple, in their mid-thirties, had a wine cooler between them, the stem of a bottle of Prosecco studded with drops of condensation.

Yes, quite a place. It was certainly a very different place from the one they'd bought seven years earlier. That first day Shaw had led her along the beach, she'd seen it in the distance: The Old Beach Café – a wooden hut, with a stone cottage behind and the Old Boathouse – a slated shed, the roof held down by rocks strung in a net. All theirs for £80,000 freehold, with no road access, no mains power and a cesspit back in the dunes. Now, a thirty-foot wind turbine turned languidly in the breeze, each blade painted a

98

different poster-box colour. (Fran's idea – to mimic the sandcastle windmills.) The Boathouse, converted to a shop, now sold everything from Hunstanton key rings at sixty-five pence to para-kites at £4,000.

She caught it then, the sudden malicious glint in Richmond's dull eyes. Now that he'd recovered his composure, Lena could see he was late-twenties, his card had listed initials after his name: BA, MBA. It occurred to her she'd under-estimated him, and that she needed to concentrate. Staying in business was about identifying risks. Suddenly she saw Richmond for what he was: a bundle of sticky red tape waiting to unfurl.

'We're minded to recommend to the licensing committee that your application be refused, Mrs . . . er, Ms Braithwaite. The timing is problem-atic. But perhaps you could explain . . .'

'I'm in business, I want to make money. It's a bar. There's more people around at bank holiday.' Lena smiled and was delighted to see Richmond's face flush in response.

'Yes,' said Richmond, laughing joylessly. 'But the pilgrimage, you'll be aware of the kind of thing that can happen. The riot of 2001 for example . . .'

'That would be nearly fifteen years ago, Mr Richmond.'

The so-called Walsingham 'riot' was a piece of local legend of a tenacious quality. Lena suspected that the sight of colourful saris on the sands of north Norfolk, not to mention ceremonial swords, had delivered some kind of visceral culture shock to the largely white, middle- to upper-class

99

holidaymakers, who provided the core of her clientele, and of every business from Old Hunstanton to Cromer. A hundred miles of old-fashioned, fifties English seaside heaven, a stretch of landscape and seascape which formed, quite accidentally, a kind of Enid Blyton theme park, a living, breathing, shoreline from a totally imaginary past.

'Mr Richmond, I'm not from around here. I grew up in Brixton. I'm a lawyer by training. I used to work for the Campaign for Racial Equality. There were riots in Brixton in 1981 – 280 police officers were injured. In 1985 fifty-five cars were burnt out. In 1995 the Met had to enforce a two-mile exclusion zone, closing down the tube and stationing helicopters overhead. I only mention this because it means that I have a pretty vivid idea of what constitutes a riot, and I'm afraid half-a-dozen tanked-up Tamils having a quick pee over someone's fence doesn't do it for me.'

Dimly a voice told her to calm down and she wished Shaw was there, because he was more objective about the business, and faced with a bureaucrat like Richmond he'd have simply sat back and played out a long rope, waiting for him to tie his own noose.

'Machetes were confiscated, Ms Braithwaite. Last year several police forces coordinated in searching vehicles en route to Walsingham. Credible information suggested that guns were being carried.'

'And what actually happened? Nothing. This isn't about civil unrest, it's about the cosy world of north Norfolk's retirees being stirred by a sudden influx of outsiders behaving with a little less decorum than the local WI. I'll say it if you won't, Mr Richmond – *black* outsiders.'

'I see,' said Richmond, blinking, calculating. 'We don't think it is a particularly good idea to open a bar all day, and pretty much all night, when certain volatile elements may be in the area. I'm sure you understand the realities of the situation.' Richmond seemed especially pleased with this meaningless gem, so much so that he couldn't stop himself saying what was in his head: 'There are, after all, nearly 160,000 Tamils in Britain.'

Even he knew he'd gone too far. There was a long silence in which a flock of seagulls overhead tried to dismember the skeleton of a rock salmon.

Lena stretched out her legs. 'Oh. I see. We're going to be inundated, are we – overrun, even? No, there's a better word. *Swamped.*'

'I didn't say that.'

'Most Tamils are Muslim, Mr Richmond. I don't want to be rude, but you might get your facts right. Less than six per cent are Christian. That's 10,000, or less, in total. Is each one a volatile element, or is it just a collective threat?'

'The bar could encourage anti-social behaviour. Especially late at night.'

'Well. Two things. This place will be shut and shuttered by 11.35 p.m. all three nights. Second: you've just walked the beach from the nearest road, Mr Richmond. If you don't mind me saying so, you don't look too pleased with the effort required. Coachloads, or even carloads, of

101

pilgrims will bring their own alcohol. Do you think they're really going to hike a mile along the beach for a sundowner at £4.50 a glass?'

Her voice had climbed a notch and she saw Leo D'Asti on the terrace of the café looking her way, trying to work out if she needed help; she shook her head quickly and he melted away.

'We're minded to recommend refusal,' said Richmond.

'I'm minded to ring the local paper and give them a rough précis of our conversation so far. Would you like to see what that means in terms of newsprint on a page?'

Richmond's eyes went blank.

'There's been threats,' he said, and bit his lip. 'Specific threats. I shouldn't tell you this, but we are concerned. There are people planning to disrupt the pilgrimage. Activists.'

'What threats, against whom? What kind of activists?'

'I've said too much. But I'm only trying to help.'

'Then be specific.'

'I can't.'

'When will I hear about the licence?'

'In twenty-four hours. Less.'

He extricated himself from the picnic table bench before pointing to the telegraph wire which ran in a loop between *Surf!* and the Old Boathouse shop. Midway along a pair of brightly coloured trainers swung on their laces.

'You should let the police know about those – they've got a shoe squad to take them down in Lynn. They're linked to drug sales, apparently, or worse. Unsightly at the very least, don't you think?'

'They're my daughter's,' said Lena, staying in her seat. 'She threw them up to celebrate her GCSE results and a new pair of trainers. It's what kids do.'

Lena watched him walk away, her reflective black Ray-Bans mirroring the first clouds of the day.

Fourteen

Julia Fortis, administrator of Marsh House, commanded an austere attic office. A set of two wide dormer windows looked north towards the sea and the sun, reflected off the flood tide, bounced and shimmered in blue and green light on the plastered ceiling. Thrown open, the windows admitted a warm breeze and the distant brittle jangle of rigging against masts. A whiteboard on the wall was covered in intricate mathematical calculations, dominated by a single equation: $w/10 + 20 = mph$, which Shaw recognized. There was very little in the room which looked personal, save a half-length summer wetsuit hanging from a hook, a fitness bike and a picture on a bookcase shelf of an elderly woman holding a spray of flowers.

Fortis, in a white blouse, sat rigidly behind a modern desk, upon which was a flipped-open laptop, listening to Shaw's brief summary of what

103

the CCTV had revealed: that Marsh House's six-camera security system was actually a five-camera system, that Camera D was effectively 'blind', or worse, programmed to simply repeat a standard pre-recorded shot; a digital facade, beyond which anything might happen, unseen between eight in the evening and six in the morning.

From the terrace below they heard the thin strains of Radio Four, and a single clash of a china cup on a china saucer, while somewhere the water pipes hummed as a shower unit ran. It occurred to Shaw that while every home had a series of distinctive noises – pipes banging, floorboards creaking – Marsh House presented a much richer soundtrack, reflecting the many lives lived under one roof.

'Your CV lists a degree in computer science, Ms Fortis,' said Shaw. Armed with a magistrates' warrant the CID team had gained access to the trust's employee records. Fortis had worked at Marsh House for five years, taking up a trainee position in 2010 straight from university. She was unmarried, lived in a harbour-side flat conversion in Wells, and had from 2007 been a member of the British Barefoot Skiing team, an extreme watersport which required skiers to ride barefoot at high speeds behind a tow boat. The sport was popular on the coast because of its wide, open, rock-free beaches and shallow, gently shelving sands. Lena sold the appropriate gear in the Old Boathouse, ranging from special wetsuits and ski shoes for beginners to padded neoprene shorts and harnesses.

'Did you install the CCTV override on Camera D?' Shaw asked.

To one side of Fortis' desk sat Guy Edgecombe, whose business card had described him as a partner in a City law firm that represented Starlight Trust, the owners of Marsh House. Shaw had rung Fortis less than half an hour earlier to arrange an interview, so the presence of Edgecombe meant either that he was on the premises anyway, or that he had been drafted in from his holiday, given his office address was High Holborn, in London's West End. As he was dressed in a pair of navy blue designer shorts and what could only be described as an Hawaiian shirt, the latter seemed likely.

'I think the answer to that question can wait,' he said. His feet were bare and, Shaw noted, still coated on the upper side with sand.

'This is a murder inquiry, so I'll decide what can wait.'

Edgecombe's narrow, equine face – deeply tanned – beamed a charming £500-an-hour legal smile at the detectives.

'We're keen to observe the proper procedures.'

Valentine, standing at one of the dormers, watched a patient being pushed in her wheelchair down towards the sea. Out on the marsh – a mazelike expanse of reed and water shielded from the ocean by Scolt Head Island – schools of training boats sailed in neat battalions.

'Proper procedures, really?' asked Shaw. 'Like obstructing a murder inquiry? I intend to make an arrest today, Mr Edgecombe, unless I get answers to pertinent questions.'

'Obstructing a murder inquiry? Really? An oversight, perhaps. But entirely innocent,' said Edgecombe, his eyes flitting to Valentine, whose narrow, skeletal frame filled the floor-to-ceiling window.

'The digital CCTV records,' said Shaw. 'Did you install the override Ms Fortis?'

Edgecombe unfolded himself from his chair and gave Shaw and Valentine each a single sheet of A4: a neat five-hundred-word statement, signed crisply in Fortis' name. Shaw, never a believer in the cod-science of reading character from someone's script, noted that the writing was expansive, even florid, in contrast to Fortis' crisp demeanor.

Shaw got the gist in a few seconds. Fortis was admitting that she knew about the dud camera and the 'overlay' images, which she stated had been used to allow staff to smoke outside and take 'a fresh air break'. She had discovered this practice shortly after the system was installed eighteen months previously. On an unexpected visit to the night nurse station during a medical emergency she'd been unable to locate the nurse on duty. Five minutes later she observed her from the French doors, outside, smoking. At the time she had been interviewing nursing staff and several had made it clear they would not work a shift system without access to regular smoking breaks. She had decided to turn a blind eye.

Shaw's team had interviewed the day staff at Marsh House in the last two hours and six of them had admitted to knowing about the blind camera. All were also regular night nurses, and all smoked. They were left with the fact that the CCTV override was a long-established workplace abuse. What did it tell them about their killer? Was he – or she – a member of staff?

Fortis, a fingertip on the rim of a glass of water, went to speak and, although Edgecombe raised a hand, she carried on: 'There are nearly thirty care homes on the coast, it's a competitive market for qualified nurses with the necessary geriatric training. A lot are senior and have worked in homes for decades. Smoking breaks help relieve tension in what is a very stressful job.'

Edgecombe beamed. 'There is no causal link between this practice and the murder. The trust has reluctantly accepted Ms Fortis' resignation. She was a highly respected member of our team, our *national* team. She will be taking owed leave from five o'clock today for six months.' Edgecombe checked his watch, as if keen to get back out in the sun.

Looking down he wriggled a big toe. 'I have agreed to represent Ms Fortis at this juncture. I'm a corporate lawyer, so it's not really my gig. But we have a criminal division and one of my colleagues is on his way north. I've advised Ms Fortis to remain silent until he is able to represent her in person. I hope I don't have to repeat that advice.'

Valentine, who'd been roaming the room, walked to the desk and lobbed a tin ashtray on to the blotter; earlier, standing at the open windows, he'd detected the engrained aroma of nicotine in the woodwork; so perhaps she didn't need to use the terrace.

107

'Sympathize with the smokers, do you? How many are you on?'

Fortis was fish-white, her lips stretched in a murderously straight line, but she wasn't sweating and Shaw sensed a deal had been made through Edgecombe with the company: her silence, the paid leave and eventually perhaps a job at one of the other care homes. None of which necessarily meant she was lying, or a killer.

'So you've known for some time that the security system had this inherent flaw,' said Shaw.

She nodded.

'A system installed, presumably, in the wake of Irene Coldshaw's death. Did you know her?'

Edgecombe had a hand up but Fortis' eyes betrayed a sudden surge of fear.

'There's no connection . . .' she said.

'My advice, Ms Fortis . . .' The lawyer's hand moved to rest on a brown envelope on the desk. The tone of voice was everything; as if he was admonishing a child who'd picked up a forbidden crayon.

'Really?' asked Shaw. 'No connection? I think there are several connections. Mrs Coldshaw got out of a secure building without being detected. How? There were no cameras then, I accept that, but there were security pads. The really interesting question is why did Mrs Coldshaw flee in the first place? What was she afraid of? Did Mrs Bright know? Is that why she wanted to write to the local newspaper?'

Edgecombe's languid bones snapped to attention, but he didn't speak, perhaps remembering the lawyers' mantra: never ask a question until you know the answer.

So instead of a question, a statement: 'I expect that any reputable newspaper would contact us for a statement before going to print.'

'You'd hope,' said Shaw, happy to allow the lawyer's discomfort to deepen.

'Ruby Bright knew something. I think that's why she's dead. That's the heart of the matter. Marsh House has a secret. Do you know what it is, Ms Fortis?'

No answer. Edgecombe opened his hands out, palm-up, then consulted the Rolex again, shaking it, so that the metallic strap made a rasping noise.

Shaw edged forward. 'I think that's why someone went to Ruby's room, got her in her wheelchair and, knowing that Camera D was blind, went out through the French doors. Then they pushed her down the track to the sea, put a freezer bag over her face, and strangled her. She put up a fight, you know. You didn't see her face, did you, Ms Fortis? You looked the other way. Or could you not bear to see it again? Did you kill her, Ms Fortis?'

She stood up and seemed unable to decide where to put her hands. Edgecombe rose slowly, trying not to appear hurried or discomforted by Shaw's allegation.

'That's it,' he said. 'Mr Paterson, my colleague, is about an hour away. Unless you wish to arrest my client, it's over, Inspector.'

'Did you kill her, Ms Fortis?'

The word 'no' was a whisper, but perfectly distinct.

'I said it's over,' said Edgecombe, to his client, not Shaw.

'Actually, it's only just begun, Mr Edgecombe. A couple of things. First, I'm told you have Javi Copon's passport in that safe. I'd like to take that with me. Javi's agreed to this, you can check with him in person, he's downstairs talking to one of my DCs. His story's illuminating. He says Camera D was an open secret with all the staff, a perk if you're a smoker, just as you have pointed out. But not just for smoking. On moonlit nights he'd run down to the beach to check out the surf. Seems to be a lax regime, Ms Fortis.

'Although I don't see Javi Copon as a killer, do you? But we're looking forward to finding out all he knows about Marsh House, he's very keen to talk. In the meantime, I'd rather have his passport in our safe. I certainly don't want it in yours.'

Shaw cast a final glance at the whiteboard, with its elegant equation.

'My wife runs the watersports shop on the beach, between Holme and Hunstanton. We get clubs, hiring kit for the day, jet skis and the like. A barefoot ski club came up last summer from West London, the instructor put that very equation up on an A-board out on the sand. The "w" is easy – weight in pounds, right? The result in miles per hour is the speed you have to reach before there's enough lift – in bare feet – to get the skier up on their legs. So, for me, that would be the best part of forty miles per hour, which is pretty scary in nothing but a wetsuit. But I guess

110

you live for that – the thrill, the sea hissing, the sky, all that space.'

Valentine was at the door, waiting to leave, but not in a hurry because he knew Shaw didn't do idle chit-chat.

'We are on the premises now and will be until further notice. The blind camera puts all members of staff under suspicion. Re-interviews will take several days. But then you're off duty at six? For good. I'm sorry to cut into what little time you have left but when your criminal lawyer arrives you might inform him we will expect you to give a formal statement at St James', police headquarters, Lynn, at four this afternoon. Sorry if that ruins any plans you had to get out on the water. Our interview rooms are eight feet by ten. All of which is positively spacious compared to a prison cell. Think about that, Ms Fortis.'

Fifteen

Detective (Grade 3) Tiffany Reason could have stepped right out of the DVD box set of *NYPD Blue*. Black, five foot three, 140 pounds, sharp-creased, slate grey pants, cap with badge and number: 455793. Shield in gold, silver and blue. Holster – minus gun – night-stick, cuffs and radio, with the mouthpiece pinned to her collar. Wet full lips, watery roaming eyes, and what looked like a permanent grin which said: 'Shucks. I'm gonna have to bust your ass.' PPC Jan Clay was sure the air of mild embarrassment, even self-effacement, was merely a screen.

'Thanks for taking the time out to come see me here now. I appreciate it,' said Reason.

The conference suite on the top floor of St James' police HQ was packed with maybe a hundred officers present, mainly uniformed. The chief constable's email had been less than subtle: he expected all ranks to attend unless on operational duty elsewhere. Jan noted that while she was still in the building an hour after her shift clocked out, DS Chalker had led a break-out to the Red House. His parting shot had been a model of its kind: 'Take a note for us, girl. We're going to chew the fat on the corner. Copy on my desk overnight.'

Jan was happy to avoid the pub. Sometimes she went along to make it clear she wasn't intimidated. But this evening she wanted to be alone in a crowd. George's news threatened the future she'd seen so clearly ahead of her just the day before. They'd meet later to talk some more, but for now she just wanted a distraction. She knew she had to get George in for an operation, because it might save his life, their lives. But she suspected he was going to duck the issue and leave the outcome to fate. She couldn't let that happen.

She sat alone, to one side, by an open window. Their affair was a well-kept secret, as they'd both wanted the anonymity and to avoid the office gossip machine. But she couldn't help thinking now that when the news did break it wasn't going to make DS Chalker's day, and that she'd like to be there to enjoy the moment. For the first time

112

since George had told her Scrutton's diagnosis, she smiled.

The room filled the east end of the main six-floor office block of St James', with windows on three sides, which had been thrown open to capture the evening breeze. The view was clear to the horizon, the sea to the north, the river winding inland past a belching power plant. But they weren't entirely above the town: Greyfriars Tower, the last remnant of the old abbey, stood next to St James' – a leaning, Gothic, octagonal turret, which came just level with the conference room, and was home to a flock of roosting crows.

Detective Reason had a fist the size of a ham-hock within which was hidden a remote control for a video screen. The first picture showed a pair of sneakers on a wire, the giant letters of HOLLYWOOD in the background, decorating LA's mountain backdrop; then a pair by the London Eye, then Madrid, Rome, Chicago.

'Yup,' she said, 'this is pretty much a global phenomenon. Isn't new – I'm not saying it is. We've got records going back to the Civil War – that's our one not yours – says demobilized soldiers, they used to chuck their boots over a tree branch on their way out of barracks, free at last. Maybe started there, maybe not. But it's here to stay, and I'm going around . . .' She mimicked a shuffle, her head down. 'Going around, place to place, just saying what we know about it in my town, that's New York. 'Cos if you're a police officer on the street, you need to know this stuff. I don't have the numbers here in *King's* Lynn . . .'

She smiled at her own emphasis on the archaic name. 'But New York we've lost 813 officers since the force was founded, 322 to gunfire. So you know, a few of us each year don't get to see Christmas. It's dangerous out there, and everything helps. Your chief constable, he's one of the police officers who thinks we should all be sharing this stuff, so that's why I'm here.'

The room's air-conditioning unit, despite the open windows, rattled. They all heard it because the room was silent now. Tiffany Reason had her audience respectfully spellbound.

'There's a website you can check out for yourselves – flyingkicks.com. They list the theories, right, but the big truth is there ain't no one reason. There's a plethora. That's a good word, I learnt it just for the trip.'

There was a dutiful flutter of laughter. On the screen they watched the images come and fade, come and fade; shoes on wires, thousands of them, in streets in every city on the planet.

Detective Reason broke the theories down into ten neat categories.

1. *Celebration:* apparently Oz teenagers throw their trainers over the wire to mark the loss of virginity. 'They lose their cherry, they lose their shoes,' said Tiffany. More generally the shoe might represent coming of age in many ways, literally sloughed off as the youngster grows and buys new ones. So brand new shoes on wires were extremely rare.

2. *Memorial:* the shoes of the dead were hung in the air where ghosts walked. Fallen gang members were often honoured with such an aerial gravestone.
3. *Bullying:* vicious but effective; the victim is simply forced to hobble away, barefoot or in socks, down the city's hard streets. The shoes remain as a daily reminder of their humiliation and the power of the bully.
4. *No-Go Zone:* documented cases in Madrid, Sicily, Marseilles and Manila point to shoes marking boundaries around neighbourhoods where the police have agreed to keep out, usually to allow organized crime to operate prostitution, drugs or illegal gaming. This is either a genuine policy, designed to limit the illegal activities, or part of a corrupt partnership between criminals and police.
5. *Drug dealing:* as a signal that a crack house is close-by, or other drug vending. In some cases – Miami 2008, Sydney 2010 – the brands of trainer were found to be significant and were used to indicate the kind of drugs for sale. Generally, this theory was seen as making little real sense unless combined with a No-Go Zone, or large numbers of shoes, in clusters, which can obscure the signal shoes. Again, colour here could be key; one New

York Brooklyn gang used purple Sky Kites to indicate drug sale points, but always on wires crowded with other shoes. (So-called shoe trees, hundreds on one tree or lamppost, were common in Latin American cities and the favellas.)

6. *Art:* often compared with graffiti, so-called shoefiti was the expression of an individual's identity in the city. One New York art house had made 5,000 pairs of wooden, two-dimensional sneakers, and tossing them had become a street performance, often greeted with applause from passers-by. Suburban residents tended to react quite differently to shoefiti, and several large cities have shoe squads to clear them away. Most residents felt they brought the neighbourhood down and depressed house prices.

Tiffany had a pair of the art shoes, green and gold, with a classic 1950s baseball design.

On the video screen they saw a young man walking down a sidewalk at night, a pair of Skewville 2D sneakers sticking out of his jeans back pocket. They watched him dash out into the street, retrieve the 'shoes', then – holding one in his left hand, one in his right – launch them expertly up and over the wires running to a set of traffic lights. Applause, off-screen, was combined with a few excited whoops.

The snippet of film brought a memory to Jan. Some nights, when George worked late, she'd walk along the river bank, then back through the graveyard of All Saints. Here, five minutes from the house on Greenland Street, lay Julie Valentine's grave. She'd see, always, a shell or a stone perched, defying the laws of gravity, and she'd imagine George visiting the spot, to think perhaps, about the past and the future. The last time she'd been on a walk she'd moved his shell aside and put her own razorbill in its place. She thought now that this was like the trainers on wires, that she was claiming territory, or – at the very least – trying to make the point, even if only to herself, that her life was important.

> 7. *Murder:* again, rare, but documented. Usually associated with gang warfare over territory. The victim was stripped of his – or her – trainers, which were often then smeared with blood, before being tossed over the wires as a warning and a statement of intent: this line will be defended. The NYPD shoe squad had five US documented cases of murder inquiries in which a so-called 'flying kicks' appeared as forensic evidence in subsequent proceedings. Interpol had two cases: one from Australia, one from Japan.

Jan shifted in her seat. She was still taking flak from Chalker and the squad for sending the

Lister Tunnel trainers to Tom Hadden for analysis. When they were officially told the result – pig's blood, no more – she'd be roundly ridiculed.

8. *Meme.* 'This,' said Detective Reason, 'is a bit like a gene. Your guy – that Richard Dawkins – he come up with this in *The Selfish Gene* which you all read about as much as we have back in Brooklyn.'

This time the laughter was genuine, spooking the crows to take to the sky in a grey, squawking, halo of wings from their roosting spot on Greyfriars Tower.

'But the idea's good enough. It's a fad, right? Or a fashion. And it just moves about between people in their heads. And it changes – *mutates*, is what the psychologists say. There's a line I remember from this report we got commissioned from Colombia. "They seem to suggest themselves to each other". That's good in there, 'cos people see the trainers on the wire and they think they'll do that too. Maybe not for the same reason at all. But it marks the fact that they're alive, that they're here, now. And every time they walk under those trainers they think: "That's me," and, of course, it marks the passage of time – what they've done since. Their lives.'

Sixteen

The Phoenix artists' cooperative, housed in a former Hanseatic warehouse on Lynn's waterfront, boasted a facade of limestone blocks and the original thirteenth-century windows, from which hung painted banners proclaiming: Festival '15. The Co-Op Café was on the ground floor, with tables outside, set between various metal and wooden artworks: a framework hung with aluminium fish, an oak totem pole decorated with Gothic gargoyle faces and a cane windmill, with coloured Picasso sails, which whirred in the stiff breeze off the distant North Sea. A visitors' floating quay had been built at this point on the water, a hi-tech metallic construction which rose and fell with the tide, offering cheap berths for yachts and inshore cruisers plying the north Norfolk coast.

Most of the warehouse windows were open after a long day of August sunshine. Spools of jazz, a sudden blast of KLFM radio, the sound of a drill biting into wood, spilled out on to the quayside. Shaw, whose degree in art had embraced months of work in the studios at Southampton, caught the distinct edge of turpentine on the air and what he could only describe as the smell of fresh air indoors, the reek of the open-window workshop. Valentine cast a bleary eye over an A-board listing 'participating artists' in the annual summer open studio festival.

Plate-glass windows opened into a scrubbed brick atrium two storeys high. A woman in multi-coloured jeans and a T-shirt made a beeline for Shaw. Clean-limbed, with a wide mouth and a sinuous step, she got close before handing him a flyer.

'For the festival . . .' she said. Yet again, Shaw was struck by the ability of art to defy time, or perhaps the regenerative effects of any obsessive behaviour. At a distance of two feet he could see her skin, the crow's feet and the thin grey roots to the ebullient hair.

Shaw had his warrant card out before she'd finished speaking. 'Sorry. I'd love to. But we're here on business, hoping to see Linas Jessop?'

A light went out in her eyes but she didn't step back.

'His studio's not open today, but he might be in. Studio eight, top floor. If you have time do look in on some of the other artists. I'm Lee, studio three – it's a video installation. I can offer tea too.'

She seemed to see Valentine for the first time. 'You'll struggle to get a cuppa out of Linas, unless he can deliver a jeremiad to go with it. Joyous welcomes aren't his style. As I say – number eight – just seek out the sound of constant laughter . . .'

The old steps in the Phoenix had been replaced with steel staircases and glass walls, the plaster stripped from the medieval brick. The third floor lay directly beneath the original wooden hammer-beam roof, exposed and artfully lit. The doors to the studios stood open and as they passed they

120

caught sight of the work within: a construction of wood and steel, a polished egg-like sculpture, a series of Rothkoesque block-colour oils.

Shaw's mobile buzzed, signaling an incoming text.

'Chief Constable,' he said, showing Valentine the message.

> *Walsingham? Just had council CEO on the line – he says neither you or George attended the last meeting. DC Twine not adequate replacement. Do we still have our eye on the ball? Joyce.*

Shaw had sent Twine to represent CID at the council offices at Hunstanton, calculating that the clean-cut DC was the ideal stand-in for a hard-pressed superior officer. He'd been told to file a 1,000 word summary of the meeting to Valentine.

'He does know this is a murder inquiry, right?' asked Valentine. 'For God's sake, Peter. I could be dead in six months; I'm not wasting my time pushing a pen around. I'm a copper.'

'I'll sort it,' said Shaw. 'Send Twine's report to me. I'll make a few calls. It's not a problem, George. Let's get on.' Valentine's mood had been poor all day and Shaw guessed he was entering the next phase in his reaction to the diagnosis of lung cancer: anger.

Studio eight was very different from the rest; a carpenter's workshop, with a series of drawing tables, framing squares, a heavy-duty guillotine, an industrial glasscutter. Against one wall stood timber and wood for picture frames and glass, while under the one, full-length window, finished work was neatly set on the floor: framed oils, sketches, prints, even a few photographs of the north Norfolk landscape.

Linas Jessop was in his fifties, lean, his jeans loose despite a leather belt. A shock of grey-streaked hair was combed back off his forehead like a Mohican. Most artists' hands, in Shaw's experience, were workmanlike, and Jessop's were no exception, short, muscular, with a single Band Aid around his left-hand index finger.

Jessop sipped black coffee from a tin mug marked: *Je Suis Charlie.*

'How can I help?' Even as he said it his eyes slipped away to a half-finished canvas. The mannerism was just a bit too smooth, Shaw felt, to indicate a genuine absence of stress, or even interest, in a visit from CID. Shaw felt a glimmer of optimism that at last they might make some real progress in the inquiry: was Linas Jessop their man?

It had been Ruby Bright's solicitors, or more precisely her last will and testament, which had brought them to the artist's studio. Shaw had a copy in his pocket, like an ace up the sleeve.

Shaw walked to one of the open dormer windows, looking out on the quayside, as a small coaster slid by on the Cut, its engines churning, trying to turn against the ebb to enter the Alexandra Docks. On a high tide the steel super-structure stood level with the window. It was like watching a block of flats slide past on invisible rails. Shaw noted a lookout on the exterior platform of the bridge, craning his neck to see the wharfside below.

'Bad news, Mr Jessop,' he said, his back to the witness but knowing Valentine would be noting how he reacted. 'You were a friend of Ruby Bright's, I'm told. You framed all her pictures – at least, I saw the Phoenix sticker on the back of the work.'

Jessop swilled coffee in a tin mug. 'She's dead. I heard, Inspector. The coast is a grapevine, if you take my meaning. The radio said there'd been a murder at Marsh House, but no name. I'm entitled to put two and two together, I take it?'

'You don't appear too upset at the news, sir,' offered Valentine.

'I've known Ruby for the best part of forty years. A good woman and a wealthy one. She married into the Bright haulage family. New money, well, Victorian new money, although they always claimed a tenuous link to Henry Bright and the Norfolk School; fifteenth cousin five times removed, that kind of thing. People think creativity is in the DNA. Hogwash, I'd say, but then my father was a bricklayer.'

The artist tipped his tin mug back so that they could see his throat, the skin stretched over a jagged Adam's apple.

'They collected art, Ruby and the family. I framed it. Sometimes we talked about art, Ruby and I. She had a good eye, especially for the landscapes.'

Valentine knew Shaw would pick that precise moment to tell Jessop the real reason they were in his studio, so he studied the man's face, waiting

123

to see the micro-emotions flood the nervous system, signifying what? Surprise, delight, guilt, avoidance?

'She left you £50,000 in her will, sir. We thought you'd like to know.'

It was the closest thing they'd found to a motive so far. Uncovering the CCTV scam had simply cleared the picture, revealing a vicious calculated murder, and an unlikely victim. They were back to question one: why kill a centurion? The dull answer was money, even if it was often the right answer.

Even the smile, the flash of joy in the jaundiced eyes, was dulled by an almost instantaneous cynicism.

'Christ. Fifty thousand – that would have actually been useful twenty years ago.' He walked to a large deal cupboard and pulled out a draw, extracting a bottle of malt whiskey, a Talisker. He poured a slug into his empty mug.

'How do you know what's in her will, Inspector, if I may ask?'

'Stapley and Howard solicitors were persuaded to share the details with us. Given Mrs Bright was murdered, and it's difficult to see a motive for that crime beyond financial gain, they were most forthcoming on the details. It's a lot of money. Why do you think she left it to you?'

'I'm a suspect? How thrilling. I haven't been anything important for years.'

Jessop drained the tin mug and re-filled it with a fresh slug. 'I suspect she left me the money because she liked my work, although nobody else shared her judgment, and therefore I have to spend my time framing the art of others, which is a faintly degrading and damaging process, if lucrative. It earns me enough money to afford the rent here but leaves me little time to do my own work. That's irony for you. She always said I shouldn't give up. She envied talent, of course – a common failure amongst those who have none.'

'Any of your work here?' asked Valentine, catching Shaw's eye and the slightest of nods, indicating that they'd give this interview the time it deserved. The more Jessop talked, the more he revealed.

On the way into Lynn, in the Porsche, Shaw had tried to dampen Valentine's excitement. 'Jessop can't be that stupid,' said Shaw. 'She's clearly been murdered, she's got her head wrapped in a freezer bag. The first thing we're going to look at is who gains. It's him. So it's crazy, unless he's set himself up the mother of all alibis. Is he really going to kill her when he could wait a year and pick up the money when she finally dies a natural death in one of Marsh House's plush armchairs? By the time you hit 100 your chances of being alive at your next birthday are less than fifty–fifty. All he had to do was wait.'

Then, parking on the wharfside, Shaw had got a second telephone call from Stapley & Howard. This time it was Jonathan Howard, the senior partner. He thought they should know he'd had a call from Mrs Bright, an old friend as well as a client, asking for an appointment to discuss *changing* her will. Howard had agreed to drive out to Marsh House. The appointment had been for three o'clock today.

Jessop had found a canvas, a wide seascape, under a winter sky. Shaw recognized with an almost visceral shock that it was precisely the view from the dunes behind his home, The Old Cottage at Hunstanton, looking across the Wash. Shaw's educated eye noted the expertise in the brushwork, the brilliant attention to shade and colour, the sheer depth of space recreated on a two-dimensional canvas.

'It's good – isn't it?' he said to Jessop. For a moment the prickly exterior softened and the artist seemed overwhelmed, so that they shared a nanosecond of mutual respect, but then it was gone.

'Yes, not bad. But as I said, times change, fashions go, fads arrive. I was out of kilter in 1960, never mind now. Most artists are in thrall to the trend, desperate to be part of a school, a movement, a generation. It goes with the territory, which doesn't make it any less reprehensible.'

He poured himself more whiskey. 'But back to Ruby. You think I killed her for money, eh? I'm a patient man, Inspector. Do you think I'd resist the temptation only to buckle on her one-hundredth bloody birthday?'

'Mrs Bright had asked to see her solicitor to *alter* her will. Which changes everything, doesn't it? Did she plan to cut you out, Mr Jessop?'

'So that's it. Mad with disappointment I kill an old friend. Is that really the best you can do? She never mentioned money. People with plump bank accounts rarely do. I can hardly know I've been cut out of the will if I didn't know I was in it.'

'You were a regular visitor, I understand, at Marsh House?'

One of Shaw's team had found the visitor's book on a small table at the foot of the stairs. Jessop's name turned up on a regular basis.

'Regular? Hardly. Once or twice, half a dozen.'

Shaw let that unconvincing statement hang in the air for a moment. 'I see. The last time?'

'A month ago.'

'At Marsh House?'

'Yes, well, no . . . I think I better stop drinking this stuff . . .' He put the glass down with a clatter on the workbench and then took a deep breath. 'I met her on the beach, a month ago as I say, below the home. Javi Copon pushed her down through the marshes in her wheelchair.'

There was an image there to savour. Is that how Bright made her last journey?

'You know Javi?'

'Sure. He was Ruby's nurse, and a good one. And we share the same politics, the radical Left. A couple of times I saw him at Trades Council meetings in Lynn, he talked about Spain, direct action. We both have a very unfashionable view that trade unions are an integral part of a democracy. Unbelievable, I know. Didn't exactly please Ruby, she was a rural Tory of the old school.'

'Artists have a trade union, do they, sir?' asked Valentine.

'No. That's the point. I'm in the GMB by default.'

127

'What time was this meeting with Ruby out on the marsh?' asked Shaw.

'Early evening, maybe six thirty.'

'And Ruby gave you no hint that she'd either left you this money in her will, or might be considering cutting you out of it after all.'

'Neither, she just enjoyed the sunset, which was glorious.'

'Was Javi Copon a witness to the meeting,' asked Shaw.

'He left us alone for twenty minutes.'

Valentine let an eye run over the frames, the tools scattered on the worktop.

Jessop turned to Shaw. 'I think it's about time I rang a solicitor myself, what do you think, Inspector?'

'Depends, sir. Where were you between eight o'clock Monday night and two o'clock Tuesday morning?'

'Monday night? That, Inspector, is the easiest question to answer, because I'm always in exactly the same spot on a Monday evening, and many others too. And at exactly the same time; well, not in clock time, but in atmospheric time, if I can put it like that. From an hour before sunset, to about an hour or an hour and a half later.'

The studio had a long wooden shelf on which were set notebooks, maybe fifty or more. Each one was leather bound, slightly worn at the spine. Jessop took a volume from the end and let it fall open in his hand.

'There's a Suffolk artist called Cotman – John Sell Cotman.' He'd hit a patronizing tone, particularly irritating as Shaw knew Cotman's work well and that he was a *Norfolk* artist. 'He had this rather laborious, if brilliant, idea. He painted the same scene, a parish church, over and over again, trying to catch its different moods, its atmospherics. In snow, in mist, in sunset light. I stole the idea.'

He flicked through a pile of sketch sheets and held one at arm's length. 'So here's Monday night. Note the moon,' he said. 'That's a supermoon rising, a rather spectacular collision of the harvest moon and the celestial apogee. I appear to have signed and dated the work too . . . which is hardly helpful to me, given that it is a worthless alibi, and puts me quite close to the scene of the crime.'

The work was meticulous and strangely magical, depicting a network of silvered reeds and a maze of marsh, the sky shaded to grey to allow the moon to shine. The only landmark, as such, was an old wooden sluice gate, standing alone like a guillotine.

'Mow Creek?' said Shaw. 'I know the spot. Near the old wharf?' The place was thirty minutes by coastal path from Marsh House.

The sketch was marked: 8.20 – 10.05 p.m.

'You were alone?' asked Shaw.

'Always.'

'And then?'

'Home – by car, I park up by the Victoria. And home's a council flat I live in alone. I'm divorced. She lives in Hampstead now, so you might like to guess why she left me. Anyway, the fact is I live a life bereft of alibis, Inspector. I'm your perfect suspect.'

129

Seventeen

Julie Valentine's grave was lit by the harsh white halogen security lamp on the wall of All Saints, Lynn's 'lost church', set amidst the ugly egg-box flats thrown up after the old, riverside streets had been demolished in the sixties. Valentine often took a seat on the bench for a last cigarette before bed. Tonight he'd promised Jan they'd talk about the future, but as he'd stood at the corner and contemplated his house, the bedroom light just visible behind curtains, he realized his thoughts might be best shared, at least at first, with the dead.

The church had been diminished by age; the tower falling in the eighteenth century, a transept in the nineteenth. What was left seemed to crouch in the shadows like a feral cat, overlooked by the balconies of the flats, a concrete waste-burner, and a single, arthritic oak. Wire mesh covered the stained glass of the church's West End, but he knew the scene depicted within well enough; Gabriel aloft, the Virgin below, the miracle of the Annunciation flooding out of her body in the form of a celestial light; a Medieval reference, surely, to the miracle at nearby Walsingham. Pilgrims arriving by boat would have prayed here, given alms, before walking on along the way.

Valentine had never thought of himself as an

angel, and besides, he had news of a different sort, but it certainly constituted an announcement.

'It's me,' he said, as if in apology. 'I've got lung cancer, so I can't see what's wrong with this . . .'

He'd bought a new packet of Silk Cut and the cellophane came off in one vicious twist of his wrist. Right pocket, left pocket, shirt pocket; he realized he didn't have a light and the tears started in his eyes for the first time since Scrutton had delivered the results of the scan.

That moment in the medical room at St James' when the doctor had dropped the word 'cancer' like a depth charge, had seemed to halt time; noontime sunlight falling flat on the roofs of the Old Town, the window open but the sea breeze spent, a car horn sounding twice on the ring road. 'George. There isn't a good way of telling you this. It's bad luck, of course. We have here' – he said, patting a brown envelope with hieroglyphics on the label – 'your scan. There's a dark shadow on the left lung. Cancer. We can operate, open you up, have a look. Then there's chemo, radio-therapy. That's the good news,' he added, and Valentine liked him just a little bit more. 'The bad news is your general health is poor. That makes fighting the cancer tough. Emphysema, high blood pressure, early signs of Type 2 diabetes. I'm not saying it's all over. But the brutal truth is that if you were running in the 1.30 at Haydock Park I'd put you at fifty to one – to finish.'

Valentine smiled again at the memory, leaning forward, as if about to share some intimate detail

131

with an invisible companion. It was then that he'd seen the shell set on Julie's gravestone, a delicate razorbill encrusted with worm casts, like some fabulous Victorian objet d'art.

'Who put that there?' he asked, standing up and taking it off. From his raincoat pocket he produced an oyster shell he'd picked up two feet from Ruby Bright's stricken wheelchair. The underside was full of mother-of-pearl colours, silvery blue, green and amber. A grammar school boy at heart he recalled the Latin adjective for such a shell-like mirror: *nacreous*, an ugly word for a beautiful thing.

Sitting down again he toyed with the razorbill.

'So that's something to look forward to,' he said. 'A week, ten days, and I'm in for the op. Or not. No waiting list, no tests, no further scans: straight under the knife. I did think I might pass, but I've thought about it and I'm thinking now I'll give it a go. Although I'm scared, really scared. I'll keep you up to date. What do they call it when the Royals are sick? A bulletin, that's it. On the palace gates. I could get mine nailed up on the dartboard at the Artichoke. I owe money, so they'll all be worried.'

The moon, now past its best, appeared above the gable end of All Saints'.

'I only mention it because I'm not ready to die. And there's a reason. The years, since you went, I'd have happily gone; planned it enough times. Pills, booze, our bed; nothing heroic or Gothic. Now, it's different, there's a future, I've got a future. I've said before, about Jan. Sorry, this isn't very tactful, is it. Do they do tact in heaven? Maybe not.'

A light flared in the shadows beside the church porch and he saw a tramp on a bench, a purple-gold can of Special Brew in his hand. Walking over he cadged a light, gave him a Silk Cut, and strolled back.

'I don't think one more will change the odds dramatically, do you? But I'll make this the last.' Trying to draw the smoke down his throat the muscles contracted and he doubled over, retching. A second breath wasn't worth the pain, so he ground out what was left into the path.

He shook his head. 'I know it sounds disloyal but I thought I might as well be honest. Eventually, if there's life after death, there'll be three of us. The philosophers call that metaphysics, I call it sodding awkward. We'll just have to see.'

Standing, he set the Silk Cut packet beside the oyster shell; full bar two, and thought for the first time that the packets were gravestone shaped, an omen he might have spotted if he'd had any kind of visual imagination. Some bright young thing in the NHS or the Ministry of Health should suggest that: each one a gravestone, with the name of a real victim on the front. It crossed his mind that he could give the packet to the tramp but then, he'd simply be giving him eighteen more chances to contract lung cancer himself.

'I better go,' he said, mumbling to himself. 'It's not fair, is it, sloping off to talk to the dead? This is the land of the living, we do things differently here. I should go home and talk to Jan. Talk about

133

the op. Although not just yet, perhaps. I need to walk. Get tired.'

A wrought-iron gateway led north, away from home. As he passed beneath, an insight came to him, that his illness would expose many of his fears as mere wraiths and ghosts, but that unexpected horrors would emerge each day, like this sudden prospect of telling Jan he was prepared to go under the knife, and the inevitable sleepless night that would follow, waiting for the dawn.

Eighteen

Valentine read the text he'd composed for Jan once more, then pressed the send button. *Gone to touch iron.*

It was an image they often shared from a long weekend in Barcelona, where they'd seen the Catalans heading for the end of La Rambla at the close of the evening, putting a hand on the elaborate railings above the sea, before heading home for bed; a ritual they'd come to mimic along Lynn's often bleak waterfront.

At eleven o'clock precisely he stood and watched the celestial clock on St Margaret's slide its stars into place, before walking down the cobblestones to the waterside and putting a hand on the metal rail. He slipped a bottle of Evian out of his raincoat pocket and took a long draught. 'Rehydration, George,' Dr Scrutton had explained. 'Preferably without a whiskey chaser.'

On the vast open square of the Tuesday Market he found five girls, the flotsam of a hen party, washed up outside The Globe. One girl lay on the ground, star-shaped, while two others massaged her shoeless feet. A police squad car stole into view from the direction of St Nicholas' Chapel and trundled round the four sides of the marketplace. The last thing Valentine needed was a late-night chat with uniformed branch so he set off further north, towards the docks.

He knew where he was going now, but still pretended the route was random; left to the Fisher Fleet, the boats silent in their muddy beds, up by the grain silo with its aircraft warning light blinking against the night, and finally into the North End, down terraced streets, out towards the rail yards. At one point he spotted a gang of teenagers on a street corner crowded round their mobile phones, the waft of alcohol palpable on the night breeze, and so he gave them a wide berth, prompting a single catcall.

Shaw and Lena had once given him a short, faintly patronizing, lecture about his habit of walking at night. Apparently, he was part of a noble tradition, a *flaneur*, a Victorian stroller, sampling the night life of the town, a poet without paper, a shadowy intellectual observer, a Dickens, a Stevenson, or worse – a latter-day Hyde. The truth was more prosaic. Even as a child he'd always found that the day got better the longer it lasted. Why go to bed just when things were getting interesting?

Lister Tunnel, when he reached it, seemed to breathe out the dank air of Parkwood Springs; a

135

toothless mouth, dank with a kind of fetid halitosis. His ears also detected a faint echo, a sigh, pulsing slowly, like a dying heartbeat. Valentine wasn't afraid; very little about the town made him anxious or worried. The unknown made him curious, but nothing more. When Jan had sent him the picture by text of the trainers they'd retrieved from the tunnel itself, he'd been intrigued. Not by the blood. The stains were too lavish, too liberal, to be human. His theory about the shoes on wires was that they marked territory, perhaps newly conquered. But who would want to celebrate capturing the Springs?

In his right pocket he always carried a torch, and he played the beam now on the power cable until he found the chalk mark she'd left to mark the spot and the initials JC.

'Well done,' he said out loud. 'You'll make CID yet.'

The brick arch under the embankment acted as a wind tunnel and, as he stood torch in hand, litter came past like tumbleweed: a page of newsprint, a paper cup, a rolling can. A smell of decay wafted from the builder's skip set on the pavement.

Valentine had a retentive brain, if not an analytical one. Recalling Beatty Hood's address precisely: 32 Hartington Street, he set out down the tunnel. The Marsh House inquiry was at a critical stage. Julia Fortis's lawyer had advised that she not answer questions during a formal interview at St James'. Reluctantly, they'd had to let her walk free, even though Shaw was convinced she knew the secret of Marsh House.

Linas Jessop would attend for questioning in the morning. Meanwhile, the team was working on the complex financial affairs of Ruby Bright, Beatty Hood and Irene Coldshaw, to see if there might be a pattern within. Had all three, perhaps, left fortunes behind? The Regional Crime Squad had made a forensic accountant available for the inquiry. DC Twine was travelling north to interview Coldshaw's niece in Scunthorpe to ask if the family had any idea why she'd so dramatically decided to leave Marsh House.

Ever since Valentine had found Beatty Hood's death certificate taped behind one of Henry Bright's serene moonlit landscapes, or more precisely, ever since Dr Scrutton had given him his scan results, he'd retained a morbid fascination for that official wording: *date and place of death*. One day his own certificate would carry this information. Every step he took brought him closer to that moment. By way, perhaps, of evasion, he walked on now towards 32 Hartington Street, the house in which Beatty Hood's life had finally passed, quietly, away.

The Spring's eight streets formed a latticework like a Georgian window, creating nine 'islands' riddled with alleyways, allowing access to back yards, although the central island had been left open as a grassed square, a great chestnut at the centre, no doubt a remnant of the old, original garden which had surrounded the manor house.

As a child he'd ridden his bike here to play football with schoolmates and lob sticks into the conker tree; recalling a sweetshop, a pub with frosted glass, a mild frisson of adventure: the

Springs was the wrong side of the tracks, and even for a boy from the docks it held an illicit thrill of otherness.

Walking the streets now he noted an upstairs bedroom light in a house on Gladstone and a downstairs light in one on Palmerston; so, despite the imminent arrival of the wrecker's ball, the Springs was not entirely deserted. True, the pub was a burnt-out shell and the Methodist chapel on the corner of Peel and Frobisher, roofless and ruined, but he thought several other properties showed signs of life, and he counted four Sky dishes on properties with no lights and one trickle of smoke from a chimney on Salisbury.

Beatty Hood's house was a Victorian throwback, with dark-blue paint on the sash windows, an ochre door with a fine dolphin knocker, the original brickwork pointed in lime, the drainpipes black and steely. Inside, the interior looked faded, respectable once, now tawdry, cloaked in dust; an aspidistra in a Chinese vase on the window ledge was artificial, upholstered chairs sprouted gouts of interior padding, while a gilt mirror, the metal beneath visible in flecks of rust, reflected Valentine's torch.

Down on one knee, he pushed open the letterbox and noted a hat stand, iron-rails holding the stair carpet in place and a framed picture of George VI. He filled his lungs with the smell of it too: polish, the cold metallic odor of a scrubbed pantry and quite distinctly fish and chips, cut by vinegar, so pungent it made Valentine's mouth flood with saliva. It was clear someone lived in Beatty Hood's old house.

He knocked twice, loud and sharp, the dolphin cracking against its metal plate. An echo came back a few seconds later, and then a third, but nothing stirred on the Springs. The street lights were unlit and, but for the moon, he'd have been in a series of dark 'calle' – urban canyons, pressing in, the soundtrack silent except for the occasional rustle of rats and pigeons. The bleak loneliness made him crave the warmth of his own bed, a comforting touch, so he tracked back towards the Lister Tunnel across the central square.

It was the tree that spooked him; his childhood horse chestnut still held its pivotal position, if dead now, a mighty forty foot of leafless, bone-like branches. But it had fruit, in the form of dozens of discarded shoes and trainers, thrown up and over the brittle twigs and boles. In the moonlight the effect was unnerving, the tree's canopy filled out with shadowy shoes and taut laces. Hanging, as if each pair had been the subject of its own, private, judicial execution. From underneath, where he stood by the trunk looking up, he could see the moon through the strange organic grid-work, and for the first time that night George Valentine looked over his shoulder.

Lister Tunnel was in sight when he heard the crunch of car wheels on the tarmac behind him. Stopping on the pavement he looked back and saw a car kerb-crawling towards him, still a hundred yards away, having turned out of Peel Street by the burnt-out remains of the Parkwood Tavern. Later, in his statement, he'd guess blue

139

as the colour, but the moonlight was deceptive and he couldn't be sure. The licence plate started with an H – that was all he could see as the moon was beyond, high now in a starry, clear sky.

The car, moving, no lights, kept up a steady ten miles per hour.

Twenty feet back he'd passed an alley between two houses, so he retraced his steps, cutting the distance between himself and the advancing car, until he came level with the alley gate, and then – boldly – he stepped out into the street, directly in front of the advancing car. He had his hand on his warrant card, ready to hold it aloft, when he thought better of the tactic: he was alone, whoever was behind the wheel had a distinct, lethal advantage.

At a distance of thirty yards it stopped, the engine idling, and then the driver slammed his foot down on the accelerator and put the head-lamps on full beam.

Valentine pushed the gate open and fell side-ways out of the path of the on-coming car, heard the thud of the tyres mounting the kerb, and saw a fleeting vision of grimy paintwork, a reflecting passenger window, a roof rack.

Back on his feet, he ran out in time to see it skid to a halt in the entrance to the Lister Tunnel. The lights went out again, plunging the scene into shadow, but leaving the vehicle in silhouette against the thin orange light of the streets beyond in the North End. The driver's door creaked open an inch and he saw a hand on the inner handle, before a decision was made; the door cracked shut, the car – still blacked-out – skidded away into the night, a single backfire echoing like a gun shot.

Nineteen

The playful naval architecture of Marsh House found its most stylish expression in what the staff liked to call the Poop Deck, a wooden balcony built out from the second floor and supported by pillars of old oak, the colour weathering towards silver. Here, behind the sturdy barrier of a brass rail, residents could enjoy the view of the sea beyond the marsh. It was possible to stand at the rail and, looking directly north, be unable to see any horizon that was not water; for here, at Brancaster, the great curve of the Norfolk coast turned from the Wash to the open North Sea, so that the 'maritime horizon' occupied all of the view ahead. Today the sea was two-tone, navy blue in deep water and a chalky green over the white sandy shallows. No waves broke the mirrored surface, which lay like mercury beyond the edge of the sands. A line of sea gulls occupied the brass rail, each one tilted into the lightest of onshore breezes, at precisely the same angle, like a set of Dutch windmills.

Shaw had just spent twenty-five minutes that morning re-interviewing Javi Copon, his third on-the-record session. The Spanish authorities had overnight provided a resume of the nurse's police record, a litany of politically-motivated

141

minor offences, including three arrests during protest marches. Shaw had requested more information: was Copon really a violent man? He was certainly a smoker and he'd known all about Camera D, which gave him the opportunity to kill Ruby Bright. He admitted going out on the night she died at least six times to smoke. Otherwise his story had not changed, and so far they'd found no hint of a motive which would link him to such a brutal killing. But he had told Shaw that if he wanted to know more about Ruby's death he should interview Christian Keyes, one of the residents of Marsh House confined here, on the upper floor. Keyes, a friend of Ruby's, had told Copon something remarkable during the night, summoning the nurse to his room. Shaw had agreed he should hear it first hand.

Shaw sat alone waiting for Keyes to finish his breakfast, flicking the card Fortis had given him on his first visit, still troubled by the euphemism 'Rest Home', which continued to remind him of one of his father's favourite blunt epithets: 'You're a long time dead.' The idea of DCI Jack Shaw spending any time in a rest home was unthinkable. Cancer of the larynx had killed Jack Shaw, but it had been that last murder case which had really brought him down, and the judge's insinuation that – in partnership with Valentine – they'd fabricated evidence to get a conviction. The corrosive label 'bent copper' had sucked the life out of Jack Shaw, and the fight. Time had shown that they'd put the right man in the dock; Valentine's career, redeemed, had thrived with his return to CID at St James'. But vindication had made no difference to the late DCI Jack Shaw. His headstone still stood in the shadows at St Faith's, Wells-next-the-Sea. Beyond the dates 1938–2008, there was but a single couplet from his favourite writer, Stephenson:

Home is the sailor, home from the sea
And the hunter home from the hill.

It had been his mother's choice, and she'd vetoed her son's suggestion that they include the preceding line: *Here he lies where he longed to be.*

Jack Shaw had wanted to die for the last year of his life, but it was a gift he was denied. Shaw had been shielded from his father's daily disappointment that he kept waking up in the morning, each dawn a reminder that he'd failed to cheat his appointed fate. It was, perhaps, a mark of the arrogance of the man, or even the arrogance of mankind, that he'd expected to summon his own death like some celestial taxi, cruising the bedsides of the dying, its 'For Hire' dimly lit.

Javi Copon slid the glass doors open and pushed out a wheelchair-bound resident, an elderly man in a tweed jacket, white shirt and tie.

'This is Christian,' he said, fussing with a blanket, which he wrapped round his knees despite the sun. The nurse's white uniform transformed Javi from a beach bum into a professional. Shaw recognized a neat ceramic badge on one chest indicating he was a SRN, a state registered

143

nurse, and another badge he didn't recognize, which was square with a red outline, containing stylized letters reading CCOO. He also noted a thin white scar across the right edge of Copon's jaw that he'd missed before, probably caused by a surfboard 'skeg'; the injury, soaked in salt water swims, was a livid badge of honour as potent as a duelling scar.

'Christian,' said Copon, placing a hand on the old man's shoulder. 'This is Detective Inspector Shaw, he wants to talk to you about Ruby? Ruby, from downstairs? And her friend Beatty Hood. Do you remember? We talked about this last night. I want you to try to remember what you said.'

Over acrid Spanish espresso in the nurses' station below, Copon had outlined for Shaw the haunted life of Christian Keyes. Now aged eighty-six, the son of a Royal Navy officer, he'd been brought up in Devonport, Plymouth. His life had been overshadowed by the fate of his father, who'd been involved in one of the great naval tragedies of the First World War: the destruction of what became known as the Live Bait Squadron.

'Live Bait – yes?' Copon had asked, expertly producing the espresso from a gleaming Italian machine, while mimicking a fisherman casting a rod.

The squadron had comprised obsolete ships, with poorly trained or reserve crews, and been stationed in the shallow waters of the North Sea.

'All the staff know this story,' said the Spaniard, his feet up on the edge of the CCTV console.

'Christian will tell anyone, even if they don't listen.'

Copon's version of Christian's tale was succinct: despite concerns that the squadron was a sitting target for German U-boat attack, it was allowed to remain on station. One ash-gray dawn in the North Sea (September 22, 1914, Shaw had checked it on his mobile while out on the poop) a German U-boat spotted three cruisers in single file. It submerged, got close and fired a single torpedo which hit the engine room of the first, breaking the ship's back and bringing it to a full stop. It sank within twenty minutes and many died. Its sister ships, thinking it had hit a mine, headed towards the wreck to pick up survivors. The U-boat, undetected, sank them both. By nightfall 1,560 men had died in the water. Midshipman Keyes was picked out of the swell by a Dutch trawler. Delirious, guilt-ridden, he seemed unable to shake off the idea that he was personally responsible for the carnage, as he'd been on watch aboard one of the ships.

Midshipman Keyes died in a psychiatric unit at Reading in 1961, killing himself by tipping an electric fire into his bath. His son, Christian, by then a lieutenant in the Royal Navy, had been his only regular visitor. In 2010 Christian had been diagnosed with Alzheimer's. As the details of his own life faded, the final hours of his father's watch that day in 1914 seemed to grow more vivid. In a nightmarish echo of the Ancient Mariner's fate, he seemed doomed, each day of the life he had left, to keep his father's watch.

His behaviour had become increasingly

145

obsessive. He told his family, and later his nurses, that it was a harmless hobby; he had a neat phrase for it, he was a 'maritime trainspotter', keeping a note in a neat log of the vessels he saw. He'd used his savings, against his family's wishes, to secure a view of the sea from one of Marsh House's second-floor suites. And so the tally grew of coasters and trawlers, wind farm tugs, oil tankers and yachts, sloops and dredgers. But Copon was not alone in suspecting that he was really searching for the ghost of the merciless U-boat.

Shaw pulled up a chair and shook Keyes' hand – which was darkly tanned, allowing the knuckles to show up as knotty bones, only just below the stretched skin. In his lap was a battered set of binoculars.

'Mr Keyes, hello. Thanks for talking to me. Javi tells me you were friends with Ruby. Why did you like her?'

Shaw was pretty convinced Keyes had heard the question and he saw the light of understanding in his pale green eyes; but then, convulsively, the old man clasped the binoculars and raised them to his eyes, scanning the horizon: once to the west, once to the east, then once more back to the west.

'The light's good,' he said, 'low. So you can see shadows. I see a lot of seals at this hour, they break the surface.'

'Is that what you're looking for, seals?'

Shaw saw that Keyes' lips were dry, cracked, like the survivor his father had once been. There was a suppressed tension in Keyes' watching, the hint of active service, rather than an idle hobby.

'Did Ruby like looking out to sea?'

'Yes, yes. That's it, you've got it. The others laugh – I know that, I see that. She had those eyes that get sharper with age. A precision, visually, that was quite extraordinary. Yes. Typically, she was gifted at that, telling people what was good about age, old age. This . . .'

He spread his hands out to indicate the width of the horizon, but somehow also encompassed his own personal predicament.

'She'd keep a weather eye for me. She loved being outside, down near the beach. It was the landscape, the art of it; the seascape as well. If she saw a vessel from the terrace she'd shout – yes, even if they told her not to. She called me Mr Christian; that was our joke, from the Mutiny on the *Bounty*. No one else remembers.'

His bony fingers tightened on the brass rail and he pulled the chair closer to the edge, looking down on to the empty terrace below.

'What was the name again?' asked Keyes.

'Shaw. Peter Shaw. I live on the beach to the east so I'm always looking out to sea too.'

He'd dropped the binoculars. 'I'm on watch.'

'Me too. I'm a lifeboat man. A pilot, actually, on the hovercraft.'

'Good God. Well done. Well done.'

He lifted the binoculars and again swept west, east, west.

'There. Coaster. See it? Fifteen miles, NNE.' He seemed excited, revitalized, but Shaw also glimpsed a genuine fear in his eyes which he thought was rare in those of such an age, who often seemed to know that death was inevitable and so life had lost its terrors. Here was a facet of the Ancient Mariner's dilemma which was subtly horrific; that the fear would be endless, because the look-out was immortal.

'I've only got the one good eye,' said Shaw, squinting. He could see the ship, a stern bridge, flat deck, probably a small container ship bound for Harwich or Felixstowe. Over a distance of more than twenty feet, having two eyes rather than one provided no actual advantage at all to anyone. Eyepatched pirates proved the point.

Keyes studied *his* face then, which was a strange reversal of roles, because the human face was Shaw's area of expertise. 'Yes, blind in one eye, I see that now.' Without warning the concentration seemed to snap, so that Keyes fussed with the binoculars, the tartan rug, his cuffs, as if he'd been overwhelmed by instant senility.

'Don't forget the ship,' said Shaw, pointing out.

As Keyes relocated the vessel, Shaw drew closer. 'Did you know Ruby's friend Beatty, Beatty Hood? Javi, the nurse, said you'd remembered something about Beatty.'

'Hood was bad, not as bad as Live Bait. HMS *Hood* – they never did know why she blew up like that. Sometimes they show it on TV – a clip they call it. A clip; sometimes modern life is so cruel, isn't it? Flippant. There she is, the *Hood*, and then she's lost, in a single plume of water. What, two seconds? 1,415 dead. It's callous, isn't it, they shouldn't do that, not with relatives watching – children, even. Still a mystery. Live

Bait wasn't a mystery. It was a scandal. Idiots thought it was a mine she'd hit. When the ship went, she rolled right over, turned turtle, with men running down the hull, like human ants. Not a sight you forget, can forget. A stricken ship is a savage sight.'

Shaw wondered then if he could see it as if he was there, if he'd taken his father's memories and made them his own. It was a kind of haunting, because his father lived on, here at Brancaster, a century after the submarine attack. It struck Shaw that this was a form of immortality, that a memory could be instilled in a family and allowed to run on down the years, so that a single image, as of the sailors running across the turning hull of the overturned ship, would be as vivid now as it was a century earlier. Odd that a man with Alzheimer's should be a vital component in the triumph of memory.

Keyes lifted the glasses but then brought them down swiftly. 'Beatty – Ruby's friend Beatty? She wasn't a resident, you know that? No, no. Just a visitor. She died, last year, year before that? No more. That was a blow for Ruby. You won't know this yet but life stops when you've got no one to tell; no one to *receive*. We're like radios, I think – transmitting and receiving, but if there's just you, what's the point? It's not death, but it's the beginning. You see something, hear something, and the joy of it rises up and then . . . dissipates, like that . . .' He raised a finger towards the large aluminium pipe which expelled fumes from the kitchens. 'Hot air. Even if you do tell someone, a nurse, a doctor, they don't listen. It's not deliberate, is it? It's just they've got their own people still. They're not on your wavelength. They're not alone.'

Using his hand, he tried to get closer to the brass rail, but the wheelchair was hard against the edge. Looking back Shaw could see Copon in the upstairs lounge, dispensing pills from a trolley.

Keyes locked his elbows into position on the arms of the chair and then clamped the binoculars into his eye sockets.

Shaw could see tears on his face, running down, as if the binoculars were weeping. Shaw waited, strangely confident that this tortured man wanted to tell him something if he could just keep in check the anxiety which drove him to look, constantly, to the sea.

'She's gone,' said Keyes, his shoulders slumping at last, the effort of concentration still holding his neat, naval features at attention.

'I'm sorry,' he said, fidgeting with the binoculars. 'I can't get my mind to work as it once did. I've enjoyed your visit. I'd ask your name, but I suspect you've told me already. But you came about Ruby – yes, of course. I told Javi, so I'll tell you.'

Dragging his eyes from the sea he looked Shaw in the face. 'Ruby said Beatty was murdered. The word she used – I'll not forget it. That's what she told me, Mr Shaw. And then she asked a curious question: "They killed her, Christian. But who can I tell?"'

Twenty

The Shack stood on the banks of the Fisher Fleet, a rickety hut built of recycled ships' boards, with a flop-down counter and a few plastic chairs outside on the quayside. High tide; so the fleet jostled with trawlers, floating free of the muddy banks, a chaos of masts and rigging, hawsers, winches, sonar and radar. The dock road, jammed with lorries to take the morning's catch, laid down a base soundtrack, as freezer units laboured to ice the fish. On the breeze Valentine detected the thin aroma of cold blood.

For the first time in thirty years Valentine could actually smell the Fisher Fleet; usually he successfully cut the stench with nicotine, the Silk Cut positioned directly under his narrow nose; a tactic so successful that he'd often been able to tackle a bacon sandwich as well as a cup of the Shack's tepid, double-builder tea. He needed the tannin, after a night in which he inexplicably slept like a child, untroubled by either his illness, or the ham-fisted attempt to scare him off the deserted streets of the Springs.

Gordon Lee, chief reporter with the *Lynn Express*, was sitting on one of the plastic chairs staring vacantly into his smartphone. Lee, a Londoner, had been part of the great sixties exodus from the East End; early fifties, bald, short, bustling, almost heroically awkward. As

Valentine pulled up his own chair, Lee glanced up – a three second appraisal – and then returned to his mobile internet screen.

'Given up the fags, then?' he said.

'All those years with the Royal Observer Corps not a waste, eh Gordon.'

Seagulls, in a screeching airborne bundle, descended on a trawler as its catch spilt from a net on to the deck.

'I ain't got a lot of time, George. Editor's conference at ten thirty. The new bloke's still keen. Jackson used to let us go get the stories, then we could have a conference to decide what to do with 'em. Teenage Boy Wonder wants it the other way round.'

'How old is he really?'

Lee shrugged and picked his mug up from the gravel by his shoe. A man of annoying habits he proceeded to aspirate his tea, drinking it at the same time as drawing in the damp fishy air, creating a sustained slurp.

'I don't care. We just want him to win an award, then he can fuck off to Fleet Street, which will then gobble him up, and spit him back out to the provinces, where he will promptly become a cynical old hack like the rest of us.'

Valentine gave him a copy of the ESDA print-out of the imprint left on Ruby Bright's blotter.

'Right,' said Lee, holding the A4 sheet as if it might be impregnated with a lethal poison. 'I told you, George, on the blower. I'm a busy man. Have I come all the way out here for a pissing cup of tea to be asked the same question again?'

'I just need to be sure, George. It's press day,

right? There aren't going to be any surprises, are there? I wouldn't like to read something you'd regret writing. Anyway, there's been developments – I wouldn't want you to miss the real story.'

Lee smiled, revealing wrecked teeth. 'Look. She never sent me a letter, all right? Think about it. She was gonna be one hundred – big deal – *not*. These days, two a penny, George. Even you'll make ninety, thanks to the marvels of modern science. I think she just planned to tip us off by letter, bit old-fashioned, but then she was born just after the First World War. But we were on to it and rang the home. The palace lines us up if there's a message from Her Maj. We'd have contacted the home sometime last month, so I reckon she just binned the letter, or never wrote it.'

The reporter sucked some more air and tea through his thin moustache. 'Why the long face?'

'It was worth a try. We had hopes, Gordon. This is a tough one to crack. But that's life. Anyway, there's a suggestion, and you can use this but no names, not even police sources, agreed?'

He waited for Lee to nod.

'There's a *suggestion* that she knew a killer was about. That he'd struck before. We're on to it, but it's just one aspect of our wide-ranging inquiries etc., etc., etc. . . .'

'Serial killer, George? Still my beating heart.'

Lee had got his notebook out and actually licked his lips in anticipation. Shaw and Valentine had talked it through and decided that floating a serial

153

killer story – especially one they could instantly dismiss as speculation – would gain the inquiry much needed attention. A high media profile would radically increase the likelihood a vital witness might step forward. They were setting up a hotline for information manned 24/7.

'You can call it what you like, Gordon. We've got one murder. But you can speculate that we are looking at two other deaths.'

'Two? At Marsh House?'

Valentine thought about that. 'Linked to Marsh House, no more at this stage. Don't go mad, Gordon. It's not the Norfolk Ripper or anything.'

Lee wasn't listening. 'And this line, the other murders, that going public, is it?'

'Nope. All yours, but as I said, no source please, otherwise your car will be unable to travel more than a hundred yards without attracting a speeding ticket.'

Valentine, bent double, dealt with a fresh bout of coughing, then ploughed on: 'In fact, *you* won't be able to go a hundred yards without getting a ticket. Just be aware that once you hit the streets all we are going to do is issue a brief line saying it's pure speculation.'

'But no denial?'

This time it was the reporter's turn to wait for clear confirmation.

'No denial, Gordon. Be careful about Marsh House, it's owned by a corporation hiding behind a trust, and they can afford lawyers, Inns of Court lawyers. So be afraid.'

Lee rubbed his left cheek, as if trying to revive a stroke victim. 'Why didn't Bright tell someone what she knew?' A light went on in the reporter's eyes. 'Oh I see, you think she told us. It would have been nice, George, but no.'

'Perhaps she did tell someone. Maybe she told the wrong person.' Valentine checked his mobile. 'As lovely as this is, Gordon . . .'

'Hold up, George. One good turn and all that, I've got something for you. Thing is . . . That's what they say now, right? *Thing is* . . . We've been getting threatening phone calls in the newsroom. Some ice-cold nutcase saying that if this 'World' pilgrimage goes ahead as planned someone's going to get hurt.'

Valentine sipped his tea. 'Precise wording?'

'Ah. Sore point. New office junior took the first one. He was on lunch duty so nobody else about. He's got a 2.1 in Applied Mathematics apparently, but his Pitman 2000 is currently thirty-five words a minute. He took a full note, but it might as well be the Gettysburg Address.

'Second time they got the news desk secretary, again at lunchtime, and she told him to ring back! Which is quite funny when you think about it. A bit like telling a bank robber to pop in next time the safe's open.

'Third call he got Eric Johns on the subs bench, what's more he got him when he was awake. Eric wouldn't know a news story if it bit him on the arse, but he's still got one hundred and eighty-words-a-minute shorthand. He took a note and promised to pass it on. By this point I'm guessing chummy's having second thoughts about the glamour associated with playing Deep Throat. But, listen up . . .'

Lee flipped open his notebook.

'Eric's description of the voice was pretty decisive,' said Lee. 'Calm, monotone, reading. A man certainly, but no way he could estimate the age beyond twenty plus, so not a kid. So this is verbatim . . .' Lee filled his lungs. 'Just get this down, all right?' Then a pause: '"Pilgrims used to travel in groups for a good reason. Wolves, wild boar, outlaws, thieves, cutpurses. That was the good old days. This pilgrimage has gone back in time. They want to outlaw gays and lesbians, they want to make abortion murder. Well, if they want to live in the past they can have the full experience. They should travel in packs because the paths are dangerous. Who knows what lies in wait on the old ways? We – reborn as the Wolves – are waiting for them. We bring stones and knives and fire and retribution. We lie in wait."'

Lee closed his notebook. 'I can email a copy.'

'Bit of a drama queen,' said Valentine, pointing at Lee's cup. The reporter nodded and Valentine went to the empty counter to collect fresh tea.

'A bacon sarnie would be nice,' said Lee.

'Yes it would. But you don't have the time,' said Valentine, returning. 'What do you want me to do with this?' he asked. 'It's pretty immature. Probably some pimply kid. The Wolves – load of tosh. And it's not the first, Gordon. Apparently someone saying something pretty similar rang the council at Hunstanton. They didn't manage to get any kind of transcript, and the woman who took the call's been off sick with stress since, but I think we can assume it's the same nutter.'

'Publication would be in the public interest, George, that's what Teenage Boy Wonder says, and he wants it all done by the book. Story runs tomorrow. We've got WAP – the protest lot, saying they disown violence of any kind, etc. I've got to try the official organizers this afternoon. If you're not bothered, a holding statement would be nice, even if it's along the lines of why should we care about some Leftie fruitcake who thinks he's Robin Hood.'

Valentine thought about that image, a forest track, a line of pilgrims, dusk falling. 'They don't go through the woods – do they?'

'Oh, yeah. It's not just one route, George. They're all on the website – www.worldpilgrim. com. Take a look. There's six long distance paths in excess of one hundred miles. That's for those who want to spend a week wasting their time and ours. Then there's two short "legs" they call 'em – for quick twenty-four-hour efforts. One of those is from Wells, your neck of the woods. 'Cause, when you think about it, that's why it's here, innit – the Holy House. It's not really at the back end of nowhere, it's a day's walk from the coast and the old ports. That's where your pilgrims landed – from France, Low Countries, Channel ports, East Coast, London even. I don't know about the rest, but last time I helped monitor the Wells leg it goes loads of places they could run into trouble – woods, riversides, old paths. And this time a fair bit's at night. So – yeah, they're vulnerable all right.'

Valentine stood, stretching, until his spine made

a series of plastic clicks. 'What d'you reckon the organizers will say? Think they'll cancel?'

'No chance. The lot who run the annual one – the National, they're reasonable; this lot, they're *zealots*. Bloke on the phone is an amateur nutter by comparison. A babe in arms. If this mob thought there was a good chance trendy Liberal Lefties were lurking in the bushes with sticks and stones they'd call for thousands more to flock to Walsingham. Martyrdom, George. That's what's on offer. Nothing better than a rock on the head when you're carrying a Pro-Life banner. They're prepared to die for the cause. No – they *want* to die for the cause, George. Looks like they might even get the chance. Only pity is we can't leave the lot of 'em to it.'

Twenty-One

'Curry,' said Valentine. 'For *lunch*?'

'It's on expenses,' said Shaw. 'Relax. Enjoy. No, celebrate. The nutter in the car last night could have broken your neck. You're alive, George. Live a bit.'

Shaw bit his tongue. Set in perspective the throwaway line sounded cruel, even brutal. But George Valentine had nothing if not a thick skin. He'd already written off the attack as payback for nosing around Parkwood Springs. Shaw's interview with Christian Keyes made him think there might be darker motives at work.

'And look on the bright side,' said Shaw, pushing open the plate glass door of the Crown of Punjab. 'Indian lager on tap.'

Scanning the restaurant Shaw thought he spotted Dr Gokak Roy – an elderly man, with frizzy grey hair, examining a tightly folded copy of the *Financial Times*. But three strides into the restaurant, he caught a movement out of the corner of his eye and saw a young man, half standing, raising a narrow hand by way of hesitant signal.

'DI Shaw? Gok Roy, good to meet you. Have a seat . . .'

Ten minutes later they were eating; Valentine having opted for the mildest korma on the menu and a pint of Tiger, Dr Roy picking at something aromatic with Naga chilli – so hot that when Shaw detected a note of the spice on the air he felt a hiccough building in his throat. He pushed some okra around his own plate, sipping iced water.

'Sorry,' said Dr Roy, 'I'm on shifts and so this is Friday night out.' The spotless, fitted, white shirt and the tall glass of fizzy water marked him out as professional, clean-cut and efficient. 'My uncle owns the place, so I get a discount.'

Valentine waved his empty pint glass at a lurking waiter.

Dr Roy, distracted by the arrival of a middle-aged man he called Ratif, appeared unfeasibly young; Shaw guessed thirty as an absolute limit. His skin, taut and toned, seemed to radiate intense life. Shaw imagined a racing blood-stream just beneath the skin, oxygen molecules

159

unloading high octane fuel to the grey cells of the brain.

'Last year,' said Shaw, 'you signed this death certificate.' He pushed a copy across the tablecloth and Dr Roy placed a finger on it lightly, the nail perfectly cut, showing a red cuticle beneath.

'Beatrice Hood,' said Dr Roy. 'Yes. I remember the house – through the archway? It was like a Victorian museum . . .' His eyes lit up. 'Not dissimilar, it has to be said, to the average British curry house. What is it with the flock wallpaper?'

'Old age is listed as the primary cause of death. Is that usual? It seems a bit sweeping, a bit flippant even.'

'Yes. Sounds odd, I admit – actually we use it a lot in patients over eighty-five. At that age, in many cases, there may be so many secondary causes, all linked to the ageing process, that "old age" is actually a very precise term. Coroners are very supportive of it in terms of the documentation. In my experience they welcome clear, common sense, certification. Beatty was ill, gravely ill, for some time. I visited her regularly that year. She'd elected to die at home, and her notes were marked to that effect. The day she passed away her condition had deteriorated markedly. I arrived at just after noon, and she was falling in, and out, of consciousness. Finally, she died in her sleep at just after three o'clock.'

'That's a good memory,' said Valentine.

'I tend to remember patients I'm with when they die, Sergeant. Especially when I'm the only person at the bedside.' He held up a hand by way of apology. 'It's stuck in my mind, certainly. That moment, the sense of being a lone witness to the end of someone's life. Do you see? In many ways it is a privilege.'

Shaw, nodding, pressed on: 'There has been a suggestion that Mrs Hood might have been killed, murdered in fact. Were there any suspicious circumstances to her death? Did she say anything which might suggest she had an enemy, or that she was in any way fearful?'

Dr Roy's face was a picture of disbelief, his eyes wide with surprise. 'Murdered? No. I was making a routine call. Her conditions were chronic. Her body and its vital organs were failing. When I got there it was clear to me she was dying. I think *she* knew she was dying. At such times the patient often retreats into an interior dialogue, with the dead, perhaps, with loved ones. I did what I could.'

'Her condition, in this final phase, it couldn't have been induced? A poison, perhaps?'

'Possibly. But I had no suspicions. Her symptoms were entirely consistent with her medical history. Death's a process, which can last months or even years. She had been on that journey for some time. There were no signals, as it were, that anything unusual, or unnatural, had occurred. No, absolutely not, Inspector.'

Dr Roy speared a piece of cauliflower baked in cumin. 'She did have problems with vandals, I know that. The house is on that old estate . . .'

'Parkwood Springs,' offered Valentine.

'Kids just run wild out there.' Dr Roy held a

161

hand to his forehead. 'That last time, I do remember now. One of the windows in the kitchen was just papered over. I went down for water and asked about it and she said they'd smashed it, these kids, and got in, and she'd shouted from the top of the stairs and it spooked them so they ran. But I think she was worried they'd come back. If she did go out, she used a white stick, so it wasn't as if they didn't know of her disability. When she woke up in bed she said she'd lie still, listening, and that sometimes she thought they might be right there, in the room, by the bed. Given her near blindness that kind of anxiety isn't going to help. Vandalism's cruel, indiscriminate and gets under the skin, even when you're young and healthy. It's like a bad dream about your teeth falling out. It reflects a deeper anxiety, a fear of intrusion, a loss of control. But it isn't murder, is it?'

Valentine made a note: they'd check vandalism, petty damage, street crime, and see if any names came up. He thought too of the picture on his phone that Jan had sent him of the blood-spattered trainers under Lister Tunnel.

'It was peaceful, then, her death when it came?' asked Shaw.

Dr Roy smiled and Shaw caught a glimpse of a crueler cast to the wide brown eyes. 'Well, I suppose people tend to imagine the Death of Nelson, everyone crowding round in the warm lantern light. The great man rewarded with a good death. The last words. *Ars moriendi* – yes? The Art of Dying. That's pretty rare in my limited experience.'

162

'It was a bad death?'

'No. She died in her bed. For her generation that's a significant comfort. She didn't die in the street, or from cholera.'

Dr Roy's eyes seemed to slip out of focus and Shaw had the distinct impression he was struggling with a memory he wished to forget.

'She wasn't cut down by a sword, or blown to bits by a bomb, or buried under rubble. So that's a small victory. Dickens is good at the deathbed scene, Little Nell, that kind of thing. Affecting, a bit sentimental. But he was reflecting something very real, you see, that most people *didn't* die in their beds. It was an extraordinary blessing to die in the home.'

He seemed to realize the subject had taken wing. 'My mother was besotted with Dickens. Very good on the poor, too. Bad deaths too, look at Sykes, swinging on his rope, neck broken. What would he have given for a cosy deathbed scene?'

'Last words?' prompted Shaw. 'Did Mrs Hood say anything at all?'

They all waited while the waiter swept the tablecloth with a set of brushes.

'Last words?' repeated Shaw.

Dr Roy shook his head. 'I think she asked me what the date was – yes. Not the time, the date. Which was odd. I had it on my smartphone. The room was half-lit, the curtains drawn, and I recall clearly her face, lit by the phone. But she couldn't read it, of course. But she held it here . . .'

He held his own phone up over his eye socket.

'After that I don't think she said anything cogent, I'm afraid.'

163

Shaw looked at the certificate. 'September the nineteenth. Why do you think she asked?'

'No idea, Inspector. I concentrate on those things I can materially affect. I made her comfortable.'

'But you were alone, after she died. What did you do?'

'Yes, I was alone.' Shaw couldn't tell if he was manufacturing the emotion but the brown eyes flooded and he snatched for the iced water, draining the glass.

'I contacted the relevant authorities. I waited for the funeral directors, I think, perhaps, twenty minutes.'

'You didn't call an ambulance?'

'No. I was able to confirm that death had occurred, Inspector. Why waste scarce resources on calling out an ambulance for no reason?'

Shaw nodded. 'And then?'

'I locked up and kept the keys, which were eventually couriered to the solicitors. The funeral directors dealt with everything else.'

'You didn't attend the funeral?'

'I did. At the crematorium.'

'You're a busy man, that was, what? Kind, dutiful?'

'Professional. The practice has served that area I think for many years. It's expected. Rightly, I think.' He dabbed the napkin at his lips.

The doctor checked his watch. 'My favourite last words are Dickens too – do you know them? His sister-in-law told him to rest on a sofa or chair and he said: "On the ground!" I can see that, can't you? Wanting to feel the earth under your back. It's as if he needed to hang on to the turning world.'

'I prefer *Mehr Licht*,' said Shaw. 'It's Goethe. More light.'

'Very good. And you, Sergeant?'

'I'll think of something,' said Valentine, holding up the empty pint mug for a refill.

Twenty-Two

Mow Creek was a tidal channel, a broad sandy inlet, opening out to the sea a mile south of Marsh House. At low tide it harboured shadows in its black, muddy depths, while high water saw it threatening to spill out into the marsh, the waves rattling the reeds. On a map it looked like an old vine, branched and curious, twisting between islands of grass and sand.

Linas Jessop was in exactly the spot Shaw had been able to predict from the artist's sketchbooks, the vantage point he'd used over the years to indulge his infatuation with atmospherics and light. A rough wooden easel stood against the sky on a grass knoll, the artist a few feet away, a separate silhouette, brush in hand. From the north a stiff tidal breeze gusted in, and Jessop stepped forward occasionally to grip the canvas. This was no delicate hobby, a bid to capture the picturesque, but something much more muscular, a kind of duel between artist and elements.

Shaw, picking his way seawards on the marsh

path, imagined the canvas as a shield, the brush a sword.

Jessop was rocking back and forth on his booted heels, his windblown head still, when he must have heard the grate of Shaw's shoe on the sandy path. His face swung round and for a moment there was a flash of obsessed anger, as if the magic of the place, the spectrum of light and colour, had been shattered and lost.

His body straightened then, the anxiety dissipating. 'Inspector. You've found my secret place, how clever of you. Feast your eyes!'

The prospect seawards was breathtaking. A vast arrow of migrating birds, thousands deep, was a mere smudge to the west. The wind, picking up, flattened the marsh grass, buffeting it down, as if an invisible giant strode inland.

'If you've secreted the chains about your person, perhaps you'd let me add time and date to this as it may be my last. This is about Beatty Hood, of course. Not an unexpected visit.'

The sketch was in watercolour washes, broad free strokes of green and blue. The sky, equally uninhibited, showed a summer chef's hat cumulus, billowing up into the stratosphere.

'It wasn't about her, no,' Shaw replied. 'It was about Ruby Bright. But if you feel the need to confess . . . You knew Beatty Hood?'

'Yes, of course, I knew Beatty. In *her* youth she was a bit of a smasher, between you and I. Art school, the Slade, I think. She was good, very good. Her and Ruby were great friends – companions really, although it sounds old fashioned now, but that was it. Husbands dead,

166

but they had each other. Odd, actually, because we all had something in common. Only children. And what that does is, I suspect, make you relate to friends. You end up surrounded by people you can actually love or admire for no other reason than themselves. It's odd, isn't it, that as a society we attack so many prejudices – colour, sex, age. But we still think it's necessary to value those who share our closest DNA. What's so *admirable* about that? You tell me, because I don't know, and never have. What's the Luther King quote: "The content of their characters". I'm getting a bit tired of that speech, but that bit's worth the preachy exhortation of the rest.'

Jessop licked his lips. 'Anyway, it was only a matter of time before you discovered that Beatty, like poor Ruby, left me a bequest. No?'

'We are exploring her financial background.'

'Ah. Well, there we are. I could have volunteered the information, but what the hell.

'A small lump sum. Five hundred pounds. Is that motive enough? I put it in the bank by the way, that's how dull my life's become. I can't even spend a windfall.'

He feigned a sudden look of horror. 'Of course. This makes me a *serial killer* to boot – preying on old ladies and then murdering them for their pots of gold. Fame at last indeed!'

'You were disappointed with the five hundred?' asked Shaw. He hadn't tracked out to the sea's edge to question Jessop, quite the opposite, but something about the lost life and lonely death of Beatty Hood seemed to hold the echo of a greater truth. Perhaps it was her death that held the key to the mystery of Marsh House.

'Disappointed? Not really. She left her house to some charity she supported. That was all she had, so I can't argue with her priorities. The Causeway Trust, I think – the name stuck because it's another one of those awful euphemisms: a narrow bridge between life and death, perhaps?

'She was a good woman,' Jessop went on. 'Given the pain of her last few years, she bore them well. She went blind, you'll know that, and it's a cruel fate for the painter – the loss of light must be difficult to take, day after day. But Beatty was always optimistic, alive to the moment. She spent a lot of time at the Phoenix, mainly with one or two of the sculptors, but form – in the three-dimensional sense – is no match for colour.' He looked out to sea. 'To the outside world she showed a brave face.'

For a minute he worked quickly with the wet paint he had on a tin palette. Satisfied, he stood back, staring into the middle distance. 'There was a little cash left over after my bequest, I recall, which caused some excitement because most of it went on some memorial to mark her family grave. It was partly her own stone work. Quite a thing, I'm told. That's out at Old Hunstanton, in the village. St Mary the Virgin. I've never bothered to visit since. I'm not a dutiful bunch of flowers kind of man, really. I went to the funeral but there's no stone at that point, is there, just a hole in the ground.

'There's a James Thurber cartoon I'm very fond

168

of . . .' He turned to Shaw then, the face relaxed, honest, and open. 'Thurber – you know Thurber?'

Shaw nodded.

'He sketched this graveyard, glimpsed through railings, the pavement crowded with determined men and women walking to the left, to the right, clutching shopping bags, briefcases, pushing prams. The caption read simply: *Destinations*. Devastating, really.'

'I didn't come to ask you questions about Beatty Hood,' said Shaw. 'I brought good news. You said you lived a life without alibis. For a while I thought that was very suspicious because it was as if you were saying don't even try to find out if I'm telling the truth. And then I thought it can't be true, because if you come here every day, or nearly every day, at the same "atmospheric" moment, then someone knows, someone sees. And I was right.'

Looking south they could see the line of high ground that marked the apron of the hill country inland. Along this modest cliff-line they could see at least two churches in the far distance, and occasional roofs and chimneys and one tower: modern, in brick, a curved observation window set just below a party-hat roof.

'I asked the local copper – PC Curtis – to see if he could find you that elusive alibi. He's one of those people who walk around as if they're under water, unhurried, but very thorough.

'For the past ten years you've been out here mimicking John Sell Cotman, while the man in that house' – he pointed to the distant tower – 'has watched you, in between tracking the flights

169

of migrant birds at dusk. On a landscape like this you need landmarks, especially if you're chronicling the movement of creatures as mobile as the oystercatcher. You're a landmark, Mr Jessop. Curious, isn't it, that you thought you were a man with no alibis and actually you turn out to be virtually on the map . . .'

Shaw produced a small tube of watercolour paint: sepia, in the Winsor & Newton 'student' range, branded under the name of 'Cotman'.

'A small gift from me. Our birdwatcher was particularly interested in the reaction of his beloved waders to the supermoon. He noted your arrival that night, the night Ruby died, and indeed your departure, setting out west towards Lynn. A perfect alibi, after all.'

Jessop accepted the paint with a small theatrical bow.

'Good news indeed. Can you keep a secret, Inspector?'

'Depends.'

'Well. If you can't I'll deny I ever said it – don't suppose we're bugged out here. Unless you've got young PC Curtis hiding in the reeds. No. I think I'm pretty safe. You see, I *did* know Ruby intended to cut me out of the will. I can say that now, of course. But at the time I thought it best to forget.'

'She told you?'

'Yes. The last time we met, down by the waterside below Marsh House. Straight to my face, too. She had guts, Ruby, you'd have to give her that. She asked Javi Copon to give us some space, so he walked off to smoke in the dunes. She said

170

I seemed to be pretty "thick" with the Spaniard. That's a good old-fashioned notion – "thick", like we were ingredients in a stew. I said we shared politics, ideas . . . ideals, even. She said I could enjoy my ideals without the benefit of her money. Fifty thousand – she told me the exact amount just to rub it in. Never said another word. I presumed she'd got round to changing the will – but clearly not.'

'I think you owe PC Curtis a present,' observed Shaw. 'Given that without your alibi you'd be an irresistible prime suspect, especially in the light of that little confession, on or off the record. He lives along at Wells, so perhaps a seascape, or even one of the sketches from here . . .'

They both considered the wide horizon.

'It's nearly sunset and I need to work,' said Jessop. 'I feel inspired, you see – energized, even. It's not the money, which is all the sweeter for knowing Ruby didn't want me to have it. It's the thought I might not leave anything worthy behind. So if you'll excuse me . . .'

Shaw walked away, inland, thinking about Beatty Hood, the artist plunged, eventually, into a world of gathering shadows, but living life to the full. Despite that upbeat picture, Jessop's verdict hung in Shaw's mind: *To the outside world she showed a brave face.*

Twenty-Three

Jan Clay had never worried about fashion, but she knew she had a sense of style. At five foot five, with a boyish close-cut blonde hairstyle, she'd always favoured trousers, rarely dresses, unless she was aiming for a 'glam' effect. She'd been able to turn heads when she wanted to, but she liked the anonymity a uniform brought. She felt compact, fit, but most of all at ease, as if she'd simply been awarded the insignia after a lifetime of working in CID. Which, in an odd way, was part of the truth. The first time she'd set the cap on her head it felt like she'd already deserved its aura of calm authority. The lace-up black leather shoes, with the low heels, gave her an intense sensation of being, literally, grounded.

So when DS Chalker had told her to write a five-hundred-word analysis of the trainers they'd picked off telegraph wires in the last week, she'd thought the request typically crass; she was a woman: it was apparently axiomatic that she could write about shoes. If there was anyone in the shoe squad qualified for the job it was PC Wolinski, who she'd spotted one evening on the Saturday Market in a complete designer outfit plus Ray-Bans. Even on patrol he wore black leather brogues which must have cost a week's wages. His haircut, while regulation, was finely layered, with a hint of an asymmetric cut.

172

But the assignment was Jan's, care of DS Chalker's prejudices, but also by way of punishment, for tying up forensics to examine the trainers recovered from the Lister Tunnel. Chalker had said it was pig's blood, and it was. Let that be a lesson to them all.

The trainers, boots and shoes were all stored beneath St James' in the old magazine chambers built by the military during the Napoleonic Wars. Police headquarters had been constructed over the ruins of the old town walls and a labyrinth of subterranean tunnels and vaults. Brick, curved, like London tube tunnels. There were six large chambers in total, three in daily use as the force's records unit. Chamber one, once a series of metal-partitioned Victorian cells, was now used as a store for traffic division's signage, but was otherwise empty. Jan requisitioned the keys from the duty officer and ferried all the shoes into the cellar in cardboard boxes. It took her twenty minutes to re-stack a set of *Road Closed* signs and the force's supply of pedestrian barriers, clearing a space twenty foot square.

Locking the door she drew an outline in chalk of the town perimeter, adding the Cut and main railway line and the inner ring road. The floor was brick too, the chalk lines wobbly, so she was relieved nobody could inspect her cartography.

Each pair of shoes had an attached label indicating where they had been found. Using an A-Z map where her local knowledge failed, she placed each pair out on the chalk map until all were in position, right down to the blood-spattered specimens from the Lister Tunnel. Then she got a chair

173

from the record office and sat looking north, the town in front of her, the sea to her right.

She checked her watch; she'd been given two hours to write the report, then she was due back with the squad in the North End. Abandoning the chair, notebook in hand, she began to pace the map. It took her less than five minutes to discern one clear pattern: the South End was character-ized by cheap trainers and out-of-date styles – Karrimor, Lonsdale, Slazenger, Everlast, Dunlop. Her iPhone gave a snapshot of a few prices – £22.99, £19.99 – the cheapest at £9.99.

The reverse was true of the North End, where most pairs fell into the categories of expensive and nearly-new. Top of the range was a pair of Lanvin crystal-embellished leather sneakers, which new cost a whopping £505. There were two pairs of Balenciaga leather and fabric trainers, retail price £276. Other upmarket brands included Nike Air Max, Asos Domino, Vans SK8 and Ash. Furthermore, all the customized trainers were found in the North End – NikEid, Kapow, Vans R, Converse. (Unfortunately, none of them customized to the point of carrying their owner's names.)

The shoe squad was due to clear the shoe tree Valentine had reported on the Springs, but Jan doubted they would in any material way alter the clear pattern she'd identified. She used her laptop to knock out a summary report, based on an initial hypothesis, that whatever lay behind the outbreak of flying kicks had something to do with class. What jarred with this analysis was the geography: most of the expensive, new shoes had been found flung over wires in the North End and the docks, a traditional working class area; while those in the south were cheap and worn, despite the fact that most were found in the leafy suburbs beyond the town walls.

Jan concluded with a possible explanation: the trainers marked 'incursions' by gang members into 'hostile territory' controlled by rival gangs. Was this what lay behind the jigsaw of footwear? A gang war? Or at least skirmishes. She printed out a copy of her report at the duty desk, pocketed it, and took a squad car out to the North End, where she found the shoe squad having a coffee break outside the North End Café, a greasy spoon famous – or notorious – for its duck egg sandwiches. The cherry picker stood idle, the council driver at the wheel, reading his latest issue of *Mayfair.*

Jan was twenty feet away when DS Chalker announced her arrival. 'Here she is, lads. Feminism's answer to Sherlock Holmes. The woman who single-handedly tracked down the phantom rasher slayer of Lynn!'

The squad, five strong, grinned, although she noted that Wolinski had the good grace to look at his highly polished black patent shoes.

Chalker gave her Hadden's SOCO report, formally identifying the blood stains as porcine, and got her a cup of tea – a real cup, with a saucer, not a mug like all the rest.

'Hard luck, love. Let's hope the chief constable doesn't spot the four hundred and thirty pound bill for spectrograph analysis, eh?' said Chalker, adjusting the tea cup just so.

The DS didn't say another word, but limited himself to whistling his signature tune: 'Young Girl, Get Out Of My Life'.

Jan gave him her report. 'If you're happy, it needs a signature.'

As he read it, Jan watched his lips move.

'Right. So it's a pissing contest between kids. The rich go north and piss on lampposts, the poor go south and piss on theirs.' He made eye contact with Jan – a rare glint of respect evident – and his voice was warmer, cosier. 'Good job. I'll get it to his office tonight. Any luck we'll be back doing something useful by Monday.' He beamed at his foot soldiers. 'She's done us a favour, boys. Someone's going to have to buy her a drink. It might even be me.'

Tea break over, they climbed aboard the police van and set off for the Springs, the cherry picker trundling behind. Chalker gave them chapter and verse. 'Wonder of wonders, we have a shoe tree to strip. George Valentine found it last night. You can all ask yourselves the obvious question: what the fuck's he doing wandering around Parkwood Springs, especially as the pub's been closed for five years.'

Jan had her face to the window, hiding a smile, so that as the van turned into Lister Tunnel, she saw two things: another pair of trainers under the arch hanging from the power cable and the skip full of rubble, still set on one side, half on the pavement. They pulled over and Chalker said that as she'd been skiving off writing reports, and as she'd spotted them, this pair was all hers.

Two minutes later she was aloft, the extension

arm juddering as it edged her upwards. The rest of the squad hadn't bothered to get out of the police van.

This pair, acid white with silver motifs, was splattered with blood like the last, and hung in exactly the same spot. Despite herself she reached for the evidence bag in her back pocket and slipped on a pair of SOCO gloves. Safely collected, she attached the evidence bag to her belt, and as she did so broke her golden rule, looking down at the cherry picker and the flagstones below.

She had a bird's-eye view into the skip: bricks and hard core, shattered carpentry, steel rods . . . and, splayed out, star-shaped, the body of a young man. The angles of the limbs were set in the semaphore of death. Three blood-red circles ran across his white T-shirt like some ghoulish motif. Luckily, when her hand shot out in shock it attached itself to the cherry picker handrail, so she didn't actually fall, although she swung out, a leg in mid-air, and she heard the echo of her own scream. Later, she told George that the one thing that stuck in her memory was not the wounds, but the feet, which were shoeless.

Twenty-Four

The *Rainbow Protestor* lay anchored to the quay at Wells-next-the-Sea, north Norfolk's miniature seaside resort. A seagoing Dutch barge, its wooden mast supported a cross-spar from which hung a sail the colour of ox blood. Brass gleamed in the sun. The forty-foot deck held a series of benches and tables, a herb garden in flower pots, a 'gyro' clothes drier and a tethered goat. Valentine walked the gangplank with all the enthusiasm of a doomed pirate; naturally averse to water of any kind, he found the concept of floating on it deeply unsettling. Once aboard, he looked up in the rigging, his eye catching a pair of trainers dangling from a cross-spa. Shaw, whistling, followed, his bones immediately seeking out the subtle movement of the vessel beneath his feet as the tide nudged it up against the stone quay.

Shaw had one foot on board when he heard Valentine's mobile pulse. The DS examined the screen. 'It's Jan,' he said, holding up the message for Shaw. *Murder. Lister Tunnel. Teenager.*

'Right. Let's get this done and get back. Ring Twine, make sure we're in on the ground floor. Beatty Hood died on Parkwood Springs. Now another victim turns up less than three hundred yards away.'

The deckhouse of the *Rainbow Protestor* held a ship's wheel fit for a trans-Atlantic crossing, but otherwise seemed deserted, except for a black-and-white collie which sat, erect and alert, in the captain's battered chair. A hatch led down into a wide stairwell, a single flight descending in twenty wooden steps into a wardroom of dark polished teak. A bar had been built, with a rack for barrels, and Shaw guessed the boat's usual trade was as a tourist tripper. Over the bar hung a banner:

WAP
THE WALSINGHAM ALTERNATIVE
PILGRIMAGE
A COALITION OF THE CIVILIZED

A blackboard listed the day's specials: Houmous, Vegetarian Lasagna, Green Salad. Two long corridors led away down the length of the ship towards the blunt prow. Piles of posters and pamphlets dotted the floorboards.

Valentine, losing patience, keen to get on the road for Parkwood Springs, rang a brass bell mounted above the bar and shouted, 'Shop!'

Somewhere, through several wooden walls, they heard a dog bark in response.

Shaw checked his watch.

A man appeared, in swimming shorts, a towel round his neck. Radiating good health, his hair spikey but unwaxed, he looked like a sea creature who'd slipped aboard from beneath the Plimsoll line.

'Hi. We're in the right place?' asked Shaw, indicating the banner. 'DI Shaw,' he added, showing his warrant card. 'DS Valentine. Lynn CID. We'd like a word with Ms Heaney . . .'

Drying his hair, the man turned on bare feet and led the way down the portside passageway; neat high-arched footprints marking his path.

Cabin doors held drawing-pinned signs: Gay Rights, Woman's Right to Choose, Labour Party, REFORM, Right to Die, Lynn Womens' Co-Op. They passed an open door and saw a gleaming photocopier producing colour posters, unattended.

At the stern the original captain's cabin had

179

been requisitioned as THE OFFICE, the double doors propped open. A genuine oak table, scoured by a century's worth of cutlery and knives, held several computer monitors and scattered laptops.

At first they thought the room was empty but then Heaney's head appeared; still make-up free, pale, with that guarded blankness, as if the clown's tear was about to begin its downward path across her cheek.

'Hi. Give me a moment – these sodding cables are impossible . . . Chris, could you?' The swimmer dived under the table to help her disconnect and reconnect a series of plugs from a long adapter. Chris, dismissed, scuttled away, followed by a small terrier they hadn't noticed.

Valentine told Heaney everything he'd been told by Gordon Lee about the threat delivered by the so-called Wolves.

'And so you've come dutifully here,' she said, dunking some kind of teabag in a wide china cup. 'I told the man from the newspaper that it's nothing to do with us.'

'It's hardly an unreasonable connection to make,' said Shaw, speaking for the first time. 'WAP is an umbrella organization, we understand that. You're coordinating the counter pilgrimage, and liaising with uniformed branch on dispositions on the day itself, we're grateful for that. But it's still a perfectly valid question: do you know who might be involved in this group – the Wolves?'

Valentine had a copy of the shorthand note taken at the newspaper office of the telephone threat.

Heaney leant back in her chair, hitching a long leg up on the edge of the table as he read it out twice.

'Charming,' was her verdict, followed by: 'Childish? It's all a bit Brother Cadfael, don't you think? Hooded monks slipping through the green forest. Wild boar in the undergrowth. WAP is many things, Inspector, but we're not into fantasy, and there's hardly time for playing games. Gale, in Woman's Right to Choose, spends her time dealing with rape victims, some of whom end up pregnant as a result of the assault. Johnnie T in Gay Rights runs a helpline for victims of physical and verbal abuse out on the estates. He's not here today; he's at Lynn magistrates for a pre-trial hearing because one of his clients lost an eye, glassed, in a pub fracas over men wearing earrings. And me? This is my annual two-week holiday. The rest of the time I am the dullest of the dull, as I said before, an NHS administrator. I work with the palliative care unit, clearly the NHS's version of Laugh a Minute. While WAP may look like a band of airheads, most of us have a pretty firm grip on reality.'

In the silence that followed this speech Shaw could see she was fighting to keep her breathing under control, disguising the moment by unfolding her long bones, to stand and stretch; one hand reaching the beam above. She wore a white T-shirt again, but this one was decorated with a map of County Antrim.

'We all live in the real world,' offered Shaw. 'We shouldn't be here, but in Lynn, where the body of a murdered teenager has just been

181

discovered. That's why we're in a hurry, Ms Heaney. So, to cut to the chase, is there an answer to my question? Can you tell us anything about the Wolves?'

'No.'

Shaw walked to the port side porthole. 'It's a bit of a fantasy boat. Must cost a fortune. There's the bus as well up at Walsingham.'

Heaney's face had set, the eyes fixed on a point over the double doors. 'A wealthy supporter, a benefactor. He hires the boat for two weeks, we change the name and it changes back when we're done. She's really called the *Delpht*. Last year, for the National, we rented a shop in Walsingham, but when the landlords found out who we were they reneged on the deal, entirely illegally, but there we are. We thought this was a smart way to avoid a repeat performance.'

'What worries me,' said Shaw, 'is that most zealots fail to realize that the other side has its fanatics too. Last year I stood in the Friday Market at Walsingham and listened to a woman – maybe twenty-five, maybe not – telling a crowd what an aborted foetus looked like. She really put her heart and soul into it. It's . . .' He searched for the word. 'Inflammable, isn't it? This cocktail of emotions and politics and personal grudges. The National is bad enough, but there's a sense of going through the motions. This time it all feels a bit less comfy. And d'you know what makes it look really dangerous to me?'

Heaney looked down at her hands, stretching a charity band bracelet, then back at Shaw.

'You see most criminals are stupid,' continued

182

Shaw. 'They blunder. That's what astute police work is all about, waiting for people to make a mistake. But all this . . .' He indicated the *Rainbow Protestor.* 'It's got what we might call an intellectual underpinning. People on either side of these arguments are clever, erudite even, articulate. That's dangerous, because people like that aren't adept at the utilization of violence, its subtle gradations. If the veneer of robust dialogue cracks someone can get hurt very quickly. So, like I said, inflammable, but also poisonous.'

'I've answered the question three times. I have no idea who these . . . Wolves are,' said Heaney.

'I hope, in retrospect, that your answer does not turn out to be less than the truth,' Shaw said. 'The pilgrimage is now only a few days away. I know you are busy, but this is a priority. Ring me, please, if you hear anything that might help us track these people down before they do something we might all regret. You might, as a favour to me, make it known to everyone that the police presence on the day will be considerable, and that any breach of public order will be dealt with by the courts. Given the high risks involved in crowd control, any magistrate – or indeed judge – is very likely to conclude that a custodial sentence is appropriate.'

'Got it,' said Heaney. 'But you need to look for your mythical wolves elsewhere, Inspector, believe me.'

'We'll show ourselves out,' said Shaw.

They took the starboard side corridor this time, passing the Socialist Workers' Party office. Several others were empty, until they had almost

183

got back to the stairwell leading up to the deck. There was one last office, door open, but clearly marked ITUC, the International Trade Union Confederation. As Shaw passed by he glanced in and saw a wall festooned with banners. The largest was white, with a red box in outline around the compact stylized letters CCOO, and a strapline in English: 'Spain's biggest trade union: working for a fairer life for all'. The last time he'd seen the motif had been on a badge, set against the crisp white nurse's uniform of Javi Copon.

Twenty-Five

The CID loos, on floor five, comprised six 'traps' and the usual rank of wall-mounted urinal bowls. Kieran Joyce, Chief Constable, was at the pissoir, legs braced, his five-hundred-pound suit stretched across a broad back. Looking over his shoulder he considered Shaw, leaning against a wash basin, sipping from a Costa coffee cup.

'I want this sorted now before I face the press,' he said, his Irish accent slightly stronger than Shaw remembered. The Norfolk Suite – the CID conference room – was packed with local media, regional TV and a couple of reporters from the nationals. 'We all need to be on the same page, all of us.'

The other occupant of the loos was DI Joseph Carney, recently of Belfast CID, now Lynn's

184

newest detective. Carney was twenty-nine years old, jet-black hair, with a face like a whippet. His thin lips seemed to hold an almost permanent half-smile which Shaw was trying hard not to dislike.

The door swung in but hit Shaw's boot. It was DC Twine. 'Paul – can you use admin's? We'll be ten.'

Twine saw the chief constable fumbling with his fly, and fled.

'Right,' said Joyce. 'Let's sort this out now. We've got a stiff in a skip. Stabbed to death. Looks like a teenage gang killing. Peter, on the other hand, thinks there may be a link to the Marsh House killing. I don't want a turf war. So let's spit it all out now. Peter – you first.'

Shaw filled his lungs, the air laced with the stench of the urinals and the little lemon-yellow deodorants in the bowls.

'Our Marsh House victim, Ruby Bright, thought that a friend, Beatty Hood, was a murder victim, and she had a copy of her death certificate hidden in her room. Hood lived on Hartington Street, less than two hundred yards from the Lister Tunnel. The doctor who attended her deathbed insists she died of natural causes, but there is a paper trail in records of complaints about vandals, petty thieves, teenagers targeting her house. Splitting the inquiry could be a fatal mistake.'

Joyce lit a cigarette, opened the window and leant on the tiled ledge, blowing the smoke out of the corner of his mouth.

'Joe?'

Carney put his hands on his hips and his feet

185

apart, staring down at the space between. 'This is a street killing, totally different. Kid has been identified by his father as Lewis Gunnel, sixteen, student at the tech college. Pathologist says he was held down and stabbed three times in the chest with something very sharp, a narrow knife, viciously sharp.

'Less than twenty-four hours earlier the shoe squad retrieved a pair of trainers from the same spot, daubed in pig's blood. A classic warning, obviously ignored, with the inevitable consequences. The shoe squad's picked up more than a hundred trainers in the last ten days and there's a clear pattern. Two gangs: North End, South End. This is about neighbourhoods, boundaries, territory. It's the Falls Road writ small. The link to Ruby Bright is tenuous at best. Coincidences do happen. That's what this is, a coincidence.'

Shaw bit his tongue. There was a lot he could have said. Coincidence was his special subject. Thanks to a decent Catholic education he knew that the word itself cropped up just once in the entire Bible, in the parable of the Good Samaritan, to describe the moment he walks down the street and happens on the Pharisee lying by the side of the road. The word in the original text was *synkyrian* in Greek, a combination of 'together with' and 'supreme authority'. So – this happened because God brought them together, so it wasn't a coincidence at all, just a plan. But, given Joyce's sectarian past, he didn't think it was the right time for a little lecture on the Bible.

'We'll do two things,' said Joyce. 'First, we'll

run two separate inquiries. Second, we'll liaise on an hourly basis. Both of you appoint liaison officers. They need to talk and share everything. NO playing games. If further links emerge, then we take action to merge the inquiries.

'For now the priority is the Lister Tunnel killing. Let's get into these gangs; close the schools down if you have to, get the trouble-makers down the nick. Every time I drive home along the London Road I see these kids, hanging around. It's the culture. We need to break it up. I want an arrest, Joe, twenty-four hours, less if you can do it. You get first call on forensics, pathology, manpower, the lot. You take the press; I'll say a few words to kick off.

'Peter. Your priority is Walsingham. These anonymous threats need to be taken seriously. Once that's behind us you can get back to Marsh House. But remember, Ruby Bright didn't have a life ahead of her. This kid did. Ruby Bright died in a care home. This kid died on the streets. It's our job to keep the streets safe. All right?'

Shaw stood back, letting Joyce blunder out, his flies still half open, heading for the press confer-ence, followed by Carney. Ruby Bright hadn't died in a care home, of course, but down by the water's edge. And, while she might not have had years ahead of her, she had fought hard for the life she had left. Who were they to weigh the worth of anyone's life in the balance?

Twenty-Six

Even in the midst of a murder inquiry Shaw tried to leave St James' at six thirty, measured by the clock on the teetering tower of the old Greyfriar's monastery. Work went with him on the journey home via a hands' free headset. He parked the Porsche at Old Hunstanton, on the sandy lane that curved down to the lifeboat house and the beach beyond. Unclipping his earpiece, he slipped into the RNLI store to change into his kit to run the mile to *Surf!*. For those precious five minutes he would be alone, two worlds slipping by, the sea to the left, the dunes to the right; alone with his heartbeat: a steady eighty beats a minute. Ahead lay home, where he could use the office PC to Skype the team. Later, George Valentine would ring, usually from the garden of the Artichoke or the Red House yard.

When they'd fled London he'd promised Lena they'd have a life outside the Job, that he'd see Fran most evenings, that they'd exist as a family, however briefly, once a day, every day. She'd left behind a high-profile career as a lawyer, he'd left the Yard's armed response unit. They didn't want to spend 'quality time' with each other, or Fran, they wanted to share a life. Trips to the cinema, celebration meals, Center Parcs, these were simply the trinkets of a childhood, gifts from indulgent uncles, or doting grandparents. A childhood was what happened every day.

As his pace slackened coming down the dunes towards the beach bar, he heard his RNLI pager buzzing in his rucksack. The readout code was 102 – the call sign for Coast Watch, which maintained a service along the north Norfolk coast from a lookout post on top of Hunstanton's red-and-white cliffs.

Kneeling in the sand, waving to Fran and the dog, he rang the landline in the lookout. An emergency call had been received from Gibraltar Point Coast Watch, twenty-five miles directly west, on the unseen Lincolnshire coast, where the Wash curved north-east on its long sweep towards the Humber. A twenty-three-year-old paraglider called Steve Thorpe had taken to the sky at 4.30 that afternoon from a grass hillside above the beach at Skegness, leaving his wife and two children on a picnic blanket. He had a registered logbook with his local club at Spalding, with more than 100 hours of flying time. Before take-off, using a backpack-powered 'paramotor', he'd registered a flight plan with Skegness Aerodrome: he planned to fly down the coast to Gibraltar Point and then return, with an estimated flight time of one hour and thirty minutes.

The first half of Thorpe's flight had gone to plan, but turning over the marker buoy at Gibraltar Point he had failed to achieve the full 180 degrees required; instead he'd headed due east, out over the Wash, a flight path of nearly thirty miles over open sea, sandbanks and tidal races. Thirty-five minutes later he passed over the automatic light

189

ship anchored on Roaring Middle. The paramotor had a flight range of 140 miles, which meant that the pilot could, in theory, make the crossing with about twenty miles to spare. Coast Watch at Hunstanton would try to track his arrival, but could Shaw provide an additional watch from his position two miles north?

Fran brought him a cold Spanish beer, complete with lime slice in the neck.

'Mum says to say she got her licence for the bank holiday weekend. So we're celebrating.'

Shaw climbed the eight feet to the high chair they'd put out in front of *Surf!*. The council provided a lifeguard from nine to six to encourage families to use a stretch of beach often deserted because it was so far from the car parks in the distant town. Fran ran to the office and fetched Shaw's telescope: a small brass antique with a leather grip which he perched on one, raised knee.

Scanning the clear blue sky three times from west to east he located nothing but a high-altitude con trail from a Scandinavia-bound jet, and a flock of geese, mid-Wash, a thousand beating wings heading south.

Sipping his beer he checked his mobile, finding a brief email from DC Twine, who had failed to track down Irene Coldshaw's relatives. The niece's last address, a small terrace two-up two-down in a threadbare estate on the edge of Scunthorpe, had new owners, who said the family had emigrated to Australia.

The contrast, between a terraced house in Scunthorpe, and a £1,200 a week room at Marsh House, held Shaw's attention for a moment, until he heard Fran's voice shout the dog's name and, glancing up, he saw them in the surf at the edge of the sea. Letting his eye rise, taking in the view ahead, he found the sun had touched the horizon, illustrating in spectacular Technicolor Hunstanton's great claim to fame: the only east coast resort with a beach facing west. The day had been hot and the warm buckling air hid the distant silhouette of the far coast, except that Shaw could just discern the needle-like column of Boston Stump – the 260-foot Gothic tower nearly forty miles distant. The sky ahead, warm and viscous, seemed almost solid, a vast block of glass, perhaps, or some fabulous semi-precious, translucent, stone – onyx, or quartz; and embedded within that jewel Shaw could now see a single dot of black, a hundred or more feet above the still surface of the sea, like a fossil insect trapped in amber.

The engine noise, labouring, came to his ear the moment he spotted the powered paraglider. The telescope gave him a neat round image: the pilot, who could steer using brake toggles and a throttle 'pedal' bar below the bucket seat, appeared to be heading directly at him. Ringing Coast Watch on the cliff he asked them to put emergency services on alert: he'd text if the pilot failed to land safely. Signing off with a grid reference for the café, he put the telescope back to his good eye.

The pilot's body stood out in sharp silhouette against the bruised sky of the sunset: dangling as if hung beneath a parachute, the circular paramotor at his back, his feet on the wide lower

191

pedal, the open crescent of the flexible wing arched overhead like a surprised eyebrow.

At a steady, implacable, forty miles-per-hour the aircraft approached landfall, its reflection tracking across the mercury-like sea lying placidly beneath. Two things were wrong: the pilot's arms hung down at his sides, whereas Shaw would have expected to see him adjusting his wing-tilt using the brake toggles above his head, and the engine was spluttering, actually cutting-out for a heart-stopping second, before firing back into an intermittent half-life.

Ten minutes later he was directly overhead and Shaw noted that while the pilot's left boot was set forward, the right was turned inwards at an angle and his crash-helmeted head lay chin-down on his chest.

'I'd say semi-conscious,' he told the emergency services op room at St James' on 999, cutting out Coast Watch, now the pilot was almost over land. 'Speed's dropping, fuel's pinking. I'll try to track him from the ground but it's going to be tough. I'd get paramedics on the road, on a line running roughly through Holme, Ringstead, Brancaster. If he stays aloft he'll be back over the sea in twenty minutes. So ring the RNLI at Cromer. They should stand by.'

He ran then, up the first wave of dunes, into the marsh grass beyond. A footpath led inland, threading the tidal channels, and he picked up speed as he heard the engine cut out again. This time he thought the motor had died but, miraculously, it fired again and he saw the paraglider soar briefly only to return to its slow descent.

Crossing the coast road, he joined a farm track which ran towards the original village of Old Hunstanton, a few cottages around the church, all set at the gates of Hunstanton Hall. At the centre of the hamlet was a mound holding an old Celtic cross, from which Shaw could see the wing of the paraglider, now half a mile ahead of him and dipping out of sight.

Hundreds of cut flowers lay in the churchyard, an elderly woman arranging them in bundles, no doubt for the altar, or to decorate the nave. The door was open, so Shaw ran in, immediately blinded by the sudden shadows after the sunlight outside. The church had run a fete to raise funds for the lifeboat and Shaw recalled they'd charged one pound for trips up the tower, with its views of the coast. The coffin-shaped door to the spiral staircase was unlocked and he counted 180 steps to the top, where an iron grid slid back to allow access to the open tower roof; a lead square, gently pitched, with a central pinnacle supporting a golden crow weather vane.

At nearly 140 feet above the north Norfolk rolling hills he found himself *above* the paraglider's wing, watching its final silent descent, a see-saw decline, the wing finally buckling as the craft swung over a small copse and subsided into a vast field of corn. The scene had a picture-book quality – the square of wheaten yellow, beside another of vivid rape seed, next to one of purple lavender and beyond a track, marked by blood-red poppies. Almost immediately he heard the siren of an ambulance, and saw it breasting a low distant hill. Asking the 999 desk to patch him direct into the paramedics in the unit, he talked them through the last 300 yards to the crash spot: across the field of lavender, over a brook, and then – blind in the eight-foot-high corn – into the centre of the final field.

Shaw had the lead paramedic on the line when they reached the spot. 'OK. Got him.' Disorientated, Shaw could hear the close soundtrack of the wing being lifted clear of the wreckage in his ear as he watched the scene unfold a mile distant, the figures in emergency jackets oddly indistinct against the corn. 'OK, we've got him out of the frame. Commencing resus.'

But Shaw had heard the subtle change in tone, the sense of tension dissipated, a despairing return to routine. The line went dead. A local police squad car breasted the hill and parked up neatly behind the paramedics' unit.

Shaw watched until they carried the body away, his own heartbeat returning to normal. Descending the cold stone steps, he went and sat on a bench in the churchyard. The grass had been just cut and the hypnotic aroma of coumarin activated his memory banks so that he saw himself, ten years old, sat on a picnic blanket on *his* beach, the stretch that now lay in front of *Surf!*, his father walking out of the sea, rough enough that you could see the sand churning in the waves, as each set fell. Conjuring up another beach, another family, he imagined the scene at Skegness, the picnic blanket abandoned, eyes searching the sky for a buzzing paraglider returning to land.

'St Mary the Virgin' read the board by the gate

and, for the first time, Shaw recalled what Linas Jessop had said about the last resting place of Beatty Hood. She'd left him £500 but the rest of her cash had gone on a stone memorial, which she'd partly helped to carve.

That's out at Old Hunstanton, in the village. St Mary the Virgin. I've never bothered to visit since.

Shaw checked his mobile. He'd give the paramedics twenty minutes before a final call, so he had the time. The flower arranger said she thought the Hood memorial was on the south wall, just beyond an ugly Victorian boiler house. The ground was mossy, dank, and the gutters had leaked over a dozen winters so that the stonework was disfigured with mould. The memorial was mounted on the church wall, a sculptured frieze of angels, with the grave below, a parallelogram of chipped marble set within miniature railings.

JAMES HOOD
Born September 19, 1919
Married Beatty, nee Farrar, September 19, 1951
Died September 19, 2008
BEATTY HOOD
Born April 5, 1929
Died September 19, 2014
'And this was our day alone.'

Shaw used a fingertip to clear moss from the numerals, double checking what looked like an extraordinary story; James Hood's birthday seemed to echo through their lives, so that they were married on that day, and then – both – died on that day, although six years apart. It was a story which seemed to indicate an almost preter-natural control over the chaos of life, particularly the gift of death. The day of a marriage lay in the hands of the couple, the day of birth the consequence of a moment's passion nine months earlier, but *death*?

His mobile bleeped and the text message from the paramedic unit was bleak in its simple capitals: DAS. (Dead At Scene.) A few seconds later a second one dropped: CARDIAC ARREST.

Shaw considered the contrast between the Thorpe family, which had got up that morning and set out for the beach confident that their intertwined lives stretched forward into the distant future, and the ageing Beatty Hood, waiting for the day to dawn when her life had, it seemed, been preordained to end.

Twenty-Seven

The Lister Tunnel was deserted, although the scene-of-crime tape fluttered in a square around the spot where the skip had stood. Dr Gokak Roy, hurrying by, was relieved the police and forensic teams had quit the spot. He'd heard a brief radio item on the local news in the car: a brutal street murder, a turf war between teenagers spilling over into violence. The tawdry, random nature of such violence made his mood plummet, and he felt in his jeans pocket for the metallic strip of diazepam tablets. Walking through the Lister

Tunnel left him apprehensive on the best of days, because it recalled vividly another archway, in another town, on the other side of the world.

Gokak had been five when the family took his grandmother Ira to Varanasi to die. The train journey took two days, and although they'd bought first-class tickets and had their own compartment, the corridor was crowded with poor pilgrims, each group with their own elderly, infirm relative. His father had explained to Gokak the dogma at issue: that if Ira died in the holy city, and her body was cremated on the sacred steps, the ghats, beside the Ganges, she would achieve moksha, a release from the cycle of reincarnation, so that she could then rise into nirvana and final, permanent peace.

The railway station lay outside the city's walls; the way ahead lay through a narrow, dank arch. The city reeked of death. He'd clung to his mother's hand on the long walk through the maze-like bustling streets. His elder brother and father had carried his grandmother on a stretcher, hired at the station. Ira was eighty-six years old and had announced a week earlier that she was ready for this final journey; she had stopped eating immediately, and her lips trembled constantly with prayer.

Eventually they came to Mukti Bhawan – Salvation House – one of the hostels which offered shelter to the pilgrims. The family were allocated one room, with Ira on a settle bed, his parents on a mattress and the children on the floor. There was a courtyard outside and Gokak played with children from other families, although

197

all the games were whispered, and there was *absolutely no running allowed!* In the hostel's other rooms, arranged on two floors, other pilgrims waited for death, surrounded by their families.

Ira's wish to die was frustrated. His father told his mother – when he thought the children were asleep – that they'd paid for two weeks' accommodation and that if Ira was still alive at the end of that period, they'd have to take her back to Mumbai. In his father's words this would be a 'conspicuous waste of money' and he certainly wasn't going to pay for a second trip. Gokak awake, watching the shadows, thought he heard his grandmother sigh. The next morning she was gone.

There was a brief, bitter inquest. His elder brother had been on watch. The owner of the hostel had reassured them the courtyard complex was secure. A bell was rung and families came to the stone balconies to look down on the family, gathered ready to set out as a posse to search the city of the dead for a woman who seemed to be very much alive.

Gokak found his grandmother on the steps of the ghats, within a hundred yards of the burning cremation pyres. His father was asking for news from a taxi driver parked up on the Lanka Road. Gokak had been sitting, watching ash fall on his feet and knees when – entirely by chance – he'd seen Ira: sitting, head on her knees, feet pressed together, a neat ball, her arms clasping her shins – no, not clasping, they had been clasping. Now the hands lay open in a classic sign of offering.

The poise, the balance of bones and flesh was remarkable, because when Gokak put his hand on her shoulder she tumbled to the side, as lifeless and haphazard as a pile of linen spilling from a basket. Gokak always thought that if anything drove his later obsession with the art of healing it was that moment when he saw his beloved grandmother splayed out unceremoniously across the hard stone steps.

He didn't remember the cremation, the smoke or the flames, or the crackle of the expensive wood his father had bought for the occasion.

Back at the Mukti Bhawan, they packed quickly and left.

On the train his mother had been forced to chat with other passengers as first class was full. Gokak remembered a brief interchange of conversation in frenetic Hindi.

'It was a good death in the end,' said his mother, puffed up with success. 'She said her time had come and it had. It is a gift.'

'Yes,' said the woman opposite, a child on her knee. 'A gift. And the name of the *dying house*?'

'It was excellent, yes. Mukti Bhawan.'

Twenty-Eight

It was not an image Shaw would ever forget; the sticky blood-red stain on the pale stone of the well, the wooden lid slid back to reveal the deep shadowy throat of the bricked shaft, the rising smell of trapped water from the circular surface below, which reflected the flame which burnt in the brass candelabra above. A steel grid prevented a headlong fall, and it too was spotted with blood, not the fluid crimson trickle from a flesh wound, but gouts mixed with crushed tissue and bone. The aromas of High Church, wax and incense and polish, were not enough to obscure that lethal edge of iron and salt, the reek of butchered meat.

Peering down, he caught the shimmering circle of light in the bottom of the shaft and looked quickly away.

The Anglican Shrine of Our Lady of Walsingham had been violated. One of the official guardians had opened the church at six that morning to discover the Holy Well, the source of the shrine's miraculous waters, broken open and desecrated; blood and gore around its edge and falling into the waters below.

The church, a functional brick thirties edifice in the neo-Byzantine style, held within it the replica of the Holy House, which in turn protected the icon of the Virgin Mary. The well stood behind the Holy House and had been cordoned off with tape from the rest of the building, where pilgrims milled, waiting their turn to enter the shrine through one of its two doors. Tom Hadden's SOCO team had been first to arrive and his speed and expertise had saved the pilgrims the grim disappointment of having walked the final mile in bare feet only to be denied access to the idol.

Hadden had met Shaw at the main door to the shrine with a glass slide, the smear of blood captured beneath a slim evidence plate. 'My guess is chicken's blood. The consistency is quite different from human blood and you can see the cellular composition is distinct. A lot of chicken's blood and some bone, muscle tissue, mucus.'

He closed his eyes, preparing to give his verdict. 'But not human, Peter. One hundred per cent not human.'

Shaw considered the possibility of a link with the Lister Tunnel trainers, spattered with pig's blood; then dismissed any connection. Blood was a popular medium of protest. Everyone was hard-wired to see red. In this case the effect had been particularly shocking.

The yellow-and-black tape, the white-suited SOCO at the well-head, the emergency services vehicles in the courtyard outside, had generated a profound sense of desecration, a palpable shock, amongst the pilgrims and clerics. Two priests stood in the nave of the small church in a tableau of comfort, one holding the other by the shoulders and being held by the elbows in return.

Shaw, circumnavigating the miniature house, saw that a window had been set in the back wall to allow those outside to view the icon and chapel within; the interior walls were covered in narrow shelves holding night-light candles, the pilgrims kneeling, the statue of Mary a blaze of gold and blue, a sunburst of silver. Pilgrims prayed, lips shivering, and one woman silently dabbed a tissue at tears on her cheeks. A young man, in a brutally unstylish haircut, edged forward towards the altar and, as he knelt, Shaw was strangely moved to note his blackened, injured feet, studded with wounds.

Other worshippers stood watching the SOCOs at work, whispering, surrounding a nun and two priests inveigled into sharing what little they knew of the discovered scandal of the blood. A large hot-water container, like those used to dispense tea at football matches or garden fetes, had been requisitioned to hold uncontaminated holy water, which was being handed out in plastic cups.

Shaw tried to find a quiet space in which to think. His priority had to be keeping this act of religious vandalism out of the media; the last thing he wanted was to escalate tensions ahead of the pilgrimage itself. Speed was the essence of success; they needed to get the blood cleaned away, the well re-dedicated by one of the guardians, and the SOCO unit back to St James' – where it was needed for the Lister Tunnel inquiry.

He'd asked to see a spokesman for the shrine, but checking his watch he saw the so-called 'guardian' was already twenty minutes late. Valentine was picking up a key for Beatty Hood's house on the Springs. Shaw, haunted by the elderly widow's gravestone epitaph – *And this was our day alone* – felt certain that if he could understand her death, and the circumstances surrounding it, the rest would fall into place. The murder team were trying to locate Hood's living relatives. Shaw wanted to see the house in which she'd died. All of which was urgent by comparison to a case of vindictive vandalism. Using his iPhone he sent an irritable text to the missing guardian: *Can we meet as planned?*

A mass had begun in the Holy House and the

202

pilgrims had edged inside until there was almost no space left. Outside several wheelchair-bound pilgrims watched through the window. Shaw backed away, around the shrine, to the west wall, where various messages were set in tiles, forming a ceramic noticeboard.

I was ill but returned home renewed
— Katherine Carty
The cancer has weakened thanks to the Holy Water
— John Maurice Forbes
My dear wife Anne came seeking an end to pain. God Bless this Holy House
— Vincent Kelly
I can live now with the life I have been given
— Fr Michael Kennedy

A hand on his shoulder made him jump. 'Inspector Shaw? I'm Jocelyn Smythe, one of the guardians. Sorry to keep you waiting. As you can imagine . . .' He waved his own smartphone. 'God may be my master, but there are several earthly intermediaries . . .'

Smythe steered him expertly towards a small anteroom which held supplies of candles, votive lights and Mass cards. Leaving the door open they were surrounded by the distorted echoes of the service being sung by the priest in the Holy House, that particular reedy tunelessness, which reminded Shaw so poignantly of his own childhood, quite a bit of which, he felt, had been wasted listening to Latin.

Shaw told Smythe the verdict of the SOCO investigation.

'I'd like you to re-open the well, as soon as the damage has been cleaned up, can you do that, Father?'

Shaw tried to remind himself that this man, and this shrine, were part of the Church of England – not the Catholic Church – but the sounds and sights were so Roman as to overwhelm the logic. He'd called him 'Father' and he hadn't flinched.

'Yes, of course. You have what you need . . . I don't know, fingerprints perhaps?'

'There are prints in the blood, our best lead. But my principal objective is to keep a low profile. I'm sure you're aware of the tensions building ahead of the pilgrimage. I'd like to keep the press in the dark . . .'

'If they ring, I can hardly lie . . .'

Smythe was very much a physical guardian, rather than an intellectual one. Built like a front-row forward, with scrubbed pale skin and black hair which, Shaw suspected, had been oiled to lie straight back from his high forehead, and matched his starched black cassock. He looked like one of Bunyan's Christian soldiers, a very muscular Christian.

'No. I understand that. I'm not asking you to lie, or even mislead, if you're asked for the truth. But we do need to keep this crime in perspective; technically, if I can use that word in this place, we're dealing with criminal damage. Desecration isn't on the statute book. I promise you we will try to find the person, or persons, responsible.

Publically, I'd like this forgotten for now. Is that possible?'

'Turn the other cheek?'

'If you will,' he said, taking a half-step back in what could have been submission. Smythe nodded once, then followed.

'Pilgrims come to the shrine for many reasons . . .' said Shaw, moving out through the door into the body of the church, running a hand over the ceramic tiles.

'Yes. To complete the pilgrimage and to take the Holy Water. It's a form of prayer, a physical prayer if you like. They may seek Our Lady's intervention for themselves, in illness, or mental distress, or sexual confusion. Or they may seek her help for others, loved ones, friends. Some seek an end to pain, or even life itself. That is a gift in Her power.'

Shaw turned to go, but again the pale cold hand touched his shoulder. The king's touch was once enough to cure the disease of scrofula, and Shaw speculated that this priest perhaps felt some of that gift lay within himself. In the modern world, however, touch was a dangerous instrument of power.

'One other thing, Inspector. We've just noticed this.' Smythe had a large book in his hand which he let fall open.

'We invite pilgrims to record their visit and add a line of prayer.'

Across the page had been scrawled, in blood, the words: *The Wolves Have the Scent.*

Twenty-Nine

Shaw took a call on his hands-free, edging the Porsche through a tailback on the outskirts of Wells. The caller ID read: FORTIS. He knew instantly from the sonar-like echo that she was outside, on a beach, if not actually in the sea, because she had to shout through the sound of the surf.

'Inspector Shaw? Julia Fortis. Can we meet?' she said. 'I'll be brief, but I need to give you something. We're on Holme Beach, it's a barefoot ski club meeting. Just head for the sound of the jet ski. We'll be here till sunset.'

Shaw said he'd be twenty minutes. The traffic crawled along the coast road until Holme, where he turned off into the car park down by the dunes and then crossed the golf course to reach the sands.

The jet ski was a hundred yards off the beach, the engine noise coming in blasts with the onshore wind, a skier behind travelling at – Shaw estimated – thirty-five miles an hour. On the beach wet-suited skiers waited their turn.

Fortis, in a one-piece costume, was walking towards him, a wetsuit over her shoulder. At Marsh House she seemed stiff and ill-at-ease, although the circumstances had hardly been auspicious. Here, on the sands, she followed a catwalk sinuous path, as elegant as a supermodel. The swimsuit was a vibrant, stand-out green.

'Gardening leave?' asked Shaw, before she reached him.

She smiled, collecting her hair in a bunch with a band. 'I spent the first twenty-four hours at home, thinking I'd done something terribly wrong. I haven't. So I thought I'd enjoy myself. And I thought I'd clear my conscience too.'

Her eyes kept flitting over his shoulder, up the long incline of the beach towards the edge of the pinewoods.

'The crime was not telling us about Camera D.'

'I know. My lawyers are dealing with that. I'm told I can expect a custodial sentence, suspended. I don't know if I should believe them, it's in their interest, you see, to keep me happy and carefree. The trust has a home in Bude, in Cornwall. I'm told the manager's job is coming up and I'm a shoe-in. I don't know what to believe.'

Shaw was in bare feet and he'd begun to sink his toes into the sand, wishing he could spend the rest of the day with this much space to savour. The thought of the CID room back at St James' made him feel tired and irritable.

'You had something for me . . .'

'A moment,' she said, dropping the suit on the sands, as if discarding a mink coat.

Shaw watched her walk away, up the beach, until she reached an elderly woman in a folding chair, with what looked like knitting on her lap. The chair had slumped slightly on one side and Fortis expertly levered herself against the frame to set it straight before rummaging through a set of bags and a picnic hamper.

She ran back with a piece of paper.

207

'Patient?' asked Shaw.

'I guess. It's my mother actually, she's at Marsh House, upstairs. Staff get a substantial discount, you see. Mum's been ill for several years. That's all part of the deal too, of course, that she can move to Bude with me. But it'll break her heart to leave. Most days she forgets my face, but she likes the view out of her room, the wallpaper in the TV room, the sunflower crockery. It's all she's got to hold on to.'

She handed Shaw the paper. 'Read this.'

It was a memo, dated, on Marsh House notepaper, with copies to several Starlight Trust executives, but addressed to Mr John E. Travis, Norfolk Regional Administrator.

Dear Mr Travis,

A brief note on Irene Coldshaw, with reference to my earlier notes. Irene is distraught about the situation she finds herself in at Marsh House. To summarize: her assets comprise her pension and a £226,000 trust fund, from which our fees are paid. Due to her condition, an inter-mittent but severe senile state, her power of attorney lies with her niece, Mrs Sarah Towton, who lives with her family in Scunthorpe.

Mrs Towton suffers from acute kidney failure and is subject to daily dialysis. They have four children under twelve, a limited income from Mr Towton's job at the ICI works in Scunthorpe, and are in poor housing. Mrs Coldshaw was, briefly,

208

housed with them after her husband died six years ago.

The Towtons are in an invidious position. They are, according to Irene, sole beneficiaries of her estate. It also falls to them to decide if she should stay at Marsh House, and incur the fees. Irene has written to them to explain that she would feel better if she were transferred into a council facility. In fact, she is very happy here at Marsh House.

However, it is obvious that she wishes the Towtons to eventually benefit from her estate, which is being diminished by the monthly payments for Marsh House.

The Towtons insist that Mrs Coldshaw is confused and they believe she would want to stay at Marsh House if she did not feel a duty to them. Mr Towton has offered to visit Mrs Coldshaw, but the offer was declined. I have to say that Mrs Coldshaw, even if this background is taken into consideration, seems peculiarly anxious. There may be other hidden pressures.

I wish to propose a possible solution. We could provide Mrs Coldshaw with a nurse for the day, and transport, so that she could visit Sarah Towton. She believes that if she can see her in person she can persuade her to agree to the transfer to council care. After all, the most important thing is that Mrs Coldshaw is happy, and it seems certain that the current situation is making her unhappy.

Mrs Coldshaw's condition is deteriorating rapidly, largely due to stress. She feels she is directly responsible for the plight of her niece. I attach an assessment by Dr Flitt, and an additional report from the psychiatric care unit.

I look forward to your response.

Julia Fortis

Administrator

'I'd like you to make me a promise which I know you can't keep,' said Fortis, waving up the beach at the woman in the folding chair.

'You can have that, it's a copy. The coroner at Irene's inquest did not request access to the documentation and the trust suggested to me that making it public would only distress the relatives. The truth, of course, was that it would put them in the dock, because they declined my suggestion. Three times. I suspect they felt *their* interests lay with collecting the fees.

'I thought it might help. It explains a lot. Also it exposes what I believe is a significant loophole in the law, which allows beneficiaries to act with the power of attorney – an intolerable clash of interests. I can't help feeling that in many cases the care homes simply play on the guilt of relatives, telling them that their loved ones deserve the very best care. Or the most expensive, which is not the same thing.

'If the trust knows you have a copy they'll know I gave it to you. And that will be the end of my Faustian pact. I can live with that – and so can Mum – otherwise I wouldn't have done this. But if you can keep me out of it by not referring directly to the letter, I'd be grateful. We'd be grateful. Perhaps you could suggest that your interviews with staff at Marsh House have uncovered Irene's story?'

Shaw looked away, out to sea, reluctant to make promises. A whistle blew and the barefoot ski club members beckoned Fortis to join them.

'My turn; I better go,' she said. 'It's a good sea, glass-like.'

'What do you think Irene was thinking that morning she drove away?' asked Shaw.

Fortis picked up her wetsuit. 'I think she was caught in a dilemma the old have to face, a sharper dilemma in her case, but essentially the same. There comes a point when they know the world would be a happier place if they weren't there. They're a burden, an obstacle in the path of the young. She couldn't live with that, so she decided to act. What was her aim? I think she wanted to talk to her niece and try and make her see that she just wanted some peace of mind. But perhaps she just needed to drive until it was over – one way or another; sometimes the weight of decision is too much, and we give ourselves up to fate.'

Thirty

The keys, two identical for the front door, and a single for the back, had come with a printed key ring label which read: 32 Hartington Street, The

Causeway Trust. Valentine, picking them up from a solicitor's office on the Tuesday Market, had asked about a fourth key on the iron ring – small, slight and gold – and been informed it sprung a padlock on the side gate which led down the tunnel-back alleyway to the yard.

Now, standing in the street, he saw that couldn't be right after all, because there was just a bolt on the gate. Shaw peered in the front window where the sunlight glinted off the old silvered mirror and splashed down on a threadbare patterned carpet. The glass in the lattice-work sash had been recently cleaned by a professional, but the sill inside was dusty and held the desiccated remains of a few flower heads. A bottle of Lucozade and what looked like the remains of a Chinese takeaway lay on the table, a spoon sticking out of a livid tray of sweet and sour sauce.

'So what's the story?' asked Shaw, putting his knee against the front door, turning the key and pushing it open. The empty hallway, bare-boarded, with a print of George VI, set a dismal note.

In contrast, Valentine appeared to relish getting inside the house. In a few strides he was checking out the downstairs front room. He seemed energized, focused and even a little light-headed. Shaw hoped it wasn't just a brief, irrational interval of post-diagnosis elation.

'She left the house to the charity – apparently it's linked to Help the Aged, but the solicitor was a bit vague,' said Valentine. 'They rent it out, fully-furnished, through a local agency, with the solicitors as agents. What's left of the rent goes to the charity. Current tenant is a' – Valentine consulted a note he'd made on his mobile phone – 'Polish migrant. Name's beyond me, but he works out of the Alexandra Dock. Currently at sea. Rent's two hundred and fifty pounds a month, which is dirt cheap, but then nobody wants to live on Parkwood Springs. Long-term strategy, according to the agents, is to sell when the developers start waving cash about.

'Current market value is sixty-eight thousand pounds, but if the developers buy up the rest of the street, it's suddenly worth a lot more. They might see one hundred thousand more.

'But that can't be the whole story. I had a look at this place from the outside a few nights back and the takeaway wasn't on the table. That night the place reeked of fish and chips. But the Pole's been at sea for a week. So, he's either sub-letting or he's had uninvited visitors.'

They split the rooms between them and then met back on the upstairs landing. Shaw had little to report save the hand marks on the wallpaper, all at the same height; Hood had been blind for the last six months of her life, and the trailing hand had left its mark, feeling along walls, finding corners, seeking out switches. That was an insight which made the trip worthwhile, he felt, solidifying an image of the frail woman, alone and blind, surrounded by the decay of Parkwood Springs.

Valentine, besides noting the cardboard over the broken pane in the kitchen door pinpointed by Dr Roy, found further evidence of burglary: a cellar door jimmied open (the cellar empty,

213

damp, but for a rustic cider press, which still gave off a faint aroma of crushed apples). And the kitchen looked strangely depleted of white goods: no fridge and the plumbing for a dishwasher, but no dishwasher.

The tenant had slept in the smaller, back box room. It was an odd choice but then Shaw raised the blind to reveal a fine view of the Cut, stretching out like a runway towards the sea. Two grain ships were passing in the mid-distance. The single bed held a sleeping bag and a girlie magazine with a Polish title. A rather fine china cup and saucer were set on the floor, containing a film of green tea. A bedside book lay spine up, splayed open: *Typhoon* by Conrad in the original English. Briefly, Shaw wrestled with the irony of the choice – the Pole who'd chosen English to write a British classic. Valentine touched the cup: cold, the tea stain almost fossilized. The wardrobe held worn work clothes, mostly high-quality thermal jackets, boots, double-skin socks, leather gloves with fur liners. Curled on the dressing table was a line and extension for a PC and a WiFi AirPort.

The front bedroom was very different.

It was dominated by a hospital bed, with hoist and stripped-down mattress, which looked almost new. The bedside table was NHS standard issue as well, as was a stand for an intravenous drip, complete with clamp and on-off metal tap. It was the only room in the house which smelt of disinfectant and the only room without a carpet.

'If you're going to die at home this is the price you pay,' said Shaw. 'Home looks like a hospital.

214

I reckon Hood died in here. No wonder chummy's taken the back room. Odd they left the gear here.'

The fourth, gold key seemed superfluous, until they got to the kitchen, which had been upgraded at some point in the eighties galley-style. The cat flap had been torn off its hinges. They let themselves out and Valentine spotted a new padlock on what had been the original toilet and bathhouse. Overhead a set of telegraph wires ran zigzag down the backs of the houses. A pair of white trainers hung above them, one spattered with blood.

Through the single window in the bathhouse, choked in cobwebs, Shaw could see a cracked mirror and a brush on a hook. Within the layered image lay something else, oyster-like and pale. Cleaning the glass with his cuff, he thought it might be the reflection of his own good eye, swimming in the silvered glass, but it didn't blink when he did.

The key slipped the lock easily, but the hinges fell away from the rotting wood when they had to force the warped door open, the sunlight illuminating the broken toilet pan, encrusted with dead spiders. Taking up most of the space was a homemade smoker – a garden brazier with the top altered to form an 'oven' in which fish, or meat, could be cured over charcoal or wood. The smell was overwhelming, the tang of salty flesh.

The body was in the tin bath, naked, its back to the door, knees up, facing the mirror, the features distorted by the plastic bag over the head, which hung loose at the neck but must have been held tight at the nape, because it still preserved

215

the shape of the fist which had crushed it tight. One arm lay outside the bath, the fingertips just touching the bare stone. Dr Gokak Roy's eyes were very white, very wide and very open, in surprise or astonishment it was difficult to tell.

Thirty-One

The killer struck the first blow in what had been Beatty Hood's bedroom. Tom Hadden, suited, taking moon steps, led them up the stairs and into the floodlit space; outside the street was dark, taped-off, the single streetlight half-shaded with black paint long ago, perhaps on Beatty Hood's insistence, to allow her some sleep before blindness plunged her into continuous shadow.

'Here, there's a bloodstain between the floor-boards, a spatter mark, so I'd say as an initial hypothesis that he came in – took a step or two – and then his assailant struck from behind. Wound's oddly jagged, so I'm thinking maybe an ornament, but we've checked everything and there's no trace. I think he took it with him, along with the victim's clothes and – presumably – valuables. A doctor you say, so maybe a medical bag, wallet, phone? He's of an age for a smartphone.'

'We're on to it,' said Valentine, out in the hall.

Hadden had his forehead almost on the floor, looking towards the bed. 'We found a series of fibres here, some from what looks like a pair of jeans and traces of white linen – so I'm thinking an expensive shirt. Sound like our victim?'

Shaw, on his knees, nodded.

'Blow to the head puts him down. Then the killer applies the plastic bag and suffocates the victim while he's either unconscious or semi-conscious. There's a little bruising on the victim's left leg and left elbow, so the second seems more likely. I'd put money on death occurring here and the clothes removed here too, because there are no fabric traces at all on the stairs or the hallway carpets, or across the yard, and you'd have to think he was dragged to the bathhouse.'

They were back in the yard a minute later, floodlit like the bedroom, a SOCO inside the bathhouse brushing the door hinges for a print.

'Question: were the trainers his?' asked Hadden, in rhetorical mode. 'We've removed some skin cells, so we'll know soon. Expensive – Emirates brand – retail at one hundred and twenty pounds. So they could be his. The Lister Tunnel inquiry has identified two gangs, clashing over territory. The gang chucking them up around here are middle class, monied, so that would fit too. They're not new, wear and tear looks like anything from a year to a few days, depends if they're just for best. Kids – they do that, have two sets. *Dress* trainers. Knockabout trainers.

'That's the best I can do. You're the detective, Peter. You work it out.'

The pathologist, Dr Kazimierz, appeared at the back door, a large leather bag in one hand, a multi-headed anglepoise lamp in the other, which she immediately attached to a cable extension. Despite being fifty, slightly stolid and big-boned, Shaw always felt her face, up close, held a glimpse of the beautiful girl she may have been. A friend of the Shaws, and a regular visitor to *Surf!*, she often walked her Labrador on the sands or braved the swell in mid-winter in a flowery swim cap.

Nodding at Hadden, she gave Shaw a buckled smile.

'Gentlemen,' she said and stood at the bath-house door, surveying the corpse. 'I see,' she said, and then remained motionless for a full minute before taking two short strides to the foot of the tub.

Shaw took her place at the door.

'Why am I reminded?' she asked. Kazimierz had been in the UK nearly twenty years but her English, while extensive, had stubbornly clung to the structures of her native tongue: Polish.

'Why are you reminded of what?' asked Shaw.

'A picture – a painting, yes?'

Shaw saw it too, then, and not just in a mental frame, but on the wall of the Museum of Fine Arts in Brussels. They'd gone on a day trip from Southampton as part of his history of art module. The pathologist's house, a clapboard cottage beyond the dunes behind Shaw's beach, was cluttered with art too; on walls, on bookshelves, frames leant against the skirting boards. He recalled a late-night conversation around a beach fire in the last weeks of her husband Dawid's illness in which she'd sought escape from tending her patient, with a spirited debate over the merits

218

and demerits of Seurat and Monet, Renoir and Pissaro.

'*The Death of Marat*. The arm's very distinctive . . .' he said, kneeling. 'David, Jacques-Louis David,' he added, using the French inflexion on the surname.

The depiction of the great revolutionary journalist's death, stabbed by a female opponent, as he lay in his bathtub, a writing desk over his knees, comprised an image full of graceful lines, especially the languid arm outside the tub, the hand still holding the quill, the unfinished paper on the writing board.

'An icon, really,' he added. 'He admired Caravaggio – *The Entombment of Christ* has the same arm, the collapsed body, almost asleep, and Michelangelo's *Pieta* of course, in the Vatican, the same arm again.'

'But the face not so,' said the pathologist, setting up the spotlights, driving out the shadows.

No – not the face. Through the plastic they could see the expression, the eyes blank but seeming to register an unbearable pain. There was no sense here, as there was in art, of a gentle acceptance of a noble, famous death. Just a young life cut short. The line of the arm wasn't a series of artistic curves, just a bone, encased in muscle, fallen away from the body.

'Tin roof,' she said, pointing up. 'Already I think the corpse begins to decay in the heat of the day.' She checked a digital thermometer. 'Still sixty-three, and it's long after dark.'

Had that been the aim? To leave the body to decay, without clothes or other sources of ID, so that when it was eventually found the evidence would have been reduced to bone and hair? They'd checked with the tenant's shipping company and he was on a long-haul container ship which would – via Mombasa, Goa, Manila and Tokyo – circumnavigate the globe via the Panama Canal and Boston. The wandering mariner would be back home, such as it was, in early summer 2016. But for Shaw and Valentine's visit, the victim's skeleton would have been old bones and little else, with only the telltale blood-stained trainers in place to offer a convenient pointer to the possible killers.

The backyard gate, unbolted, opened to the alleyway and DI Joe Carney appeared.

Shaw left Dr Kazimierz to her work.

'What do we know?' asked Carney, trying to pull off a brand of effortless superiority, but falling short, taking a step back, yielding the floor to Shaw.

'What we don't know is more interesting. Why did Dr Roy return to this house? What possible reason could he have to re-visit the deathbed of a woman who died last year of natural causes? A woman who our Marsh House victim, Ruby Bright, insisted was murdered.'

'Blood-spattered trainers over the wires, that right?' said Carney, looking up, but the shoes had been cut down by SOCO. 'So that links it to the Lister Tunnel.'

'And a plastic bag over the head, which links it to Marsh House.'

Carney just shrugged. 'The CC's been on, he wants us at St James' at seven tomorrow morning.

His office. My guess is he's gonna merge the inquiries. Not much choice. Thing *is* – who's in charge?'

Thirty-Two

Dr Furey, district coroner, lived in an old Georgian house which stood just beyond the London Gate, its facade boldly confronting the ring road – although there was a *cordon sanitaire* provided by a long garden, a grove of birch trees and a high wrought-iron railing. The building, three storeys high, with dormers in the roof, stood narrow and alone, as if its supporting neighbours had been bulldozed away. Tonight, lights blazed from the sash windows on the lower two floors and from a pair of converted gaslights on either side of the door, the wooden pillars of which had become curiously warped by age or winter damp.

Shaw noted a modern electric doorbell and heard the distant buzz within, competing against an interior soundtrack which he could not identify with any confidence, but felt sounded like Mumford & Sons, a reel transformed into a rock and roll riff. Dr Furey opened the door, his round asymmetric face slightly flushed, the eyes catching the light. The hallway beyond was full of light and voices and laughter, coming from a room to one side with a half-opened door, which revealed a glimpse of armchairs, and a set of playing cards laid out on the carpet as if for a game of patience.

'Shaw. Good man. Let's cut to my office, unless
. . . is there time for a drink?' Shaw liked Furey,
enjoyed working with him, because whatever the
medium – telephone, email, face-to-face – everything he said was infused with a kind of convivial
energy.

Shaw declined but Furey retreated to fetch his
own glass of red wine, and then led the way up
the stairs two steps at a time, his orange cords
striding out, showing the heels of his worn leather
brogues as they ascended to the attic.

The office had the same shabby-chic typical of
the rest of the house; an old bureau writing-desk,
a hat stand, fitted bookshelves, but also a flat-
screen TV, three grey filing cabinets and a desktop
PC set on a plain deal table, surrounded by neat
piles of paper. On the wall hung the doctor's
medical degree certificate, issued by Trinity
College, Dublin.

Despite the hour the internal shutters were
thrown back and the curtainless window gave a
view which made Shaw laugh out loud: the town's
cemetery ran to the edge of sight, lit by the
peripheral street lights and the passing cars on
the distant ring road.

'I know, I know,' said Furey, booting up the
computer. 'It's a profound embarrassment. My
wife says it makes us look like bodysnatchers.
Burke, Hare and Furey! The coroner who takes
his work home – eh? We fell in love with the
house from the front gate. I don't believe in
ghosts, Shaw, do you?'

Shaw didn't want to be drawn; he was still
struggling with the sense that the headstones of

the dead seemed to represent a crowd outside the window, looking up at the house, edging closer to share the light or to listen.

'A cousin says it makes the place look like Joyce's "dark gaunt house",' said Furey, selecting documents which chugged out of a printer on the table.

Shaw didn't get the reference but, intrigued, wanted to know more.

'*The Dead*,' said Furey. 'Fine story, set in a house just like this one. Which didn't help really – Catriona hates bloody Joyce, but she liked the film.' He pronounced 'film' in the Irish manner, squeezing in two syllables. 'Gabriel, the hero, looks out the window, you see, and thinks of the snow falling on the grave of his wife's young lover. It makes him wonder if it's best to die young when we're still strong, our vital emotions undiminished by the passage of time. There's a phrase there . . .' he added, putting thumb and forefinger to the bridge of his nose. '"Or die old, when the threat of error grows more with every year."'

The doctor collected up the freshly printed pages. 'No ghosts, Shaw, but we're haunted by that, yes? That we grow towards a time of error. But not yet, hopefully . . . .'

Furey straightened, taking an inch off his wine. 'I keep an eye on the dead. But some are more interesting than others, eh? Just like the living. Several years ago I created an ongoing digital log of the death certificates issued locally and, to some extent, the information provided on the medical certificates which support them, each one

223

signed by the doctor who attends the deceased. Your man Twine rang and said you wanted to look at Dr Gokak Roy's recent certificates. Given the outcome, that was a very smart question, Inspector.'

Furey stopped then, the manic activity instantly stilled, his eyebrows arching. 'A strictly unprofessional request, of course. And no doubt you'll fill me in on precisely why we need to answer such a question . . . Although I suspect that the fact Dr Roy's body is currently in the morgue at the Ark awaiting my professional attention will have something to do with it, eh? But first, results . . .'

Furey summarized the document trail he'd investigated: Dr Roy had signed six certificates over a period of eleven months, covering patients with a wide range of ages, conditions and treatments.

'Here they are,' said Furey, brandishing the certificates.

'Three of the deceased were women, two in receipt of ongoing respite care, one aged seventy-three, the other eighty-one. Mrs Beatrice Hood, who died first, was eighty-seven. In addition there were three adult males – two men – both under fifty, suffered degenerative neurological diseases. The third, aged eighty-seven, had spent some time at Marsh House care home – a detail I thought you'd appreciate. Two of the six were, additionally, psychiatric patients on day care. So, pretty much the usual hotchpotch, if a little on the grim side. The causes of death are exactly what you would expect given the secondary causes listed, and the background outlined in the medical certificates, which is why the coroner's office would not be informed.

'These deaths are neither violent, unnatural or unexpected. In a profound sense of the word I'd say, from the documentation, that all the patients died a natural death, given their conditions. Nothing, on the face of it, is suspicious at all.

'I've got a bit of software which simply tracks data and searches out patterns – repetitions basically, although it's a bit more sophisticated than that. For example, it might point up a relationship between the profession of the deceased and a certain medical condition, say asbestosis and building contractors. Or between respiratory disease and a particular postcode, an area along the bypass, for example. You see? Useful for my work, which is tracking the medical condition of the poor, especially the homeless.

'The postcode analysis is particularly illuminating when you're looking at big cities, I don't know, say Dublin, or Manchester, or London. You'd never think it but a lot of illness has a geographical basis, a spatial dimension; that's interesting to me, you see. That's the heart of it. We love patterns, don't we, Shaw, being logical men, and the patterns within the patterns.'

He put a printout of a GPS map of Lynn on the table, upon which were six stars, in a cluster.

'This is the pattern I wanted you to see.'

'This is the old Parkwood Springs estate. Frankly, I'm poleaxed anyone still lives there, I thought the place was in ruins. But you can see here all six of the stars, and each is the address of one of Dr Roy's deceased patients. All are within an area of less than half a square mile.'

Furey studied the GPS map. 'Could this pattern be the result of chance? Maybe. It's a rundown part of town, full of the elderly and infirm. Dr Gokak is a GP for the local practice.

'But you see Shaw, the point is, this is not the *only* pattern.'

Furey's cheeks had flushed redder and he gripped the six certificates roughly in his hand.

'As well as listing the home addresses of the deceased, and their causes of death, these certificates stipulate the *place of death*. In each case, Shaw, *in each case* – it is listed as 32 Hartington Street, the home address of Beatty Hood, the first of the six to die. Now that, DI Shaw, is very, very, odd.'

Shaw thought of the Lister Tunnel, the stale breath of it, seeping out into the rest of town.

'And this pattern went *unnoticed*?'

'Yes, well – unnoticed until now. But yes, fundamentally. Dr Roy was perfectly entitled to sign the death certificates, and they appear entirely valid. I only found the correlation when alerted to the possibility that there might be a pattern in the certificates signed by Dr Roy.'

'It's fifteen years since Harold Shipman, Britain's most prolific serial killer, murdered fifteen of his patients, and you're saying a doctor can still just sign death certificates and the coroner isn't involved at all – or anyone else?'

Furey held up both hands. 'I've no idea what's happened here, Shaw. I point the finger at no man. Let's give Dr Roy the benefit of the doubt, shall we? But I concede he would have questions to answer, if he wasn't on a mortuary slab. Most of the legal changes proposed after Shipman have been kicked into the long grass – a scandal, yes, but there it is.

'On the other hand, there have been changes – profound changes, to procedure. The NHS looks for clusters too. But I'd have to admit that a determined doctor could still avoid detection, especially if they had accomplices within the system – either complicit directly, or just willing to turn a blind eye to breaking bureaucratic procedure. And after all, Shaw, the health service is under huge strain. Shortcuts save money, time – frankly, even lives. We're all human.'

'What about simple data collection? Surely this pattern just screams at you?'

'Certificates end up stored at the General Register Office, at Stockport. It's a paper-based system, you see, so unless data is input specifically such patterns do not appear. Also, data analysis tends to concentrate on other aspects of the certificate, not the place of death, which is often a hospital, or a home.'

Furey drained his glass. 'And there's one more pattern. All six were buried, Shaw. That's odd in itself these days. But the crucial thing is that post-Shipman one of the processes that *has* been tightened up is that concerning cremation. You can see why. No body, no evidence, no possible way of finding out what really happened. Burials, we can just dig them up. So you see, if someone wanted to subvert the system, they'd favour the graveyard. Fewer questions, and no extra awkward forms to complete.'

Furey led the way out on to the landing.

Shaw, pausing, looked down the elegant circular stairwell. 'You're saying that, according to these certificates, six people died in this one house – 32 Hartington Street – in eleven months?'

'Correct. As the Americans like to say, Shaw: go figure. And that may not be the end of it. I tracked these six down by searching for Dr Roy's name on certificates where the address of the deceased is local. He may have signed others. And note this: he may have signed others, but the *place of death* might still be this one house. Do you see? This shows you the major flaw in the system, Shaw. We trust doctors too much. We defer. We even let them insist they have a title beyond plain *mister*. And we're not going to reform the system because money's short. That's the root of it, Shaw. Always is.'

They were on the doorstep a minute later, the light overhead throwing their silhouettes down the path. Dr Furey gave Shaw copies of the six death certificates.

The doctor produced a slightly battered silver cigarette case, took one out, and let the door close gently to behind him, but not so far that the lock clicked.

'Any thoughts?' asked Shaw.

'I can see no possible medical explanation. That's as far as I go. I'll leave speculation on Dr Roy's motives to CID. Shipman killed himself, Shaw, and he never told us why he killed his patients. Money, was it? Or treasures filched

– paintings and jewellery? Or did he want to play God, or stop the pain; or did he just think his victims were in his way, bureaucratic nuisances, clogging up his surgery. We'll not know now, Shaw.'

The evening was so still that when he lit the cigarette the wisp of sulphur hung in the air, curling round the lighter and his slightly thick fingers.

Shaw lingered too, looking up at the stars turning over the cemetery.

'And if there's no reason?' he asked. 'No logic behind the pattern?'

'You'll have not done your job, Inspector. Or the world's full of dark chaos. One of the two.'

Thirty-Three

Barbecue flames flickered like Bedouin camp fires along the beach as Shaw ran the mile to *Surf!*. The chosen path, up through the dunes, sucked the energy from his legs as his feet sank into the sand. Cold sand, chilled sand, the sun long set, leaving sharp stars in a yet moonless sky. Ahead he could see the fire pit outside the bar, the bright yellow glow of the logs, sparks rising in clouds as the sea breeze blew them into life with an intermittent breath. Lena, grill chef for the evening, stood at the gleaming aluminium gas range flipping venison burgers, prawn and mackerel, twisting kebabs of peppers, shallots and mushroom.

Shaw, kissing her on the back of the neck, felt the heat of her skin, as if she'd absorbed the sun's rays and was re-radiating them as the night air cooled. He ordered a burger with couscous and sat eating with Fran, checking through a page of Spanish vocabulary for a school test. The heat of the fire pit was intense and *Surf!*'s clientele, about thirty strong, edged closer as the wind picked up, making Shaw shiver in his T-shirt and shorts. By the time the moon rose, long past its super phase, he had Fran in a gentle hug, looking out to sea.

Lena called her daughter in for bed and Shaw took the opportunity to spread Dr Furey's GPS map of Parkwood Springs out on the picnic tabletop, then rang Valentine on his mobile.

'Peter.' Valentine managed to make the single word sound exhausted. Then Shaw heard footsteps, a door squealing on unoiled hinges.

'Working late?'

The couple on the next table to Shaw pulled a bottle of Prosecco from an ice bucket and popped the cork.

'Thought I'd make a few calls. Copon's done a runner. Marsh House says he missed his morning shift – first time in five years. Control room has put out an alert. Girlfriend says he's gone AWOL.'

There was a pause and Shaw could hear Valentine's laboured breathing as he climbed the steps at St James' towards the CID suite on the fourth floor.

'There's a lift, George.'

'Not tonight there isn't, Peter. Out of order.'

Silence on the phone and Shaw imagined him resting on the landing.

'Think Copon's our man?' asked Valentine.

'Yes. I do. Is he our *only* man? That's the question.'

'Motive?'

Shaw gave his DS a brief summary of his interview with Dr Furey.

'You think Roy killed them? Why? Money? Mercy?'

'Maybe,' said Shaw. 'But why bring them all to the one house? Why do they all live on the Springs? And you saw Ruby Bright, George. Not much mercy there. Dr Roy was young, gifted, driven. I know doctors help people on their way – in the final hours, but this is something very different. This is organized, cold and brutal. So perhaps it is money. And Irene Coldshaw – what drove her out of Marsh House?'

Given Valentine's penchant for late-night wandering he was not surprised when his DS volunteered to check out the five addresses on the Springs.

'And George . . .'

'Peter.'

'Don't forget to talk to Jan. Make the time. I know it's your decision, to go for the op or tough it out, but it's her life too, right? You got a date yet?'

He'd turned his back on the sea, waiting for a reply, but the line went dead.

By the time Lena had ferried out his coffee he

had his laptop open, the screen lit, the broadband signal flowing in via *Surf!*'s AirPort connection – password SUNSETSTRIP.

Lena sat on the end of the bench, long legs outstretched, bare feet insinuated into the sand.

'What yer doing, copper?'

Shaw hesitated, but Lena insisted. 'Tell me.'

Leo, her business partner, arrived with two glasses of chilled white wine and set them down. 'Compliments of the house,' he said, then fled.

'It's work,' said Shaw, shaking his head. 'Sorry.' It was their most jealously guarded house rule, to avoid talking shop after dark. But it wasn't a total ban. Shaw's father had never discussed the police, either generically or in terms of individual cases, and the result had been his son's burning ambition to find out what he'd been shielded from, what exactly lay beyond the wall of silence. Shaw tried hard not to blot out the job, merely to reduce its allure by making sure Lena and Fran knew the facts: he'd summarize his cases, leaving out the low-life detail, the gritty forensics, the corrosive motives. Sometimes he felt detectives deliberately created a mystery out of their working lives, a half-glimpsed fantasy much more alluring than the real routine.

Lena had a good brain, a forensic logic, a talent for objectivity. Over the years she'd provided countless, subtle insights, which would have been beyond Shaw.

One aspect of the case which was disturbing Shaw was Beatty Hood's gravestone. He told Lena what he'd found, the curious coincidence of birthday and wedding days, and for want of a better term, death days. Earlier, he'd asked Mark Birley to track down some family background.

'I thought it was all a bit weird,' said Shaw. 'Turns out weird is just the tip of the iceberg.'

He swivelled the laptop round so that Lena could see a homepage, in livid blue and red, with the banner heading: HOOD DAY.

'This webpage appears to be some kind of online home for the family,' he said, bringing his legs up, perching higher on the bench. 'And by family I mean the wider clan, if you like. Thousands of them.'

He drilled down into the site until he found a page showing a black-and-white archive photograph.

'Turns out this is all about these two . . .'

The portrait would have been taken in the early years of the twentieth century. A man and woman, both in the rather stiff clothes of wealthy settlers, sat in wooden captain's chairs on a verandah, sub-tropical fronds intruding. The woman held a parasol despite being depicted in the shade, and the man held a gun across his lap.

'To cut a long story short these two were born on the same day – September the nineteenth 1875. They decided, presumably, to marry on that day, in 1900. Things get sinister, or charming, depending on your point of view, on September the nineteenth 1944, when they both died on the same day, just two hours apart, according to the family history.

'Since then their descendants have celebrated family events on Hood Day. All these emails and

233

posts are from the family, mostly sent around the day itself . . . take a look.'

> *#HoodDay Yeah! Findlay Garcia born two minutes after midnight. We made it, kidda. Another one for the record book.*
> *#HoodDay Married today in the Special Memory Chapel, Las Vegas. Go you Hoods! Telling no secrets but we might be back to tell you even more amazing news next year.*

'And this,' he said, 'from last year.'

> *#Livia Jane McCartney, nee Hood, died today, on her day. On our day. She knew that God had smiled on her and she rests in peace. Obit online at Adelaide IN-DAILY.*

The page was decorated, there was no other word for it. Bells, flowers, storks, doves of peace, all pulsing, a line of fairy lights twinkling.

'Celebratory is the word,' said Shaw.

'Or gross, that's another word,' said Lena. 'This is an unhealthy obsession. I can see that getting married on the day might be cool. Being born on the day is, I guess, something you could aim for if you were the parents. Even that's a bit . . .' She rolled her shoulders as if a cold drip of icy rain had fallen down her spine. 'Controlling. But dying on the day. Imagine what that's like if the family's all downstairs and you're the one on the

234

death bed. Like you wake up and think – it's *the* day. I really ought to go.'

She drew a circle round the wine glass, tracing her finger through the condensation, then put it down next to Dr Furey's GPS map of Lynn. 'And this?'

Covering his eyes, Shaw yawned, then disentangled himself from the bench to put another log in the fire pit.

'Tell me,' said Lena. 'It looks like a puzzle.'

Shaw spread the map flat with his hand, the wedding ring catching the firelight. Dealing swiftly with the death of Dr Roy, he summarized Furey's documentation.

'We have six deaths, starting with Beatty Hood's, and these are the home addresses of the dead. In each case the death certificate is signed by Dr Roy – the place of death being the same in each, 32 Hartington Street. We know that our murder victim, Ruby Bright, thought Hood was murdered. Now Dr Roy is dead. A puzzle? You said it.'

Shaw stared at the six red dots on the street plan.

Lena sipped her wine. Since opening *Surf!* up after dark for drinks she'd been working too hard and she'd lost a few pounds, which made her face – normally an array of curves – less sinuous and slightly harder, as if the skin was revealing the bone structure beneath. Her eyes, in contrast, had taken on a sparkle which had once been intermittent. They shone now, studying the street plan of Parkwood Springs.

'You know me and maths . . .' she said.

235

One of the reasons she'd gone into partnership with Leo D'Asti was that his skill set – banking, accounting, enterprise – had neatly plugged her own fear of numbers. And it was a fear, or a kind of phobia, rather than innumeracy. It was as if the numbers danced before her eyes, in a statistical form of dyslexia.

'But . . .' she said, splaying her hand out over the map. 'Randomness: it's the absence of a pattern. I look at this and I see a pattern in the fact that there's no pattern. If you said to Fran sprinkle six red dots on the map evenly, they'd look like that. So randomness can betray an underlying logic, right? These dots are all on different streets, they're all mid-terrace, they're all "middling", except there's just one on a corner, as if that proves they're random. That's what I see, Peter, but then I'm not a mathematician.'

Shaw's phone rang, *Valentine* came up on the screen and he put his voice on speaker.

'Peter, I'm outside one of those addresses on the Springs. You need to see this.'

Thirty-Four

The house was gone: mid-terrace, a stone step, then a gap like a rotten tooth, the space held open by two wooden beams which, at an angle, supported the dividing walls on either side, protecting the neighbouring properties from tumbling in on the cavity left behind. To the right

236

was a boarded up house with a chalk 21 on the door, while to the left 25 still had its numerals, although one of the nails in the 5 had rusted free, so that the number hung upside down.

'This is twenty-three, Salisbury Street,' read Valentine from his notebook. 'According to you the death certificate of Roland True, aged forty-three, stipulated this house as his home. Signed by Dr Gokak Roy. But Mr Robert 'Bobbie' Pauley – number eighteen – where the light is . . .'

Valentine pointed down the street, unlit except for a single lamppost, to a rectangle of light marking a downstairs window.

'He's been here since 1953. So he remembers the night this house blew up, in 1986, due to a fractured gas main. Christmas was early that year for glaziers, he reckons. Took out every window on the Springs. It's been a pile of rubble for nearly forty years.'

Valentine set off towards the dimly-lit corner, where a pub, boarded up, still displayed a sketchy hanging sign of an ornate Victorian water pump: the Parkwood Tavern. Then, taking the next left, he doubled back down the parallel street to Salisbury – Stanley Street.

Outside number 31, Valentine stopped again. 'Fire this time. I can't find a light around here, but old Pauley says he thinks it was back in the nineties, arson to boot, although there's nothing on the local rag's website. We'll have it on file. Not that it matters, point is that it was in this condition, apparently, when Arthur Ridge was supposed to be living here three months ago.'

Shaw walked up to the door and pushed it open

to reveal the blackened bricks and timber. Somewhere in the darkness, impossibly, he heard a faint sound so reedy, so redolent of a human baby's whimper that he could not stop his heartbeat picking up. The pitch changed, faltering, on the very edge of the range of the human vocal cords. Shaw's good eye widened its aperture and from the darkness shadows and shapes appeared until finally he discerned what he knew would be there; the curled, taut body of a feral cat guarding a nook in the rubble, waiting, no doubt, for a rat to lose its nerve, and then its life.

A stone flew past his head and rattled in the rubble, so that the cat fled.

'Christ,' said Valentine. 'Can't stand it. Talk about a caterwaul.'

'The other houses?' asked Shaw, carefully closing the door despite the fact that the downstairs window frame had long gone, exposing the charred shell of the front room and, incongruously, a square yard of pristine wallpaper in arts and crafts colours, depicting spring flowers.

'Two just empty – one, on Palmerston, did have a tenant but she said the place was refurnished by the landlord when they moved in and the neighbours, now gone, told her it had stood empty since the Coronation. So that's a clean sweep, but at least there's a pattern. All we need to do is work out what it bloody means.'

At the end of Stanley Street stood the Methodist chapel, as big as a cinema of the Gaumont era, its attenuated windows shadowy blanks, the glass long gone. A single iron cross clung to the apex of the roof. The doors, once a heart-warming eggshell blue, were daubed with slogans – *We rule the Springs, fuck off Polskies* – and half-a-dozen personal tags, in spray-can curls.

Parkwood Square lay beyond, the great tree at its centre, still decorated with trainers, like some grunge version of a counter-culture Christmas tree. The discovery of the body in the skip by Lister Tunnel had derailed the shoe squad's orders to strip it bare. Samples had been taken, to back up Jan Clay's sound theory that the middle-class kids of the South End were trying to muscle in on the North End. But the rest had been left to rot until uniformed branch had time on its hands.

In the docks a whistle blew on a coaster and, eerily, they saw it moving between the distant silhouettes of grain silos, edging out to take the night tide.

'I think this all began with Beatty Hood, George. If we knew why she died, we'd be able to see the way ahead. Let's see if we can get to this charity that owns the house.'

Valentine made a note. 'I'll get on to it first thing. The team needs to run down the other five too: background, relatives, the lot. If they didn't live here, where did they live?' His phone buzzed and he took the call. 'Hi. Yeah – Parkwood Springs. I'll be ten minutes, less. Sorry, I know. Look, I've decided.'

In the silence, Shaw watched a skein of mist off the Cut entangle itself in the shoe tree.

Valentine stared at the mobile screen as if he'd been cut off.

'Decided what?' asked Shaw. 'As if I've got a right to know.'

Valentine pocketed the phone and shook his shoulders free of the damp of the night. 'Things have come to a head. The hospital came up with a date. I was thinking I'd go for it, but I've decided now, and I won't. In theory it was easy – saying yes. But now it's real: a hospital bed, the operating theatre, waking up, not waking up. Or radiotherapy, chemo. I don't want that. I'm scared too. She knows, she's guessed, she's not happy. So I better face the music. I'm going to play my life out the way the cards fall, Peter.'

Thirty-Five

Shaw, in the half-light of their bedroom, pulled on swimming trunks and the summer wetsuit, bundled his work clothes in his rucksack and ran the dune-line to the Porsche. The day promised a tourist-brochure sky but with a hint of autumn cool on the air, which made the marram grass smell sweet. The coast road was empty but for an early bus, its lit interior deserted, the driver in dark glasses, braced to face the rising sun as his route took him east.

At Holkham, the small wooden kiosk inhabited by the car-park man was locked, so he left a single pound coin on the sill and put the car at the end of the carriageway by the National Trust information board, which held a wide, coloured map of the woods, leading into the funnel-shaped inlet of Holkham Bay. A chalk board marked 6.05 and 19.13 indicated the day's two high tides.

The sound of the sea filled the air, polar breakers, as white as ice, thudded down on the sand. Running along the duck boards through the bird reserve, he tried to focus on the reason for his choice of beach: Javi Copon, the elusive Spanish nurse, who'd seemed to have such a genuine insight into the plight of his elderly patients. Why had he disappeared? His connections to their first victim, Ruby Bright, were intimate. Now, thanks to Dr Furey's documentation, there was another direct link to one of the other Parkwood Springs deaths – the elderly man who'd once been a resident, but had eventually died at the house on Hartington Street. Did Copon's nursing duties take him further afield than Marsh House?

The sea filled the view ahead, a 180-degree sweep of surf lines, running back towards the horizon, six deep, ten deep, twelve. He left his rucksack and clothes on the high-water mark and sprinted the last three hundred yards into the shallows, then – spear-like – he sliced through the glassy wall of the first wave, surfacing to savour his favourite sound, the hiss of the spume on the surface, nature's own Alka-Seltzer, the air freighted with ozone and oxygen, salt and a hint of the crushed quartz of the sand beneath.

On his back, floating, buoyant in the suit, he let his eyes widen to allow the blue light to soak into his brain. A few seconds, and then the water bore him up as the next set approached, hissing, and washed him down into a darker shade of ocean, from green into the blue, with a distant, heart-stopping glimpse of the black that seemed to lurk just beyond his paddling feet.

Free-thinking, he centred on the compact, self-contained face of Javi Copon. The single fact which had stuck in Shaw's mind from that initial meeting with Copon and his girlfriend concerned Garrett McNamara – the surfer pictured in the large poster in the VW camper. 'That's the great hero,' she'd told them.

Shaw judged the waves, which were currently pounding his body into a numb coma, were, perhaps, seven feet in amplitude from the wave crest to the trough base. The wave that McNamara had ridden was more than ten times bigger; Shaw was no physicist but he understood that there was a relationship between the wave height and its speed as it teetered and then fell. Surfers were physically brave, often very fit, but could they really survive such an encounter on a slim board, encased in a single extra skin of neoprene?

The night before, out on the beach as Lena locked up, YouTube had given him the answer. Footage from a beach on the Portuguese coast was, in the surfer's hackneyed phrase, awesome. Cameras on a clifftop held a foreground shot of a lighthouse, a constant crowd soaked in spray, while beyond, approaching from the Atlantic with an unseen fetch of nearly 4,000 miles, came the mighty waves, tripping over the edge of the continental shelf, falling towards Europe. And on the shimmering face of the waves were the tiny figures of the surfers,

242

poised just ahead of the lethal fringe of the breaker, racing down the glassy tunnel, speeding towards the light.

But these surfers were not alone and were far from the image of the lonely knight of the sea. Circling in the choppy water beyond the surf line were jet skis, the pilots of which were twinned with the surfers, providing what the aficionados called a 'tow in'. This is how McNamara rode a eighty-nine-foot wave – the jet ski pulling him into the right spot at a high enough speed to catch the wave while also giving him the chance to stand on a much larger, safer board.

This, then, had been Javi Copon's dream, to ride the big waves, but it came with a price tag. This wasn't beach bum surfing at the cost of a tub of wax. Shaw had checked out prices on a website and found the jet-ski pilots, as prized as golfing caddies, could charge £200 an hour. A lot of the surfers doubled up as pilots, which meant buying the jet ski, at something like £8,000, and then purchasing fuel. It was a rich boy's obsession, and Javi Copon was no rich boy.

Shaw let the next wave take him inshore. His knees weak and his arms deadweights, he walked towards the curtain of Scots pine and his clothes, to find the path through the woods, his bones accommodating the unwelcome return of gravity. The VW camper van stood in its clearing still, the door open, the sound of KLFM a tinny waspish soundtrack. Gail appeared in what was nearly a uniform: white blouse, black skirt, black tights, her hair up and pinned back with regimented determination.

'Day job?' he asked, standing still, feeling the blood-warmed water percolating in his suit.

She locked the metal door, slipping the key under a stone in the sand. 'If you're still after Javi, forget it. The last time he just upped and went it was Cornwall, to catch the tail-end of typhoon Glenda. He's obsessed, so it's not personal. That's what he'll say when he gets back.'

Her face was set hard, the eyes without light, and Shaw thought then that she didn't really think he'd ever return.

'He missed a shift,' said Shaw, looking away as she rearranged her tights by slipping a hand under the skirt.

'I know. The mobile's been buzzing.'

'He left his mobile?'

She had brown eyes, a complement to the tan, and he could see now how worried she was, feigning a cynical worldliness she didn't feel.

'We've got his passport.'

'That won't stop him,' she said, then bit her lip. 'Javi's got friends – brothers, he calls them. They work on the boats, the ferries – if he needs it he can slip in, slip out.' She shielded her eyes against the sun which slipped through the trees. 'He's in politics, right? A union. So they all help. It's a big part of his life, not as important as surfing, but loads more important than me.'

She had a small gold watch on a little leather strap which Shaw guessed was an heirloom, her mother's perhaps, because it was workaday, solid and dependable.

'I have to be at work for breakfast: The

244

Sandcliffe.' Shaw knew it well, a Norfolk stone mansion, now a hotel, with sky-blue woodwork and its own golf course.

'Javi's got dreams,' said Shaw. 'My question is how can he afford them. The sea's free, but the hundred-foot waves aren't, are they? He needs to get there, he needs to pay for a tow-in. Not just one – hundreds, right, hoping each one will build, become *the* big one.'

'He saved.' Shaw noted the past tense and thought that this little ritual – of dressing smartly for work – was perhaps the first step she had to take to re-build her life alone.

Shaw looked at the VW, the slightly rusted wheel spokes, the battered pot grill over an ash fire.

'When did you meet?'

'Two summers back,' she said, checking the watch a third time. 'He said he loved me – turns out the blonde girlfriend is part of the essential gear: Ray-Bans, espadrilles, six-hundred-pound slim board, diver's chronometer. He loves all of that – the apparel. My dad's a fisherman, works on the quay at Wells selling crabs and mussels. So he says that's what apparel means, right, all the stuff you need to fit out a ship. So that's me, I'm a chandler's girl. Least he loved something. And he never made any promises.'

They'd started walking, and Shaw could feel the pine cones in the sand with his toes.

'Javi ever talk about a place called Parkwood Springs?'

They'd emerged from the trees and found a

dusty Fiat parked on a sandy track. She threw
her bag on the back seat and shook her head.

'Think he was capable of murder?'

She didn't look surprised, or shocked, or even
indignant. The question had made her think, and
as she worked at the idea, turning it in her mind,
Shaw could see the colour flooding out of her
skin. 'I don't think he would ever take what
wasn't his to take. That's part of the code too.
Out on the water, what do you need? A board, a
smoke, a suit. They're sacred – you don't touch
those. So I don't think he'd take a life, unless it
belonged to someone who stood between him
and the sea.'

Thirty-Six

The Ark's lone angel, but for its shielding stone
hands, looked down on the four bodies, laid out
on the aluminium tables in the morgue. Or, as
Dr Kazimierz, the pathologist, liked to call it, the
dead room. She scuttled and fussed between her
lifeless patients, checking and cross-checking.
Each lay with their feet to the west wall and the
angel, their heads to the glass partition which
separated the pathology suite from Tom Hadden's
forensic laboratory.

Shaw had assembled the team for a briefing
and given them a short summary of Dr Furey's
findings, expertly boiled-down by Paul Twine
into a two-hundred-word handout. He'd seen the

chief constable for a meeting which took precisely ninety seconds, in which Joyce had given Shaw control of the whole inquiry, including the Lister Tunnel killing. 'Frankly, I've got no choice, given Furey's intervention,' he'd added, gracefully. 'We need to know what's been happening on this estate. It's your job to find out, Peter. Don't let me down.' DI Carney would continue to investigate the Lewis Gunnel murder, but under Shaw's direction.

The team considered the dead. Sometimes it was too easy for detectives to forget the reality of murder, the simple binary distinction between life and death. Shaw had brought them here to make sure that they understood why the inquiry was so important, not in an intellectual sense, in their heads, but in their guts.

Mid-morning, but the squad stood bleary-eyed and, Shaw sensed, disorientated. Not one of the team had put in less than an eighteen-hour shift in six straight days. The investigation had struggled to construct a narrative since the discovery of Ruby Bright's body in her wheelchair at Marsh House. It was Shaw's job to restore clarity, to dissipate the complexities which threatened to obscure the way ahead.

'Let's just think about the dead in the order in which the inquiry encountered them,' said Shaw, standing to one side, so that they could all see the aluminium tables beyond.

'Ruby Bright, suffocated with a freezer bag at the age of one hundred . . .' Bright's head, covered in wispy grey hair, seemed incredibly fragile, like a large exotic egg. But Shaw

247

reminded them of Dr Kazimierz's observation that she'd fought ferociously for life. Of the dead laid out, Ruby's body seemed the least substantial, as if the mottled skin was corrupting as they watched, completing the transformation from dust to dust.

'Lewis Gunnel next. Seventeen years old. A random victim of gang violence, or a key part of our jigsaw? I've still got an open mind, but consider this: Ruby Bright died believing her friend Beatty Hood had been murdered, at home, on the Springs. She'd been the victim of a studied campaign of intimidation and theft by teenage boys. They'd got into her house, they terrified a blind, elderly widow.

'Is Lewis part of our story? Read Justina's preliminary report . . .' Shaw waved an A4 file and then tossed it on to an open desktop. 'The kid died with three stab wounds in his body and several pints of his blood were in the bottom of the skip. But the autopsy told a different tale: Lewis was suffocated first. Not only does that put him in line with Ruby, and our last victim – Gokak Roy – but someone was keen to disguise that connection. Keep that in mind.'

'And our third victim, Dr Roy,' said Shaw, inviting the team to get closer to the glass partition. The colour in the young doctor's skin saved it from the death-like pallor instilled in the room by the overhead neon lights. 'Someone squeezed the life out of this young man. Think of the strength that requires. The *application* of violence. Why did he have to die?'

'Did he kill Beatty Hood?' asked Shaw. 'Is that

what Ruby wanted to tell the press? And what of the other five people who – according to the death certificates he signed – died in Beatty's house? Why one house? Why the false addresses on Parkwood Springs? We're still working on the background checks, and they may provide the answers. For now, one of them will have to represent the rest . . .'

Shaw walked to the partition and splayed a hand against the glass. 'Of the six deaths recorded by Dr Roy all were buried. So far, we've managed to get permission for one exhumation . . .'

The fourth table held a skeleton, not entirely bereft of flesh, the knuckle-like skull still supporting a mat of what looked like light blond hair. The cadaver was enclosed within a plastic see-through body bag, with a Y-shaped red zip.

'This is Richard Brook, despite his name, a UK national of Polish descent, who was in the advanced stages of a rare neurological disease when he died just eight months ago. We need to know if his certificate statement, signed by Dr Roy, is an accurate representation of his death. That's Justina's job.

'We have to think of Richard as representative of the others – the five others, who died under Dr Roy's care. All victims, perhaps.

'Paul's summarized what we know about Brook. There's three things to note. He had no real address, as he'd been in a private hospice until shortly before his death. Dr Roy visited him there three times during his last six months of life. Brook was married, but they'd been separated for ten years. On his documents he usually lists his next of kin as an uncle living in Warsaw. The hospice is checking his file but it looks like he discharged himself, saying only that he'd found "alternative provision" – his precise words. So, if he's typical of the other victims, then he's a loner, someone who can just fall out of the system. He was, subsequently, allocated one of the fake Parkwood Springs addresses, presumably by Dr Roy. The burial plan was pre-paid. The internment, at East Sowerby, was attended by two relatives – or friends – and Dr Roy.'

Shaw leaned his back against the glass.

'So: Bright first, in the wake of Hood. Then Lewis in the Lister Tunnel, then Dr Roy – who points the way to the other Parkwood Springs deaths, represented by Richard Brook. That's the picture.'

Shaw tossed his empty coffee into the bin. 'Motive, or motives, are still unclear. Mercy killings? Hardly. This feels much more like a hard-edged scam. Identity theft? We need to check that out – see if their names have lived on, see if their IDs are being re-used after death. Murder? Here's a thought. Let's find out how much these people were paying for care. Their bank accounts were bleeding away. What if someone decided to cut short their lives to get at that money? They may look like loners but there's always someone in line for a windfall. We've got forensic accountants crawling over the paperwork. Let's keep a sharp eye on what they find. They're not detectives. We are. Let's make sure they have access to our expertise.'

Shaw checked his diver's watch. 'And, while

we may still be struggling on motive, we have a clear suspect in Javi Copon. His disappearance is eloquent of guilt. Let's touch base again right down the line: Interpol, Madrid, the ferry ports. Make sure they know how much we want to find Javi Copon. We need to know why he's decided to run.'

'I'll sort it,' said Twine, scratching a note with his trademark Montblanc fountain pen.

Mark Birley, sitting down, stretched in his seat, linking his hands and cracking the joints. 'Just on the practical side. And thinking about the Parkwood six – we're saying that they all died at Hartington Street? There's a missing link here, how did the body get to the undertakers for burial? By hearse, presumably. But like, you'd blow the whistle if you turned up at the same house *six* times. Are they in on the scam?'

Twine shuffled papers, put the cap on his pen, and checked his laptop. 'Good spot, Mark.' He scrolled up and down twice, checking the certificates and his notes. 'Yup – six different funeral directors. Four from Lynn, one from Gayton, one from Peterborough. So none of them would have found anything inconsistent in being called to the same address in a short space of time. And there are no neighbours to keep a nosey eye out. It's a system – it has to be. A conveyor belt.'

'And but for Ruby Bright's murder it might be running still,' said Shaw.

Thirty-Seven

DI Joe Carney phoned Jan Clay at seven that evening. Sat in an armchair by the gas fire, which was off, she'd been so still she jumped at the sound. Valentine had sent her a text saying he was on his way home an hour earlier, but had not appeared. His sullen retreat into the role of stricken wanderer had at its heart, she felt, a selfish streak. His announcement that he'd decided to turn down the chance of an operation when the date was offered had not been open to discussion.

Angry, dejected – *rejected* – she had decided to leave. A trundle-case on two wheels stood in the hallway, and what was left of a fish and chip supper was in the oven. She'd simultaneously decided that she wouldn't go until Valentine was back in the house. She'd tell him to his face why she couldn't stay. Stupidly, she couldn't stop herself worrying about the cat. Zebra lay curled listlessly beside its untouched food. She'd booked an appointment that evening with the vet, but doubted Valentine would be able to inveigle the animal into its carrier.

'Look, Clay,' said Carney, as soon as she picked up the call. 'This is good work on the Lister Tunnel. It's been noted. Well done. We've got a suspect. I want you in for the interview, that's in twenty minutes, St James'. You can make that?

252

Stow the kids, do whatever you have to, just get here.'

'Sir. On my way.'

She put the phone down. 'Tosser,' she said, so loud the cat looked up.

The arrest had been made that afternoon at St James'. Like so many criminal cases the apparent breakthrough had involved luck and routine in equal measure. There'd been a brawl in a town centre shopping mall between two sets of kids: North End versus South End. The security guard in the Arndale saw it start on CCTV and rang the police control room. By the time a squad car arrived on the scene there was only one teenager left: Jacob James Dunne and he was lying in a sticky, smudged pool of his own blood. The extent of his injuries suggested the fight had been about more than territorial rights.

While Dunne was receiving treatment in A&E, DI Carney had persuaded him, despite the fact the victim was half senseless with painkillers, to agree to the police entering his home address to pick up a change of clothing. An old trick, it had worked to perfection. By the time Dunne's mother had summoned the wit to ask for a warrant the forensic team had found a blood-stained T-shirt.

DI Carney was desperate for an arrest in the Lister Tunnel killing to undermine Shaw's inquiry. He hadn't moved his family from the stunning Irish coastline to a dead-beat north Norfolk commuter village to get lumbered with a petty gang dispute, while some one-eyed whizz kid was left to run a multiple-murder inquiry. He planned to dutifully inform Shaw of the arrest and interview, after the fact.

The suspect 'Jake' Dunne, sat beside his lawyer – a legal aid regular Jan recognized from court called Ashington. No one had spoken for ten minutes. Dunne was staring into the lap of his jeans. When he looked up Jan could see the extent of the beating he'd taken. The original shape of his skull was not discernable, as he was so badly bruised the eye sockets and nose were misshapen. One eye was closed, the skin darkening to black, his top lip so badly broken it appeared in two separate sections, separated by a blood-red gash. She had to admit Carney was right. This was no teenage spat over a pair of trainers.

Ashington, the lawyer, kept checking his watch.

'The doctor was entirely clear,' he said to Jan, breaking the silence. 'Half an hour max. He needs to rest.'

The echo of his words, trapped in the tiled room, circulated and then, finally, died. DI Carney's footsteps clattered outside and he burst in with a swagger. Flicking on the digital recorder, a cigarette behind one ear, he asked them all to identify themselves. When Jan heard herself declaring her own name and rank, she felt a genuine thrill of achievement, wanting Valentine to be there. In a single moment of telepathic certainty she knew he was in the building, over their heads, in the CID room.

'OK. Now. We've done the dull stuff, haven't we, Jake?' said Carney, affecting 'hail fellow, well met' conviviality. '*You say* this fight was

254

just a dust up over name-calling. *You say* you didn't leave your house on the night Lewis Gunnel was strangled, then knifed to death. *You say* the blood on your T-shirt was a mate's who cracked his head in a game of street footy.'

Carney waited for a response. Dunne nodded.

'We've taken statements from your mother, step-father and half-sister to the effect that you were upstairs in your bedroom . . .' Carney cast a glance over a statement sheet. 'Doing your homework, it says here. Very commendable. You're at West Anglia College right, doing a GCSE in business studies?'

Dunne nodded and a gasp of air slipped out through his lips, as if breathing, the simple raising and lowering of his ribs, was a pain in itself.

'I'm afraid there's going to be a short break in your studies, Jake. Ten to twelve years is my guess. Or you could carry on, studying inside. You'd have the time.'

Carney laughed at Jan and she was ashamed to find her lips creasing in a supportive grin.

Ashington leant forward. 'If you've got any evidence which would secure such a conviction perhaps you'd present it, Inspector. Your predictions on the future are fascinating; however, there's a fortune teller on the Tuesday Market. She charges five pounds for reading tea leaves. If we wanted to listen to tripe we could have opted for her. I think the name's Pellecano by the way – Madame Pellecano.'

A ripe smile disfigured Dunne's beaten face.

Carney opened the folder and produced a forensics report.

'Forensic examination of the bloodstains on the T-shirt removed from Jake's bedroom has provided a match with the victim. I'm looking into the future, Mr Ashington, completely free of charge, and I can see your client in the dock, unless he can tell me how this happened . . .'

Ashington, mid-fifties, gaunt, slightly beaten himself, if in a less obviously violent manner than his client, put a hand on Jake Dunne's shoulder. 'That's convenient, Inspector. I do hope you haven't imported working practices best suited to the Royal Ulster Constabulary.'

'What the fuck does that mean?'

'It means you're on the record as mouthing obscenities, Inspector. Tut tut. But if you really don't know what it means, I'll spell it out: I hope – and it is just a hope – that this evidence has not been fabricated. Or, possibly, fraudulently placed in my client's bedroom. And I understand no warrant was in force? I can assure you that fact will be on the record . . .'

DI Carney was having trouble sitting still and Jan wondered if he was used to a more physical brand of police interview. It was with a visible effort that he sat back, and began to read the forensic report.

'Why is the victim's blood on your clothing, Jake?' he asked, eventually.

'You've got this all wrong,' said Dunne.

'Jake. Remember. There's a strategy and we agreed it,' said Ashington, but he was looking at DI Carney and Jan noted with a thrill that there was a glint of genuine hatred in that tired legal eye.

'I'm here to learn,' said DI Carney, legs stretched out under the interview table.

Dunne looked at Jan then, perhaps sensing an ally. 'The South End kids come up to piss on our patch. We give as good as we get – we go down there, make ourselves felt, whatever it takes.'

'Jake,' repeated Ashington, his hand tightening on the teenager's shoulder. 'Think, please. I am your solicitor. I have your best interests at heart.'

'They're middle-class, right,' persisted Dunne. 'They've got stuff, and it's quality stuff. Mobiles, trainers, gear. Haircuts – that's what you notice first off. Latest cool look, instant, on every head. So they don't need to steal, right, and so like, what do they do when they want to hit out? That's the thing about needing money, it sort of soaks up why you're angry. It's a goal, right, something to go for. We get stuff, we're happy.

'Not them. This kid – Gunnel – was one of the kids with everything. Looking for something that'll hurt us. Looking for a way to get his kicks. So they'd pick on the lonely, old folk squatters. Stand there in their front rooms and piss in the fireplace. You ask about, copper, find out. 'Stead of sitting there scratching your arse.'

A grin fell off Carney's face like a landslide.

'Yeah. You. Find out,' said Dunne and Jan thought that if his real IQ had been unleashed he wouldn't be doing a single GCSE at the local tech.

'They'd start fires too, upstairs, or in the yards, just to watch. And pets, they'd pick on them. Hang up a kitten, chuck a brick at a dog. And they'd tell 'em, these people, the old folks, You

257

tell the police, we'll burn your house while you're in your beds. You'll die screaming. Nice, right. I'm not saying we're angels, but that's not us.

'I'm saying, the thing is this kid, Gunnel, might have picked the wrong house. The Springs is for the lonely, but there's others. That's all I'm saying. Others.'

Ashington had taken a note and he popped the cap back on his biro, as if to say that was a nice, convenient place to pause.

'Nice speech,' said Carney. 'But the question stands, Jake. Why's his blood on your shirt?'

Ashington was on his feet. 'We'll break there. I'd like a copy of the forensics, Inspector. You know the drill.'

'That's the story is it, Jake?' persisted Carney. 'That Gunnel, sixteen, fit, brimming with attitude, gets strangled, knifed, by some old dear who can't sleep nights. Give us a break, kid.'

Carney stood too, but the tape was still running. 'I'm not the only one thinks you killed him, am I, Jake?

'You didn't get those bruises . . .' Carney pointed his pen at the teenager's injuries. 'All that, in a punch-up over pissing rights. They think you did it, the North End kids. They think you killed their mate. Their brother. You get out of here, which isn't going to happen, but for the sake of it, you get out of here and they'll finish the job.'

Jan, studying the beaten face, was appalled to see that the shape of the skull, especially around the left eye, was actually changing by the minute, as the injuries swelled, the tissue inflamed and torn. The eye, clear when the interview had started, was now blushed pink.

'Gunnel.' Dunne shook his head and then had to raise both palms to each temple to cool the pain. 'Fuck. We found him in the skip. Dead as meat,' he said, shaking his head at Ashington's pleas for silence.

'I climbed in the skip to see if there was anything worth lifting and there he was. The knife, right, it had gone in his chest. He just looked kinda stunned to me. I tried to lift him up, to get him out, but there was blood underneath too – loads of it, sticky and clotted. I just dropped him, right. Coz I thought, like what's the point here.

'I left him, I admit that.' His voice rose to a shout, 'Like he wasn't going to get any deader, right. No deader than that.'

Thirty-Eight

Valentine felt as out of place in a vet's surgery as he did in a hospital. The clinical surfaces, the bloodless efficiency, made him feel feral by comparison, and – overwhelmingly – guilty. The bright lights hurt his eyes.

Standing at the table in the examination room he ran a hand along the spine of the cat and it flexed under his touch, but he noted – again – that a large amount of the dry black fur came off on his sweaty hand.

'We could keep him in and try an ultrasound scan,' said the vet, 'but I can feel the problem . . .' She held the cat with that expert vice-like grip that vets used to somehow hypnotize wild animals. 'Just here, in the lower abdomen, there's a definite lump. I'm guessing it's a tumour, which is why he's got no appetite. We could operate, but that would involve Zebra staying with us for a few days. And there would be the post-operative care.'

Valentine was already in a foul mood because Jan was missing and she'd promised to help with the vet. Oddly, for once his own illness made the decision easier because he actually didn't give a toss about the money. If cash could solve the problem he'd have gladly paid up. In fact, he'd been fantasizing that if things moved inexorably towards his own death he could start issuing post-dated cheques, just for the hell of it.

So it genuinely wasn't about the money. He just had to decide what was right. And he knew what was right because he could tell the vet didn't think an operation was worth the pain, or . . . Valentine searched for the right word in his head and came up with 'indignity', because that's what cats always managed to preserve, their sense of independent grace.

Zebra looked disorientated, but worst of all, groggy. The real heartbreaker was not that the animal looked unwell, but that it had begun, very slightly, to lose its innate beauty. Everything, thought Valentine, dies ugly.

'It's cancer?'

'Or he's ingested something, a chemical.

260

They're very sensitive to that and they don't have to swallow the stuff. They can take it in through their paws . . .'

She held up her hands as if Valentine was a simpleton.

'It's a two-way membrane,' she explained. 'Anti-freeze off a car bonnet, or petrol on a garage floor. That kind of thing. It's just bad luck.'

'It's in pain?' asked Valentine.

'Yes. Certainly. I can give you painkillers but as you know they're murder to get down if they're off their food. So we could give him injections, but you'd have to bring him in for those. And they have side effects. Or we could scan and operate, as I said. A major procedure, highly invasive.'

Valentine thought that in the vet's code, or whatever, there should be a rule that they have to mention the euphemism first – the one about *sleep*. It wasn't as if there weren't ways to avoid the word death when it came to animals – although, personally, he'd always thought 'destroying' a racehorse was a unique euphemism in that it sounded worse than using straightforward English. But all that stuff about an operation being 'invasive', and a 'major procedure' was there to prompt Valentine to use the forbidden word. Why couldn't they say it first?

'You think it's best to put him out of his pain?' he said, bitter that it had been left to him and that he'd opted for a euphemism himself. Something of his own predicament seemed to loom then, casting a shadow over the brightly lit room, and he wanted, desperately, to be out on the street, jostling with the living.

The vet's voice was far off. 'Do you want to stay? You could hold him.'

A minute later Valentine had both hands on the cat, one under the chin, one on the abdomen, both of them hot, while the vet did something with a small bottle and a syringe. Then they both stood there for a while until it was all over, which, Valentine had to admit, was painless, in the sense that it didn't hurt the cat.

Brisk, businesslike, he said he thought that charging eighty quid to dispose of the body was a bit steep, so he'd take it with him and put it in the back yard, where there was six square feet of flowerbed.

Which was why, a bit later, he was stood on the corner of London Road, waiting for the lights to change. Red. Amber. Green. None of the colours seemed capable of releasing him from a strange trance, until, holding the custom-made cardboard box with the dead weight inside, he thought that, actually, he'd like to change his mind; not about Zebra's options, but his own.

Thirty-Nine

The pilgrims made their way through the woods. Shaw, watching from the hillside above, felt an extraordinary, atavistic sense that the scene below had been played out a thousandfold, as if all those

who had ever used the ancient path had material-
ized on this one evening, at dusk, to make their
way up from the coast towards the Holy House
of Walsingham, through the woods of Holkham.
The old way, here a deep green lane, was a millen-
nium in the walking; a curving, graceful track,
hugging the low contours beyond the marsh,
before setting off uphill, beside a small stream,
a tributary of the Burn. The line of guttering
lanterns which marked the pilgrims' latter-day
caravan snaked its way forward, accompanied by
the sound of plainsong, just audible, adding
another layer of the past, an audible memory, to
match the visual.

Cutting in a zigzag path across open grassland,
Shaw slipped into the trees and joined the old
path, the line of pilgrims ahead now beyond sight
around a slow curve. The tunnel vision, up the
green lane, with the branches over-arching,
seemed to crackle with the energy they'd left
behind, a kind of electrical trace, like the after-
image of a lightning strike. Shaw expected to see
the ghost of a medieval monk perhaps, leaning
on a crook, sandals slipping on the worn flagstones, fading into the half-light.

He set off in pursuit. The enfolding glaucous
light took Shaw back to his first holiday with
Lena. They'd driven the Porsche to Portsmouth
and taken the car ferry across the Bay of Biscay
to the north coast of Spain; a voyage of blue
ocean, the rolling ship accompanied by sudden
leaping dolphin and long-backed fin whales.
Hiring an isolated farmhouse in the hills of
Asturias, built into the rock side, they'd waited

263

for the clouds to lift, revealing the distant coast. The first evening Shaw had followed the painted clam-shell signs on the roadside to a set of stone steps, which led between two old houses, until he fell out, unexpectedly, on a branch of the ancient Camino itself: the sprawling network of pathways which had led millions to the tomb of St James at Compostella. Dusk again, the stone path leading the eye into a misty distance, completely in the shadow of the trees. Shaw's hair had stood on end as he felt the presence of those who had gone before, walking east, returning west, the millions who had stepped out on that rocky track, wearing it down, inscribing it into the earth. He'd never believed in life after death, but that moment on the Camino showed him another possibility, that you could make a direct, emotional link with the past. As he'd stood that evening in the falling night on the Camino he'd not been alone.

Ahead, a voice, baritone, threaded its way between the ash and the elder, its musical pattern mazy, hypnotic and sinuous. Shaw felt something of the fear of the stranger; the eyes watching from the woods, the danger of approaching night, of roaming boar or hungry wolves, and worst of all, the outlaws who must have watched, and waited, their prey striding into traps which they could lay with confidence along the many branches of this pilgrims' way – Norfolk's Camino, heading for England's Nazareth.

This pilgrims' way was, like its Spanish cousin, many-branched. This 'leg' – the 'Wells leg' – had thrived thanks to the ships which brought pilgrims from Europe and the north. At this point it was within two miles of the shrine itself. The pilgrims had 'landed' two nights earlier and camped just outside the town, before covering three miles and camping again. This one-off 'World' pilgrimage route was popular with the infirm, families and the disabled, as it offered the opportunity to complete the way, without covering more than six or seven miles over three days. The 'camping' provided was hardly 'glamping', but it was superior, with camp beds and some night heaters and food provided from a mobile kitchen on site.

This last site lay just outside the Holkham Estate, which owned the great house, the Elizabethan chimneys of which were just visible a few miles along the coast. At a point on the upland track, where the hillside held a narrow vale, the old woods cleared to form a natural clearing known as Foghanger, and, as Shaw cleared the brow, he saw the fire pits, freshly lit, and the trestle tables laid out for the evening meal, volunteers carrying water jugs and bowls from the catering vans parked in the shadows of the wood.

The Met Office forecast, a vital component of the modern pilgrim's digital pack, was dry and clear. Leaves and moss, litter and boughs, had been spread in 'dormitory' lines to provide makeshift beds for the younger pilgrims, while a row of canvas tents stood back in the lee of the trees for the elderly and infirm.

A uniformed PC walked out of this medieval throng, a radio crackling at her chest. It was Jan Clay and, when she saw it was Shaw, her eyes

265

flitted quickly beyond, expecting Valentine to limp out of the shadows too.

'No George?' she said. 'Sorry, forget that, not very professional.' A practised movement of the head flicked her blonde fringe out of her eyes.

'I got a text. He's back at St James' running the team. We might have five more murders on the slate. I'm only here because the chief constable's got the idea north Norfolk's the next Ulster: barricades and Molotov cocktails next. And now there's what, food poisoning?'

'Medical officer's here . . .' She led the way towards the kitchens.

Louis Snow was the assistant medical officer for the district council based at Hunstanton: mid-thirties, earnest, a keen cyclist who specialized in turning up at St James' for press conferences in the full lycra outfit. Shaw spotted his cycle now, a top of the range Dutch & Wolf, £10,000 worth of kit, carefully locked to an ash tree bole. Now they were in the wood Shaw could see two ambulances parked beyond the catering line.

'One minute,' he said, leaning back on the bonnet of one of the catering vans, filling in a report, his mobile set on the clipboard. 'Just let me get this done and dusted, Shaw. If you're hungry the food's good. Just don't touch the chicken.'

They had thirty seconds so Shaw repeated to Clay what he'd told Valentine to pass on, but suspected he hadn't. 'Good work on Lister Tunnel,' he said. 'DS Chalker's a dinosaur. It was smart work all round and you don't need me to

266

tell you it's been noticed. Has DI Carney got his man?'

'You heard? I've done you a short report . . .'

'He rang me to update. Perfunctory, but what the hell. He doesn't like me, I don't like him. Sorry, unprofessional . . .'

Snow was ready for them. 'Hi. Right. We have what the authorities like to call a sequence of events. First night of the journey two elderly men complained of stomach cramps. One of those, an eighty-three-year-old, is in the QE2 now. I got test results an hour ago on him and it's salmonella. Chicken, probably. Which is odd because according to the catering company they didn't put chicken out. It's an open buffet, some hot, some cold. Where did the chicken come from? That's your department. Thing is the second batch of patients all said they had prawns on the second night, but again, that wasn't on the menu either.

'They collect all the food at the end of the evening and bin it and I've found some chicken and prawns and isolated the evidence . . .' The pannier of the bike held a small plastic freezer box. The lid made a small hermetic pop as he flipped it open and held it out for them to see. Shaw, unable to suppress his instincts, took a step back.

'It won't kill you, Shaw. Well, actually that's not true, is it? It might, if you ate this you'd get the full range of the usual symptoms: cramps, nausea, vomiting, diarrhea. Then you'd get better – unless you're vulnerable – like the elderly, who can't rehydrate quickly enough. So it could kill. And it's deliberate all right. Take the chicken;

each slice of breast has been left out – I'd say for twenty-four hours – then half-cooked. You can't be sure it will produce the bacteria, but there's a bloody good chance. In this case it was a bull's eye, these samples are rife.'

The trick with any crime, Jack Shaw used to say, was to see it – not just hear about it, or read about it, but to see it actually happening. Shaw tried to imagine the buffet table, the volunteers putting out bowls. 'Someone must remember where the chicken dish came from?'

'No,' said Jan, consulting a notebook. 'Both nights they put out more than thirty bowls of food, plus salads, fruit, bread. It's like a banquet, there's people everywhere. The victims seem to think the chicken was mixed in with salad leaves in a wooden bowl. Nobody seems to recognize that dish, not amongst the volunteers anyway.'

'Do they know each other that well?' asked Shaw.

'Not that well,' said Jan. 'But I think they'd spot an outsider.'

'OK. So our culprit's probably on the inside.'

'Most of the volunteers are bussed in with the caterers,' said Jan. 'They bring rucksacks, so it would be easy to secrete the food, then simply serve it out.'

'Tonight?' asked Shaw.

'Chicken's on the menu, but it's been vouched for,' said Snow. 'Plus they'd have to be blind not to see we're on to them. And it's done now; eight in hospital, including two kids. A couple of the pensioners who fell ill are soldiering on . . . I think it's all part of the pilgrim experience.'

As if by stage direction the back doors of one of the ambulances opened and two nurses helped an elderly man negotiate the fold-down steps. Walking towards them he took a series of paces, each one taking several seconds, the moving foot held perilously horizontal to the leafy woodland path. It was an illusion, Shaw recognized, but it was as if they could hear bones creaking, joints stiff with arthritis.

'This is Miles Thomas,' said Snow. 'Despite my advice he has decided against a night in hospital. I think you could say he was determined to finish the trip, isn't that right, Mr Thomas? Just two more miles now, then I think a period of rest, don't you?'

'Tomorrow's enough for any man,' said Thomas, the voice stricken with a weak reediness. He held his back straight and his head up, but Shaw noted the almost imperceptible vibration of the jawbone.

Thomas had those blue, almost colourless eyes that can turn milky with age, but still retain a shard of ice. A life force burned out of those eyes, thought Shaw, which was at odds with the almost broken body. The combination of spiritual determination and physical frailty was not entirely inspiring. It was as if Thomas felt, on some higher level, that his body was a superfluous detail; nothing more than a necessary burden, supported by sheer willpower.

'I will make it to the shrine,' he said. 'It's my last journey, God willing.'

Shaw thought this sounded like a disguised invitation to ask a question, so he simply smiled.

'Pancreatic cancer,' volunteered Thomas. 'I

269

won't let them touch me now. I've got days, weeks – but that's what they said a month ago. I have prayed for a release from pain and it will be mine soon. These last hours are a blessing.'

'Do many pilgrims come to die?' asked Jan Clay and Shaw detected a belligerent note.

'Yes. Oh yes. Many of us here have reached the ends of our lives, but we still breathe, still wake. So we must wait. There are, what can I say, other routes. Christ's anger at such weakness must be sublime. A flight to Switzerland, a hypodermic. And they call *that* Dignitas.'

The passion with which he spat out the word almost unbalanced him and he would have fallen but for his stick.

'They pay for death, counting out silver to the devil, in my view.' When nobody agreed his eyes narrowed and he focused on Shaw's mooneye. 'It's a package too, like a holiday to Spain. A flight, the room, the nursing care and, most vitally, the lethal dose of *pento-bar-bital*.' He enunciated each syllable. 'I'm told the current rate is eight thousand pounds. That's it then, the price of death. They say we have a society in which *everything* has a price.'

Shaw found the sermon almost intolerable. A Catholic education had left him with a short attention span when faced with a one-way polemic. But something about that one word – Dignitas – made his skin cool, the hair prickling on the nape of his neck. The word stem was *dignity*, of course, and it brought to mind the clinical front room of 32 Hartington Street, with its NHS bed and the steel drip-holder, poised above. Dignity

270

at a price. Shaw had missed this obvious truth; that faced with pain, or an apparently shameful descent into dependency, many people would pay handsomely for death on demand.

Thomas, impatient, shrugged off a helping hand from the nurse who'd helped him out of the ambulance. 'What would you prefer, Inspector: the Geneva clinic, with its pretence of science, or the woods of Holkham, a night breeze, and tomorrow – God willing – my last sight of the Holy House?'

'That's up to God, isn't it?' said Clay. 'That's why you pay your money for a trip to Switzerland, Mr Thomas – the certainty of euthanasia. The pentobarbital always works,' she added, with a brutal logic Shaw admired. 'God's ways, by comparison, are a bit more unpredictable.'

Thomas shuffled his feet, then sought out Jan's eyes. 'Euthanasia, assisted suicide, weasel words, don't you think? It's not our gift, of course, that's the trick of it.' He got a little closer. 'You can pay for death, young lady, but you can't pay for a good death. That's what I live for, what I walk for, each step. A righteous death, and a timely one.'

Forty

Gunning the Porsche west Shaw did what he never did: he went back to his office at St James'. The canteen, open for the night shift, provided

271

coffee and a bacon sarnie, and by midnight he was at his desk, the anglepoise lamp burning a bright circle on Furey's map of Parkwood Springs. The pious arrogance of Miles Thomas had provided the key to the mystery of Marsh House. All he needed now was to amass the necessary evidence.

A late email from Tom Hadden added two more pieces to the jigsaw. Toxicology on Dr Gokak Roy had revealed a high concentration of amphetamines in his bloodstream. Further analysis would follow at the Home Office's London laboratory. But all the signs were Dr Roy had a serious, chronic, habitual need for drugs.

So Javi Copon needed the money to chase Atlantic waves and Gokak Roy had an extremely expensive addiction. Shaw saw them as a team: nurse and doctor, both adept at providing the necessary 'care' on offer at Hartington Street and the insiders' knowledge needed to manipulate the documentary system. Crucially, Gokak Roy brought the magic word 'doctor', qualifying him to be the unquestioned signatory of any death certificate. Javi Copon had fled and Gokak Roy was dead. What was missing from this emerging picture was organizational brainpower.

From his office window Shaw could see that the lights were still on in the Ark, so he sent Hadden an email. Could the forensic scientist check the bones of Richard Brook for traces of pentobarbital, or any related drug used in assisted suicide, or euthanasia. Then he left an email for DC Paul Twine. Inquiries into the Causeway Trust, the charity to which Beatty Hood had left

272

her house, needed to be fast-tracked; also, could he check through all the constituent organizations affiliated to WAP – the Walsingham Alternative Pilgrimage – and see if there was any reference to EXIT, or other campaign groups which supported a legal 'right to die'. In addition, CCOO, the Madrid-based trade union, was supporting WAP – who provided the link with Spain? Finally, via the Charity Commission, he needed the name of WAP's mysterious rich bene-factor, responsible for bankrolling the *Rainbow Protestor.*

By dawn he was on the road home, the Porsche purring, and he thought of the pilgrims waking in their tents and hostels, congregating on the paths and tracks and green lanes, excited at the prospect of walking towards Walsingham and joining forces in their thousands for the final Holy Mile.

Forty-One

The town of Walsingham radiated a kind of reli-gious tension, like a miniature Vatican City. The main pilgrimage procession, an amalgamation of the various 'legs', had reached the Slipper Chapel at nine, and was now resting, before making its way down the final Holy Mile, a narrow lane, shielded by hedgerows. The two airborne police helicopters estimated the crowd below awaiting its arrival at between 2,000 and 2,500 – far less

273

than the alarmist figures mooted by the chief constable, who had made an unannounced visit to the police mobile control room in the station car park, and finding everything quiet, had promptly announced he would return to St James'. (His civilian driver had tipped Valentine the truth. Joyce had a tee-time of 7.15 a.m. at the West Norfolk golf club.) Shaw had noted DI Carney, in the back seat of the chief constable's official car, getting out for fresh air, his golf shoe spikes scraping on the tarmac.

The chief constable took Shaw aside for a personal debrief. They stood by three plain wooden crosses set on a miniature Calvary for the day, in the shadow of the Russian Orthodox church's single onion dome.

'The food poisoning?' he asked, bristling with impatience, as if Shaw was wasting his time.

'Four still in hospital. None in danger. A deliberate attempt to injure, certainly. Kill? No. Although that could have been the outcome and the perpetrators were reckless as to the consequences of feeding salmonella to the frail and elderly. Forensics have the tainted chicken and prawns, and some hope that they might have the culprit's fingerprints on one of the bowls, because there's a match with a blurred partial on the welltop in the shrine. If we're close to an arrest I might even try using a bit of the budget to get a handwriting match off the note. My guess is we're dealing with one zealot, maybe three – but no more. Committed, ingenious, but strictly limited in scope. The poisoner's got to be one of the twenty-six volunteers who served out the food.

We'll get them all into St James', but not until Monday. Today I need the manpower here, on the street.'

'Parkwood Springs?'

'Copon is our prime suspect,' said Shaw, deciding he'd give the chief constable what he wanted to hear, but at this stage, nothing more. Shaw had theories, evidence, and a new prime suspect within his grasp, but he wanted the chief constable on the golf course, not on his back. 'I've got ports, airports, main rail hubs on alert, and later today we're Skyping CID in Bilbao, they want to know where he is too. The girl-friend thinks he's off riding the perfect wave in Cornwall, or Wales – so we've got local uniformed units checking the beaches, life-guards, RNLI. He's done a runner, and he's done a runner because he's involved. But we've got his passport.'

Joyce gave him a very cold eye. 'You better hope he hasn't slipped the net, Peter. Got it?'

'Sir.' Shaw nodded, beaming.

The chief constable's Rover slid away past a crowd of pilgrims coming down from the hill, their excited, exultant, faces reflected in the black, mirror-like paintwork.

Forty-Two

By noon the town, expectant, was bulging with sightseers, pilgrims, and the WAP protest group,

275

which had set up its banners and billboards on a grassy triangle on the edge of Common Place at midnight, and spent the night singing tuneless protest classics, from 'We Will Overcome' to 'Ninety-nine Red Balloons'. At the one o'clock police briefing the uniformed DCI in charge of crowd control estimated the total numbers – including the 'incoming' pilgrims from the Slipper Chapel – at 3,000–3,500. A small contingent of Tamils – largely from Coventry – had arrived in four cars and a multicoloured van. One of Shaw's team, DC Jackie Lau, had been deployed to discreetly track the group. She'd ditched her usual leather jacket and wrap-around sunglasses for a tie-dye shirt in mauve and green, and a bling silver crucifix studded with fake stones.

Shaw, briefing the thirty plain-clothed detectives on duty, was worried only about complacency. The self-styed Wolves had so far struck twice, and in both cases revealed a distinct aversion for direct action. There was little doubt they would mark the day with a third attempt, but Shaw suspected the role of the police would simply be to discover the damage after the fact. The most worrying scenario, given the town's medieval streets and ancient buildings, involved fire, so he'd called in the brigade's senior operations man on the ground and put two officers on a rooftop watch for smoke or flames. A small explosive device could not be discounted either, so he made sure that the emergency services and the St John's Ambulance Brigade were ready to deal with the consequences: burns, shock, trauma. An army bomb squad unit near Sheringham stood on amber alert.

'So what are we looking for?' asked Shaw.

He'd got everyone outside the mobile control room, in the shadow of St Seraphim's. 'I have no doubt the Wolves are in the crowd. Or at least, on its edges. Look for familiar faces, in the wrong places. They'll want a *symbolic* triumph, so the icon itself is the key, let's concentrate on the statue of the Virgin Mary under the portable canopy; the Holy House itself, although attacks on either would have to be public, possibly violent, and would certainly result in arrest. So, maybe not. There are six other churches at risk, so we need to check them out on a regular basis. George has got the rota.'

Valentine, standing at Shaw's shoulder, waved a piece of paper.

'The abbey ruins are crowded, the gardens full of picnicking pilgrims. But our principal problem is that the focus of attention – the icon – is a moving target. It's brought out to meet the pilgrims as they process in, then carried back to the shrine, and then on to the abbey, before returning back to the shrine. All eyes are on her. That's their chance. So while we must track the icon, *our* eyes must be on the pilgrims. Look relaxed, enjoy the crowds, mingle, but remember, we're here to do a job.'

A radio crackled. 'Procession's in sight at the south end.' DC Lau's voice was mildly distorted, charged with an unmissable tension.

'OK. Good luck. And keep talking. The radios are our lifeline.'

Shaw took his set and slipped through the crowds towards the High Street, dropping sharply down Station Lane into Common Place. The protestors of WAP, on their slight mound, were delivering sporadic radical chants: an elderly woman, with a banner reading A WOMAN'S RIGHT TO CHOOSE, was trying to inveigle pilgrims into a discussion on the issues. 'Why do you want to oppress women? On what authority do you claim jurisdiction over my body?'

Shaw noted that Nano Heaney was absent, although uniformed branch reported that she'd been into the control room to confirm that 208 protestors had assembled by ten o'clock. Overnight, Tom Hadden had answered his questions and Paul Twine had tracked down the Causeway Trust. Shaw had questions for Nano Heaney, but for now, they'd have to wait. Around the protestors various pilgrims, avoiding eye-contact with their protagonists, made preparations to greet the procession, hoisting banners and crosses. Applause rippled along the route.

Looking down the High Street, Shaw glimpsed the on-coming pilgrims, the icon of the Virgin Mary at their head, wavering slightly from the horizontal and the vertical, as it was borne along in the vanguard on its platform; a pulse of clapping, like a wave falling on a beach, grew loud, almost raucous. A group of men in the square, in white robes, began to chant in plain-song, the stone walls of the town museum as a backdrop, below its crenellated mock-medieval roof. The first flower was thrown, in a graceful arc, into

278

the path of the barefoot pilgrims. Herbs followed; sprigs of rosemary, bay and thyme, immediately lacing the air with a culinary, exotic scent.

'Why does the church ignore the rights of gay people?' shouted a man on the grassy knoll and Shaw heard a woman to his own right 'tut' with a tight smack of the lips.

Ahead of the procession a TV film cameraman walked backwards, balancing an extraordinary gyroscopic gantry, which supported the camera and a sound boom, and a series of three floodlights. This crude blast of illumination fell on the leading pilgrims, making them hold their hands up in defence, leaving blinded eyes in shadow. The richness of the icon attracted even Shaw's eye: the gold rays radiating from the head, the silver-edged gown, the richly embroidered canopy, the lifelike hand-painted detail of the Virgin's face, feet and hands, one of which was held up in stiff benediction. The gentle rocking of the wooden figure, above the heads of the passionate, was deeply Latin, a tiny glimpse of a festive street in Assisi perhaps, Rio, or Tarragona.

Shaw, feeling himself beguiled by the spectacle, made himself look away and let his eye rest on the reflections opposite in a shop window; an old-fashioned butchers, the plate glass clean and unsullied by offers or enticements, revealing the meat within: a long neck of beef, a collection of crusted pies, a brace of partridge hung from a rail. In the rest of the window the reflection was perfect, so that Shaw could see himself, and then at the back of the protestors, in between a set of banners, a familiar face. Shaw knew in that

279

moment that he had been recognized too, because the face immediately disappeared from view.

Javi Copon had fled.

Turning away in pursuit, Shaw sensed a change in the air: a vibration perhaps, but more – and this in retrospect – a change in pressure, as if the door on a jet had been closed ahead of takeoff, a sudden compaction of the atmosphere, so that one of his eardrums popped, and he began, in the second he thought he had left, to duck what he thought must be an explosion. Head down, he kept his good eye on the swaying icon, the scene caught in frozen frame, and instead of the blinding flash of a bomb, he saw the splash of blood red, the icon's neck shattering, the arterial fluids spraying out over the crowd, leaving shocked white faces blotched with crimson.

A static second of silence, then the screaming, then the concertina effect again, the air compacted as if for a sonic boom, but this time blue and white exploding, a Miroesque nightmare of the spectrum, leaving gouts of dripping colour on the shoulders and coats of the pilgrims, matting heads, falling in veils of pigment from the icon's decorated mobile shrine: one pilgrim, a teenage girl, stood screaming, arms rigid with fear, and the only feature of her whitewashed face discernible was the mouth, stretched in a tortured oval – a sickening reminder of Ruby Bright's last breath, glimpsed through the misted freezer bag.

In slow motion the Technicolor chaos lasted, in fact, half a dozen seconds, in which a pure, wild panic gripped the crowd. Shaw locked on the colour red: a primeval signal of blood. From that one assumption all else followed, leading inexorably to gunfire. The icon's plaster head lolled from its broken, blood-drenched neck. Using the kerb and a Victorian lamp post Shaw hoisted himself up above the heads of the crowd, swinging round to look back at the rooftops. The periphery of his vision was blurred, a physiological symptom of the adrenalin pumping round his body, but the centre, the clear focus, was preternaturally sharp, as if he could discern each of the split flints in the facade of the old museum, or the waft of the linen cowls on the monks who had been, until a handful of seconds earlier, executing a mesmerizing Gregorian chant.

Along the crenellated roofline of the museum one of the clear notches held a figure, with a gun. Because panic still had a grip on his brain, he saw the transparent, tubular object as a gun. One of the uniformed officers in the crowd was pointing up, an arm as straight as an archer's. Instantly the roofline figure was gone. Sirens began to wail and the street, now thronged with the crowd which had filled the pavements, seemed to divide of its own, collective will, giving Shaw a view again of the stricken procession. It was the woman in white, or rather the woman *drenched* in white, who broke the spell. The horror had gone from her face, to be replaced by shock, but she held out her hands, watching the sticky fluid drip from her fingertips.

Shaw's eye, at last free of the spell cast by the word 'gun', moved rapidly over the scene picking out a new set of clues: the blue paint sliding down a shop window, the priest lovingly attempting to reconstruct the red-spattered figure of the shattered icon, the sticky puddle of colours on the cobbles, even now producing odd hues of green and brown, on a palette of stone.

Shaw hit the open channel button on his radio: 'Paint-gun attack, calm everyone down. Culprit male, on the roof of the museum, now not visible. Let's see if there are any injuries, and get emergency services in from Back Lane and up from the shrine. Repeat: not gunfire.'

Shaw needed to get to the rear of the museum, so he ducked under the medieval gate into the old abbey gardens. Through the dank archway lay the ruins, and a great field of grass, edged with trees. A crowd here had been waiting patiently for the icon to process down the High Street, past the shrine and into the parklands from the riverside. The Stiffkey, a brook, wound its way like a corkscrew through the grassy estate. To the south lay a house, in the Palladian style, built from plundered abbey stone.

Shaw climbed a tower of masonry which had once formed the base of one of the abbey's great pillars. The screams from the High Street had precipitated a division in the waiting crowd: some, curious, thronged the gateway; others, retreating, often in family groups, had fled to the edge of the grass, marked by a high ridge. Shaw's eye sought out the attacker, trying to pick out an individual not in tune with either of these two basic responses, to draw close in curiosity, or flee danger. Instead he spotted George Valentine, striding towards him though the crowd.

'No sign,' he said. 'He's come down that fire

exit . . .' They could see an iron zigzag escape route from the roof of the museum to the park below. 'Lock's been forced. Some injuries in the procession, one woman got a paint ball in the face and it's broken some bones, and one of the wheelchair-bound pilgrims has caught it in the eye. A few cases of shock. Otherwise, it's just fear.'

Shaw listened, but still watched. 'Organizers?'

'There's another statue at the shrine they can use. They're going to get everyone down there and then carry on. Bloody-minded doesn't come into it.'

'Javi Copon's here. I saw him in the crowd just before it all kicked off. He saw me too. So that means we've got two on the run.' He turned back to Valentine. 'Get Mark Birley to check the CCTV, there's a live feed in the mobile control room. One camera is outside the shrine and there's two traffic cameras on the road to the Slipper Chapel. There might be something . . .'

'Big question,' said Valentine. 'Is that it?'

'Probably. It'll make every paper in the country, plus the TV news. So I guess that counts as a success. Chief Constable's going to get a text soon, if he's not in the club house already. He might even see it on the TV news, which'll be a nice surprise. I'll ring his driver.' Shaw checked his watch. 'Then I'll meet you at the control room in ten.'

An ambulance siren pulsed, the sound magnified by the Gothic archway of the gate. Shaw heard another, circling the abbey ruins, but couldn't see it until the blue light appeared

283

running briefly above the distant ridge which marked the edge of the gardens. He understood then it was not simply a ridge, but the first bank of a ha-ha, designed to shield the owners of the Palladian mansion from the sight of peasants using a hidden road: the bank would rise, then dip to the track, then rise again, even higher, tricking the eye.

Jogging away from the ruins, he ran up the slope and looked down on the sunken lane; a single-track, in red tarmac to reinforce a twenty-miles-per-hour speed limit. To the north it ran to the shrine, to the south towards the parish church. A stand of pines and a great cedar dominated the graveyard, creating a pool of deep shadow. By the churchyard wall he could see two men, circling a small two-door car, the boot open. A door slammed, the sound travelling the acoustic curve of the ha-ha. As the car drove off, with a slight skid on gravel, the man left behind scanned the horizon, appeared to miss Shaw, then turned away, running easily, back around the gardens towards the High Street. The high-step running action was that of a surfer, leaving the shallows, a moving, kinetic signature.

Forty-Three

It took an hour to create a sense of order out of the chaos in the streets of Walsingham. A police helicopter circled constantly overhead and

Common Place, below the battlements of the old museum, was taped off. The procession had been routed directly into the abbey grounds and an icon, hastily attached to a replacement 'litter', was blessed, and then led by a line of priests and monks into the gardens. An open air service, under a white billowing canopy, began only twenty minutes later than scheduled. St John's Ambulance brigade vans, at each exit road, treated nearly thirty pilgrims and tourists for minor injuries and shock. Two pilgrims, a young woman and an eighty-four-year-old man, were taken to the QE2 hospital at Lynn. Eight bales of straw, teased out, were used to cover the wet paint on the roadway and pavements. The 'sniper's' eerie, on the museum roof, was checked for forensics.

The chief constable had asked Shaw for briefings on the hour and had agreed to appear on *BBC Look East* at six, excerpts of which might be used on the national news. The cameraman ahead of the procession had secured decent footage of the moment of the attack and the film had also been offered to ITV and foreign outlets and cable news. Shaw told Joyce to emphasize the fact that the service, the principal event of the pilgrimage, had gone ahead, and assured him that he'd seen a BBC camera crew capturing the event. The paint-gun attack was reckless and had showed no regard for the disabled, the infirm, or the elderly. The police were confident arrests were imminent.

Joyce's sign-off was ominously brutal: 'They better be, Peter. I want someone for this, and I want them today.'

285

Less than ten minutes after their first conversation Shaw rang back, to tell the chief constable that a traffic unit had stopped a silver Ford, registration DNIO HZK, matching Shaw's description of the car he'd seen leaving the scene, and arrested a twenty-two-year-old male on suspicion of a breach of the peace; charges were indeed imminent and likely to include affray, which carried a maximum sentence of up to three years. Aggravating factors, including so-called 'group action', the presence of vulnerable individuals, causing injuries and using weapons, would – the police hoped – secure a stiff penalty. Not for broadcast, Shaw also had details on the arrested suspect: the man, Jonathan Parry, was a civil servant with a local address and a record as a gay rights activist.

In the minutes after the attack there had been scuffles between members of the procession and protestors from WAP. For their own protection uniformed branch had moved the group out of the village centre to their rainbow bus. There was still no sign of their leader, Nano Heaney, although two protestors said she'd been in place, on the grassy rise, just before the attack.

Shaw noted again the motif painted on the side of the bus – a single-decker. 'The Walsingham Alternative Pilgrimage: *A Coalition of the Civilized.*' Climbing aboard, he looked down the aisle. At the back the seats were piled with protest boards, loud hailers and banners. One of the protestors, a teenage girl, was nursing a bandaged ankle. Two others, an elderly couple, were trying

286

to remove paint stains from sun hats, while still wearing them. Several others just sat, still shocked, one or two clutching handkerchiefs to their mouths.

'What can anyone tell me about Jon Parry?' asked Shaw. He spelt the name out, twice.

The girl with the injured ankle buckled first. 'Jon's a member. Well, he comes to meetings but we don't see that much of him. He thinks we've sold out, that a street protest is a poor substitute for the principle of direct action.' She delivered the end of the phrase in a deadpan tone, as if mimicking Parry's own voice.

'Bad tempered,' said another alternative pilgrim, cradling a thermos cup of coffee. 'Angry. Not like Nano, not channelled anger, just like spilling out. It's him isn't it, on the rooftop?'

'Probably,' said Shaw. 'He's in custody. Anyone like to volunteer some useful information? We're thinking this is not a campaign organized, or delivered, by one man. If there's still people out there we need to know about, now is the time to speak up.'

No one spoke. A bee, heavy and drugged, hung in the hot air.

Shaw thought of a white nurse's uniform with the red trade union badge CCOO. 'What about Javi Copon?' asked Shaw.

'Javi's a sweetheart,' offered one of the elderly women. 'He wouldn't hurt anyone. He's not been to meetings for months.' Everyone shook their heads, agreeing.

Searching faces, Shaw asked, 'Has anyone any idea where Ms Heaney might be?'

One of the pensioners raised a hand. 'She slipped away . . . a text, I think. She said she wouldn't be long. Sometimes I think we're all a bit too much for her. She needs her own space. She'll have found somewhere quiet.'

Forty-Four

The door of St Seraphim's, a rectangle of cool shadow, stood open as it had done the day Shaw had met Heaney inside; she'd said then, half in irony, that it was a wonderful place for an atheist to contemplate the mysteries of life. It was one of her hidden, quiet places.

The sunlit vestibule, no more than a glass-fronted porch, gave quickly into the velvet darkness of the chapel. Icons glinted in the light of two candles, stood in sand within brass dishes, the image set against a reedy soundtrack of Orthodox chant.

It was the beauty of this which made Shaw pause, and in that silence, his footfall poised, he heard a strange sound: a distinct guttural click; the noise, perhaps, a thirsty man might make drinking a glass of iced water. From behind the wooden painted screen which shielded the priest's inner sanctum, the sound came again, slightly louder, and this time repeated twice.

The small iron lock was broken, so that when Shaw touched the double doors they both swung open. A table held some simple chalices, a bottle of wine in a silver tracery holder and a plate of ashes. The light here came from an intricate candelabra which, when fully lit, must have supported fifty candles, but just one burned now, illuminating a bare concrete floor, on which lay Nano Heaney, the Pierrot still, in her white trousers and milky T-shirt and a pair of what looked like white ballet shoes.

In one hand she held a wristwatch, unstrapped, on her chest, so that she could see the luminous face.

As Shaw knelt beside her, she raised her wrist so that he could see a pinprick injection mark, a trace of blood smeared over the hidden veins and arteries beneath the pale skin.

Her hand gripped Shaw's arm with great force. 'Listen,' she said, the tongue slightly sluggish, so that the word was smeared with sibilance.

'This is what they need to know. Forty-five milligrams of pentobarbital at 2.35 p.m. precisely. I need . . .' Her voice failed and she had to haul in air before forcing herself to go on: 'I need . . . a vasso suppressor – any will do. Medics, St John's. Shaw' – she pulled his face close – 'just get them.' She looked at the watch face. 'I've got eight minutes – less.'

Outside, Shaw found Valentine on the doorstep, drinking from a bottle of mineral water. The DS ran to the mobile control room and briefed three uniformed constables who set off in different directions to find the St John's Ambulance units, Shaw used the radio to get direct to the ambulance service; he gave them location and deadline: eight minutes and counting. Finally he rang the

St James' control room and told them to raise local doctors and the Magpas Air Ambulance. Again, he reiterated the deadline: now seven minutes and counting.

Heaney's pallor was tinged with blue and a sickly fish-like green. Taking her hand he got his lips close to her ear: 'They're coming. Who did this?'

Looking at the watch face she seemed to make a decision, so that the tension eased in her neck and she turned her head, letting the weight of it fall on Shaw's arm, which he'd insinuated under her shoulders.

'Javi. It's a lethal dose. Death within twenty-five minutes. I might have longer, Javi's hand was shaking, I don't think he'd got the vein cleanly. I think Gokak always did the incisions. So there's a chance.'

Her eyes rolled back in her head. With what looked like a supreme effort, she refocused on Shaw's face.

'But you're not the innocent victim, are you?' said Shaw, gently. 'You're the supplier. Through the palliative care unit, the NHS admin, you found them, with Javi, the vulnerable and the desperate. And Gokak Roy administered the drug. And you provided the house, because Hood left it to the Causeway Trust, which bankrolls WAP.'

'I only wanted to help, to enact the principal, that it's their life and they can choose. They don't have to live in pain. Many do, now. Hundreds. It's not necessary.'

Her face distorted and Shaw realized she was

trying to smile. 'I don't want to die, Shaw. It's not my time, not my place, but Javi thought you were close. He panicked when he saw your sergeant outside the house. He didn't want loose ends. Gokak was a loose end, and so was I.'

Her eyes locked on the single candle flame.

'Don't talk. Save your energy. They won't be long,' said Shaw.

She shook her head. 'Javi found the Coldshaw woman. He knew her well, she trusted him, but he pushed her too hard. It was a decision she couldn't face. So she ran. I'm sorry for that. Then he found Beatty. It was an act of pure pity, because we didn't know she'd leave us the house. It was a mercy. I'm proud of that.'

Shaw thought then that she felt death was close, and that this was her chance to set out some justification for what she'd done, and to shift, in part, the blame to others.

'Gokak said it could be our Dying House, a place for them to find peace, a way-station. But we needed to finance the project, the cause, and so if there was money, we took it.'

She swallowed hard, her eyes closed.

'We'd talked before, we all *believed,* Shaw,' she said, suddenly brighter, engaged. 'We all *believed.* We wanted to do good by our own rules. Finding others was easier than it should have been. We never pushed.' She licked her lips. 'I never pushed. But money corrupts. Boundaries, principles, were compromised.'

A sudden convulsion made her body hinge at the waist, the legs rising, and she gasped for air.

For the first time he saw abject despair in her face, the fear of death.

When the fit passed she looked at the watch.

'Once we'd begun we couldn't stop. They said there were costs. The money was a drug, I can see that. It became . . .' The eyes closed. 'Businesslike.'

Somewhere close they heard a siren wail.

'Poor Beatty Hood. She told Ruby she didn't want to go, even though the blindness was a nightmare. She said Javi was pushing her, telling her it was for the best, telling her she could choose the moment, the day, and that seemed to help. In the end, at the end, Gokak said she accepted it, embraced it even.

'But Ruby thought we'd killed her. Murdered her. It's a cruel word.'

Her eyes closed and for a moment Shaw thought she'd gone, but then she suddenly gasped, the air whistling between her lips. 'Javi took her down to the sea that night because she wanted to see the great moon, and he tried to tell her about Beatty, tell her how it had ended. And about the principle, the freedom. That it was about people's right to choose, that thanks to Shipman most doctors were too afraid to help, too scared to ease the pain.'

Her eyes locked on the wristwatch. 'She said she'd tell the press, so Javi killed her. It was never planned, never. That ended the pretence, I suppose.'

Her body stiffened and she gripped Shaw tighter by the fingers. 'That's the evil,' she whispered. '*Persuasion.* I see it now, Shaw. It's their

292

choice, the choice of the dying, but they know what others want: family, friends, those who care. It's not a decision they take for themselves. We don't seek the death we wish, we seek the one expected of us.'

Distantly they felt, rather than heard, the base thud of a helicopter's rotors.

'My share of the money was set aside, even when I said I didn't want it. I had it transferred to WAP. I thought that one day we'd use it to campaign, a change in the law, perhaps. We should all have the right to die.'

'Jon Parry?'

'Unstable. I told Javi not to encourage him but, after he killed Ruby, he wanted to keep you busy until he was ready to disappear. So he wound Jon up, helped him with the practicalities. Javi's cool, cold. Jon's a hot-head, a cat's paw. I told them to stop, Shaw. I pleaded.'

The eyes again, rolling back, slipping away.

Shaw felt the pressure shift in his ear before he heard the swish of the blades, much closer now, right over the town. The vibrations made the icons shake and dust fell from the candelabra.

Two paramedics were at her side within seconds, pumping adrenaline into her blood system. For the first time Shaw noted a thin trickle of blood crossing her left temple. One of the paramedics pushed back her hair to reveal a bruise forming, a blue shadow, swelling.

As they strapped her into a stretcher she seemed suddenly desperate to finish her story.

'Once Ruby was dead they both wanted out. We had to cover our tracks. Javi went back to the house to clear up because that was the plan, to sell, and bank the cash. The teenager was in the house. They'd left stuff about, Gokak's hypos, the drugs, the bed set up with its drip. The kid was smart, said it was drugs, and he'd tell the police if we didn't pay. Javi said they fought but I don't believe him. It was out of control then, we were out of control. Dumping the body in the skip, and throwing the shoes over the wires, was clever. It nearly worked.

'After that Javi was still worried. He thought Gokak and I were weak. I think he sent Gokak a message to meet at the house. Then he came for me . . .'

They hoisted her up and her arm hung loose, the fingers seeking out Shaw.

'I don't want to die,' she said, gripping his arm.

To one side, for the first time, Shaw noticed a small door covered with a red velvet curtain and realized it was a confessional box.

As they ran towards the helicopter, which had come down in the old station car park, the noise was shattering, the blades turning just above their heads. Shaw stayed with her, holding her hand, as they rose up and then swung out over Walsingham, and the pilgrims below at the open air mass covered their ears and looked up, the strobe shadow playing over the landscape as the helicopter cut across the sun.

'I don't want to die,' was the last thing she said before the drugs plunged her into darkness.

Forty-Five

Six days later

The CID room looked empty, until Shaw spotted his team crowded round Mark Birley's PC, and a flickering grainy image of a CCTV camera shot. Not Marsh House, but a grey dockside, lit by the flat shadowless light of security beams, a few HGVs parked in a line like a wagon-train pitched for the night, and beyond a distant security fence, a stream of car headlights on the wrong side of a road. The silhouette of a castle stood against a starless sky, as did a single tall pine, in the shape of an exclamation mark.

'We're in triple time,' said Birley, and as if to prove the point the moon rose rapidly, care of a celestial props department, towards the stars. Cars, caravans and camper vans began to fill the wide expanse of tarmac, directed into line by Day-Glo clad officers with reflective bats – the narrow lanes marked in giant letters: A, B, C to K, L, M.

'Here she is . . .' said Birley, tapping the screen with his biro.

The left-hand side of the screen had remained black, Stygian, with just a faint reflection of the speeding moon. It churned white now as a large ship's stern came into view, ropes thrown from steel crow's nests to port and starboard. Exhaust fumes, rising from the car decks, made it appear the ship was boiling on the inside, its heated guts seeping out into the cool night air.

HGVs first, the ship began to disembowel itself, until the line of vehicles became simply small cars, the faces of excited travellers peering out at a foreign quayside.

Birley noticed Shaw for the first time. 'Sir. Dockside, Santander, night before last. Interpol released it to us an hour ago. You need to watch here . . .'

At the roll-on roll-off exit there were two gangplanks, metallic covered walkways, disgorging people. Birley scaled back the fast-forward to x2. One line carried rucksacks and climbers' sticks, the other comprised a stream of men and women in the corporate livery of the ferry company, neat uniforms or overalls emblazoned with a dolphin motif.

Birley keyed a precise digital time into the frame finder on screen and they watched the crew file past until the automatic stop facility froze the image: then, defining a small rectangle with a cursor Birley magnified the image. 'That's him.'

The only crewman with a hoody and a pair of silver-white trainers. 'Watch carefully, this is a bit of a three-card trick which I suspect he's done before . . .'

The crew snaked their way around the waiting line of cars towards a one-storey building beyond which waited a coach.

'This is Crew Alpha, just off a three-day stint, so they're heading home after briefly checking out with customs and border security. All except our friend here . . .'

The single-file crew line began to coalesce into small groups, chatting, hugging, excitedly discussing plans for leave. Ahead of them the doors of the single-story reception building had opened and a uniformed police officer stood waiting. 'Hoody', a hundred yards back, stooped to tie loose shoelaces until he was last in the line, then, with purposeful steps, he slipped to one side between two large shipping containers.

The video stuck, then buzzed, before cutting out.

'That's it. The customs staff on the main gate watch this stuff live, especially during embarkation. At least that's the drill. This time they spotted our friend and sent out a plain-clothed guard, who located him hiding in a large waste bin, where he was detained by two police officers. Interviewed on site at 20.35 hours, Spanish time, last night. This is the mug shot.'

It was Javi Copon. The jawline looked different; tauter, as if he was determined not to show any emotion other than inner strength to the camera.

'They interviewed him for sixty-five minutes but got nothing. The crew was dragged back off their courtesy bus, but they all claimed that they thought he was a deckhand, and they change every crossing, so nobody thought an alarm needed to be raised. Copon was arrested and put in a cell in the reception block awaiting re-interview by immigration officials. The block has three cells. When they went back for him at 23.30 hours he'd gone, a hole kicked through the

297

partition, the window to the next cell off its hinges. They closed the port for two hours but there was no sign of him; by which time the unloading lorries had all gone through the gate. Their guess is he had a mate on board, an HGV driver. Anyway, long and short of it is, he's gone.'

The team seemed to let out a collective sigh. The inquiry's big breakthrough, the arrest of Nano Heaney, had opened up the case like a magic key. They now knew that while Dr Gokak Roy was guilty of illegal euthanasia in the cases of the six Parkwood Springs victims, Javi Copon had brutally murdered Ruby Bright, Dr Roy himself – and had attempted to kill Heaney. It was all very well knowing what had happened, but the public and the chief constable wanted someone to pay. Heaney's appearance in court, due in ten days, would spark a media circus, as her legal team sought to portray her as a principled campaigner for the right to die. The case itself, destined for the Old Bailey, could make legal history. But what Shaw's team wanted, no, *needed*, was to put Javi Copon in the dock: a cold-blooded killer who might have been drawn to ending the lives of those in pain on a point of principle, but had soon found himself beguiled by the fortune that could be made.

'We need to find him,' said Shaw, simply.

'We don't know if his family is aware he's back in Spain,' offered Twine. 'I've got the local police to watch their house at Zarautz. But he can't be that stupid, especially now he knows the police are on his trail.'

'I'll try the Home Office,' said Shaw. 'We need

298

to pull strings, apply pressure. The Spanish need to know what this man did: extortion, murder by knife, strangulation. I don't want Madrid thinking we're tracking down some kind of angel, a man who brought peace to the troubled and infirm. We've got this close, we need to lay a hand on him. We *will* lay a hand on him.'

Out the window Shaw caught sight of the Cut, the distant surf line of the sea. 'Let's remind Madrid he's a surfhead too. They can alert Lisbon. Let's have them scouring the Atlantic beaches.'

'The bank's come through, sir,' added Twine, the Montblanc poised over a list of figures. 'Copon had a hire car out on the day of the Walsingham attack. He used a bank in Cromer to clear out the Causeway Trust's current surplus of sixty-two thousand pounds. All in fifties. The Met put a round-robin out at mainline currency exchange points and one at Paddington said they'd done a sterling to euro transaction for fifteen thousand pounds. So he's got resources. Can't help thinking he's got something specific in mind, why change that large a sum?'

'Pay off the HGV driver?' suggested Birley. 'Buy himself a ticket that gets him further away.'

'We lose him now, we'll never get him,' said DC Lau. 'It's not about money. He's got what it takes to disappear: a language he can use anywhere in the world.' Lau was first-generation British-Asian, armed with at least three useful languages, not including immaculate English. 'The girlfriend's made it clear he doesn't need a passport anyway. He's got friends on the ships, in the union, so he can come and go. South

299

America, the Philippines, North Africa, Mexico; he leaves Spain undetected, he's a new man. An innocent man.'

Shaw closed the door of his office and put a call into the Home Office. Then he rang a former colleague from New Scotland Yard now at Interpol in Brussels.

As he waited for the call to be put through, he picked up a lurid seaside postcard lying on his desktop.

A slogan in blue read: BUDE FROM THE BREAKWATER.

He'd rung Julia Fortis after hearing Nano Heaney's confession and told her he would not need to use the Coldshaw letter in the on-going inquiry. The postcard had arrived three days later. A neat hand in blue ink said simply: 'A break with Mum. She loves the place. The job's mine pending the court case, so we'll see. Local bare-foot ski club needs new members! Best. J.'

He finished his calls, adding one, with the chief constable's blessing, to ACPO – the chief constables' organization – requesting that their international secretary ring Madrid to put extra pressure on the senior officers in north Spain.

It was all he could do. It wasn't, unfortunately, going to be enough.

The final call made he sat looking out over the rooftops, the window ledge crowded with dusty pigeons.

Valentine, knotting a tie, appeared at the door. 'Peter. If you want to go it's time.'

Shaw had put the Porsche through the St James' car wash and was admiring the reflection of his

300

charcoal grey suit in the paintwork when he heard his name called: Tom Hadden stood at the door of the Ark, one hand beckoning them inside.

'Peter, George. A few loose ends. And maybe, a new beginning . . .'

In the centre of the old nave of the Ark stood the hospital drip stand retrieved from 32 Hartington Street, bagged in cellophane and labelled as a forensic exhibit. From a metal filing cabinet Hadden produced another bagged item, a hard plastic paint gun.

'We needed to cross-match the prints on the gun with Parry's, which was fine. Positive. There's no doubt he pulled the trigger.'

He slid the cellophane off the drip stand and showed them the small aluminium tap which had been used to administer the lethal drug.

'There was a print on this tap, a nice clear crisp one. The tap is lodged in the "on" position, by the way. We could surmise, although it would only be a surmise, that this print belongs to the person who precipitated the death of the last of the Parkwood Six victims, by allowing pentobarbital to flow into their bloodstream . . . You turn this tap, walk away, and your patient is dead in twenty-five minutes.

'The hand that turned this tap, gentlemen, was Nano Heaney's. We took her print under warrant when she was admitted to intensive care at the QE2. There's no doubt, I'm afraid.'

Which, subtly, changed everything. Shaw still hoped that one day a court would deal with Javi Copon. Apportioning guilt, or blame, in the six Parkwood Springs' killings required the wisdom of Solomon. He'd always imagined Copon as the enforcer, Dr Roy as the technician, capable of the coldest of cold-blooded killing. And Nano Heaney? He'd seen her as aloof, the creative force, striving for what she thought was merciful, working in the background to provide organization and finance. She'd denied ever being in the house at all. The fact that she'd been there, at the moment of death, transformed the crime.

Forty-Six

Nano Heaney had been transferred overnight from the QE2 hospital at Lynn to a private clinic near Sandringham. A prominent, wealthy campaigner for the legalization of euthanasia had stepped forward, publicly, to pay the bill for her care. The police were secretly delighted to be offered a chance to increase security around Heaney, who had been arrested and charged in connection with the six Parkwood Springs deaths. A large crowd had mounted a vigil of support at Lynn from the moment the story broke, occasionally taunted by Pro-Life counter protestors. Fleet Street had, largely, portrayed Heaney as a hero, who'd tried to bring peace to tortured souls, her good intentions corrupted by Dr Roy and Javi Copon: a view reinforced by casual racism. The quality press had devoted feature pages to the problems faced by doctors in the wake of the

Shipman scandal, too nervous of prosecution to provide the kind of palliative care which had allowed so many in the past to die peacefully in their sleep.

Shaw let the Porsche swing past the photographers at the gates of Orchid Lodge Hospital, and Valentine adjusted his tie for the TV cameras. The BBC news that morning on Radio 4 had suggested that there was now a majority in the House of Commons, across all parties, for a change in legislation to approve euthanasia and assisted dying. There was also growing support to enact, immediately, changes to the law suggested after Shipman's arrest which would create a new post – of Medical Examiner, a kind of investigative coroner's officer. An un-named source in Downing Street had indicated that a vote might take place in the new year. The case of Nano Heaney was cited, and indeed credited, with sparking a wider public debate. The BBC's *Moral Maze* would tackle the subject in its next edition.

Shaw and Valentine had interviewed Heaney twice under caution at the QE2, and established a clear picture of her role in the six Parkwood Springs deaths. She had never been to Marsh House, she had never been to Hartington Street. She had helped Dr Roy and Javi Copon identify possible candidates for euthanasia: those in chronic pain or mental anguish. She had never, personally, approached patients. She denied, point-blank, that any other health care officials were involved in the conspiracy. Her share of the financial proceeds had been transferred to the

303

Causeway Trust. The price of euthanasia, in each case, had been set after a discussion with the patient and reflected their resources. However, in no case was it less than £9,000. In several cases, including Beatty Hood's, it was in excess of £80,000. The victims were assured, Heaney said, that most of the proceeds would be used by the Causeway Trust to campaign for a change in British law.

Heaney had been allocated a room on the first floor, decked out with flowers, with a view over Castle Rising woods. A heart monitor beeped as they entered. Heaney herself was sitting up, cushioned by pillows, a laptop open. The duvet cover was littered with cards and letters, and a complete set of daily newspapers.

'Shaw, Valentine . . .'

Shaw noted ice white pajamas, with thin blue stripes. Six days of medication had reduced her weight, so that her bones looked heavier, as if her skin was slightly wasted.

'I always saw you as a NHS supporter, a stalwart . . .' said Shaw, his eyes scanning the room: the coffee table with fresh fruit, a glass cafetière, an Indian rug, the faint echo of classical Musak.

'The law needs to change, Shaw. The NHS is standing in the way, it represents the Establishment's red line, across which we cannot step. The private sector's got a lot to offer in radical, innovative procedures.'

'Lucrative procedures,' offered Shaw, taking a seat. 'Not for your personal gain, for sure. But it was for the campaign, the cause. So it is difficult to argue that you did not profit at all . . .'

A silence followed. 'Are we under caution?' she asked. 'The lawyers are downstairs in the conference room. A statement's being drafted on today's news from Parliament. I should ask for a representative to be present.'

According to that morning's *Daily Telegraph* a London law practice had offered to act for Heaney, pro bono.

'I just wanted to ask a question,' said Shaw, as she reached for a bedside phone. 'I wondered, really, if it was straightforward perjury, or if there was a degree of self-delusion, or even *clinical* delusion. My money, for what it is worth, is on a straightforward lie.'

She looked disappointed and the blood showed in her cheeks, but she said nothing as she slowly replaced the telephone receiver.

'When I held your head up so that you could speak, in those few minutes which might have been your last in St Seraphim's, why did you waste what time you had on a lie? Self-justification, perhaps, even so close to death?'

'Riddles, Shaw. Valentine looks embarrassed. I hope there's some factual basis to these allegations.'

Shaw tossed Hadden's forensic report on to the duvet. 'You can read that at your leisure. In summary your fingerprint was found on the drip stand by the deathbed in Hood's front room. A clear, primary print. That means you were there, and you were the last to touch it. Which suggests you were there for the whole procedure; there for the moments of final persuasion. Did you have to calm last-minute doubts? Ignore, perhaps,

305

last-minute nerves and questions? The court, I'm sure, will want every detail.'

'I really do think I need one of those lawyers present.' Something like anger flooded her eyes. 'But does it matter, I mean really *matter*? This is an idea, a principle, not a parlour game: this is about life and death, Shaw. It's not Cluedo.'

'I'm not sure the criminal law works that way. But you'll find out soon enough. Matter? Yes, I think it does. I think a jury will think it matters. I'm pretty certain the chattering classes will think it matters. That's the thing about a mercy killing, fine in principle, but someone has to do the deed. At the point of death it's a very personal relationship, between victim and killer. People seem to think that euthanasia is simply a policy you can enact, and then the deed is miraculously done. It isn't like that, is it? Did Gokak refuse to turn the tap? Is that why your prints are there?'

She picked up and dialled a single digit.

Shaw carried on speaking. 'People, most people, will see you in a different light. I think that's going to have repercussions for what we can now call your public persona. Angel of mercy, angel of death. The debate goes on. Let's see what a jury thinks.'

Forty-Seven

Did they see Javi Copon die? They certainly saw the precise moment when he was lost to view, which might, in Shaw's opinion, not be quite the same thing. The Policia de Seguranca Publica in Lisbon alerted New Scotland Yard to the website film, having briefed the GNR – the local gendarmerie at Nazare – to take statements at the scene. Emails from the Portuguese resort began to arrive at St James' early that morning, so the facts were clear enough. Javi Copon had arrived the day before the film was shot and slept in a beachside house with three friends, having completed the purchase of two jet skis from a local supplier – a Yamaha Waverunner, at 13,500 Euro and a Seadoo Rxt at 11,200 Euro. New winter suits and four locally made 'long boards' came in at a further 12,000 Euro. All transactions were made in cash, from Copon's wallet.

The Atlantic sea state was perfect for an attempt on the world record, set by Garrett McNamara exactly a year earlier, at precisely this spot. A swell of fifty-two feet was building to sets of waves in excess of seventy-five feet off Nazare's North Point. A fresh offshore wind was due to peak at dusk, creating perfect conditions to hold waves up, like glass walls, waiting to trip over the rocks of the continental shelf, and fall – headlong – on to Nazare's sands. Copon and his three comrades took to the water at 6.35 a.m. from the Old Port. A woman in the beachside chapel, frequented by surfers, said all three had prayed and lit candles, leaving twenty Euro notes in the collection box. Her statement included an odd addition, the observation that surfers seemed to require more holy water than other visitors, splashing it on to the forehead like a fresh, daily baptism.

During the first hour Copon piloted the jet ski, towing his friend along the crest of the brewing waves, darting forward at speed to release the surfer into the path of the breaking water, hurling them down the glassy front of the great waves; recorded by officials from the Nazare Surf Observatory, stationed in the old lighthouse on the point. During those first few hours, in which they took alternate shifts at the controls of the jet ski, they rode waves measured at seventy-seven feet, along with dozens below the seventy foot mark. Their twin pair recorded seventy-six feet and seventy-six-and-a-half feet. Despite higher off-shore wind speeds and a persistent Atlantic swell, afternoon heights declined as the weather deteriorated, a heavy sea mist creating dangerous conditions in the rock-strewn approaches off the point.

At 3.30 p.m., as a premature dusk began to gather, safety marshals called surfers in using a fog horn on the lighthouse. Copon, noting a series of deepening wave troughs, persuaded his comrade to make one last run in the jet ski. This run, with Copon on his long board, was put up on the website and remained captured in thirty-one seconds of film. It showed the grey towering wave front, the plunging white wake of the surf board, Copon's angled body, the accelerating foam crest, descending under the weight of millions of tonnes of seawater, curling over the frail figure, then obliterating him. For two seconds he reappears, a fleeting image of the arms outstretched, arrow-like, hurtling down the glassy 'tube' of the wave, speeding desperately for safety. The tube closes, the wave breaks, the water explodes in plumes and geysers as it runs through the rocks.

The wave height was recorded at eighty feet – a new *unofficial* world record – because Copon's body was not found, sucked out by the undertow, plucked free by the coastal drift which no doubt took him north out into the vast expanses of the Bay of Biscay.

A verbatim account of an interview undertaken with Cheyne O'Brien, Copon's partner, by the local GNR officer, surname Barroso, was forwarded to St James' via Lisbon.

BARROSO: Why did Copon ignore the marshal's signal – why did you ignore it?

O'BRIEN: Javi said there was a chance of the record. He said his time had come. God offers you this opportunity, he said this often but he meant it today. The swell of the ocean, the wind off the cliffs, the last few great waves before the darkness falls. He asked me to do this for him, and then wait out at sea. We gave him to fate – yes. Fate did not give him back.

BARROSO: There was no sign of his body once the wave broke?

O'BRIEN: None. I used the searchlight on the jet ski, but the sea then was in shadow, and his body must have slipped past. It was a risk but we always talk about this risk. In the chapel on the beach there is a motto, carved on the door. *It is not when you want, it is when God decides.*

Forty-Eight

Jan and Lena walked in the shallows, towing Fran on an inflatable raft. Shaw and Valentine sat at one of the picnic tables, a barbecue sizzling a few feet away, across which had been set a dozen kebabs: scallops, prawns, hake and artichoke, sprinkled with olive oil. Shaw tended it before refilling Valentine's glass with Sancerre.

'There's been a series of unfortunate events,' said Valentine.

'OK,' said Shaw, sitting down, facing him across the table. There was something in the tone, and the rehearsed phrase, which made his blood run cold.

'Not for me, for others,' said Valentine. 'Death makes you see things differently. Makes you think,' he added, heaving in some air. 'But I'd never thought about my name – the surname. From *valere* apparently, Jan looked it up, means strong and healthy. There's loads of saints, of course, droves, going back to God knows when. The romance thing's modern, well, Chaucer. One of that crowd. Apparently it's all about the day – February the fourteenth. It's when birds pair up.'

He looked Shaw in his good eye. 'Anyway. Point is I didn't want to lose Jan in the end so I rang the Great Eastern and said I'd like to go for the op after all. Could they get me in under the knife. They had to check the paperwork, see if it was still possible, and I had to hang on. I hung on, like I've got a choice. I thought, I've missed the slot. One chance, and I've just ballsed it up, all because I just wanted to curl up and die. This nurse came on and I had to repeat my details, spell it all out, and then he said he'd call back if I could just sit tight for a few minutes.'

Valentine shook his head, the narrow skull going from sunlight to shadow and back again. 'I aged, Peter. Right then. I sat on a public bench and watched the clock on the Customs House: eight minutes it took them. A doctor, this time – no, a surgeon, a *mister* – and he says he's sorry but there's been a mistake.

'I knew then, but I didn't know if it was good or bad. I remembered the day of the scan, how I'd met the man next to me on the appointment schedule: Juan Roberto Valenciana. I told you about him. I thought then I'd never forget the name, now I'm sure I won't. The scan that showed the carcinoma, you see, that's his lung, not mine. I've got chronic emphysema, but I knew that. So I said, "I'm all right then." And this surgeon says, "Yes. You can walk free," like a joke. "But I have to ring Mr Valenciana and tell him the bad news."'

Valentine's facial features struggled to represent

311

a single emotion. 'Which means that if I hadn't changed my mind I'd have gone on thinking it was over, and I'd have just waited to die, and Jan would have walked out, because she's not a quitter, is she? And Juan Roberto would have struggled with the symptoms – the nausea, the vomiting, the fatigue. So it wasn't bad news at all, because now he's got a chance, and even if it fails there'll be palliative care. Although that's a euphemism I don't like the sound of anymore. But overall I'm glad I rang. What do those two Aussie's say on the Foster's XXXX ad? *Good call.*'

Shaw turned, watching Jan kicking a splash at Fran.

'Does Jan know?'

'Not yet,' he said. 'She knew I'd made my mind up to go for the op, which is important, at least it feels like it's important, that she knew I was up for the fight. But the rest, no. I don't know where to start. I'll tell her now. She might have a drink. Only she doesn't usually, but if not now, when?'

Valentine smiled, the full hundred-watt version, which was so rare Shaw decided that this was the moment *he'd* been waiting for ever since he'd returned to the coast from London and the Met. They had unfinished business, and it couldn't wait any longer.

He refilled the DS's glass. 'I'd come back for the weekend to the house,' he said, knowing Valentine knew the street well; a playful Victorian villa, on a hill going down to the pier head at Hunstanton, built like the rest to be a guest house, the house he'd been brought up in, the house Jack Shaw died in. The window opposite held its little hanging sign: VACANCIES.

'It's hard to recall precisely . . .' Valentine was looking out to sea, his face set hard. 'Dad was in the final stretch, and so what weight there was seemed to pin him down in that bed in the front room upstairs, like he was made of lead, sinking. Mum said you'd stayed with him at night, so she could rest. I tried to help but I got in the way.

'There were nurses. They didn't call it palliative care then – that's new, slicker. I felt excluded, envious really, they came and went with their own key, talking, making cups of tea. I felt like an outsider. And you were part of the mystery, part of what was going on in that bedroom. It was like being a kid again, with you and him in the Job, and never saying what it entailed, what was really happening.

'I just wondered, George. I know it's late, but was he ready to die? I can't imagine he wanted to linger. It's brutal, isn't it, but he knew when he wasn't wanted. Not in that state. That's what he always told me about the booze . . . That if you're not enjoying it, go home.

'Did they hasten the end? I'm not angry, or vengeful – it's just I left, and he was alive, and then I got the call, the next evening. Mum had it pat – died in his sleep, just floated away. I've seen a few people die, George. It's never looked good. This last case just made me think again.'

Valentine re-filled his own glass from the bottle in the cooler. Taking an inch off the top, he held the back of his hand to his lips. 'The pain was

313

bad – he could hide it for twenty minutes, then he had to be alone. At night it was worse – a sort of delirium, I don't think he knew I was there.' He looked at Shaw. 'He did ask. Not for the end, not directly, but he said he wanted the pain to stop and he didn't mind how it stopped. They upped the medication, the morphine, we didn't ask questions. Hours, they said, but they'd said that for weeks. Your mum stayed up til two, maybe three. I took over.

'I'm not making this up. I should have said this all to you, one day, that day, but the moment passed and we're all different people now.

'There was a picture on the fireplace in that room, of you on the beach as a kid. This beach. You in a hole with a spade, Jack on his knees.

'That night he asked me to put it by the bed where he could see it, by the glass of water and the whiskey. I did it straightaway. Then he fell asleep. The window rattled – there was a storm off the sea – so I got up and opened it out wide. I don't know why. I stood there breathing in the air and when I looked back it was over. You can tell instantly because the lines of the face fall away, I've seen it before, like you're watching a time-lapse film. I should have said before, Peter. It was a good death.'

They had a party then, on the sand, until dusk, when the conversation came back to St Valentine. Fran, using her smartphone, found a picture of the skull of the saint, encased in a glass and gold reliquary, in Rome. The Wikipedia entry said he was the patron saint of happy marriages, which prompted Valentine to announce that he'd asked

Jan to marry him, although that had been against the backdrop of his – possible – imminent, death. She confirmed that the date was still in the diary.

Valentine stood, and they expected a toast, but instead he put his left foot on the bench and eased off his black slip-on shoe, followed by the right, then his socks.

Barefoot, he walked away in the sand until he was directly under the power cable which ran from the apex of the roof of the shop to its counter-point on the roof of the café bar.

Lacing the shoes together he launched them up, one from the right hand, one from the left, so that they passed the cable on opposite sides, the laces jerking them back, crossing in mid-air so that they hung down, spinning together, to form a single thread.